HOW NOT TO BE A POLITICAL WIFE

SARAH VINE

HOW NOT TO BE A POLITICAL WIFE

A MEMOIR

HARPER
element

HarperElement
An imprint of HarperCollins*Publishers*
1 London Bridge Street
London SE1 9GF

www.harpercollins.co.uk

HarperCollins*Publishers*
Macken House, 39/40 Mayor Street Upper
Dublin 1, D01 C9W8, Ireland

First published by HarperElement 2025

1 3 5 7 9 10 8 6 4 2

A catalogue record of this book is
available from the British Library

ISBN 978-0-00-874657-5

Printed and bound in the UK using 100%
renewable electricity at CPI Group (UK) Ltd

To Bea and Will

'Lasciate ogne speranza, voi ch'intrate:
Abandon all hope, ye who enter here.'

– Dante Alighieri, Inferno (1300)

'So go on, be vulgar. Love yourself madly,
for all your faults.'

– Sarah Vine & Tania Kindersley, *Backwards in High*
Heels: The Impossible Art of Being Female
(Fourth Estate, 2009)

'Recollections may vary.'

– Statement from Buckingham Palace, March 2021,
often attributed to Queen Elizabeth II

CONTENTS

PROLOGUE

For nearly 20 years, I was inside the rooms of government, a sanctioned eavesdropper on the rise – and fall – of the Cameroon style of Conservatism. At the same time, I was building a career in journalism, raising two children and doing my best to support my own husband, Michael Gove, on his political journey. I was both an insider and an outsider; observer – via my journalism – and participant in the cut and thrust (mainly cut, if I'm honest) of frontline politics.

After my divorce from Michael and the demise of the Conservatives' old guard, that all came to an end. So, I am no longer officially a Westminster WAG. But you won't find me mourning her demise. Politics trampled my health, my happiness, my marriage, my sanity; it placed intolerable pressure on my loved ones, especially my children; it twisted my sense of self and others' sense of me; it tainted everything I did or said. I can't say I miss it.

I thought long and hard about writing this memoir. I've done so not to settle old scores or plead my case, more because I hope it's a tale worth telling, not just for those who are interested in the political events of the past few years, but also because it's about the people and characters behind those events, and why things ended up the way they did. It's a story of high hopes and dirty tricks, broken friendships and divided loyalties, dodgems and dunderheads, heartache and regret, human failure and, ultimately, my own inability to be the person I should have been.

Recollections, as a great woman once said, may of course vary, but this is my story, the way I remember it, written with no fear, no favour – and, frankly, no fucks left to give.

Buckle up.

CHAPTER ONE

THE EYE OF THE STORM: 23–24 JUNE 2016

'A quick flick of the remote control revealed a surreal scene: our house was live on Sky TV. "You were only supposed to blow the bloody doors off," I said to Michael, in my best (i.e. not very good) Michael Caine Italian Job accent. In other words, you've really torn it now.'

Sarah Vine, *Daily Mail*, 29 June 2016

It is still dark when I open my eyes. I've been dreaming, a dream that the house is on fire. For some unknown reason I'm trying to reach the children by phone to warn them, but my eyes won't open and I can't see the numbers on the keypad. I'm stumbling, blind, through the house desperately looking for them, the smoke bitter in my throat …

My anxiety shakes me awake. Unfamiliar noises drift up through the open window. They're not the usual sounds of a

West London dawn – the angry buzz of scooters, the ragged shouts of drunks, the hiss and sigh of the No 7 bus carrying sleepy domestic workers from the outer reaches of Acton to the mansions of Paddington and Notting Hill.

No, these are conversations, hushed and excited, a steady hum of educated vowels, punctuated by the occasional suppressed laugh. For a few seconds, I hover blissfully between dream and reality. Then my memory kicks in. It is Friday; Friday, 24 June 2016. The morning after the EU Referendum. I check my phone: 4:45 a.m.

Someone is smoking a cigarette, sour in the clear morning air. Maybe that explains the fire in my head. A phone goes off and is quickly silenced. There is a very faint smell of coffee. I take my phone off airplane mode and it explodes in a barrage of notification alerts.

I can't bring myself to check Twitter. Instead I get up, walk around the bed and into the upstairs hallway. In the bath-room I put my contact lenses in, the night sliding into focus. The house is dark; children and dogs sleeping. I open the door to my daughter's attic bedroom and climb the stairs, picking my way over to the window through the debris of her teenage existence.

From here I have a bird's eye view of the street. I can see them, but they can't see me. A forest of cameras and microphones, reporters yawning and stretching in the faint morning light. I know by their very presence that some-thing big has happened. And that something can only be one thing.

I briefly contemplate curling up next to my girl, burying my face in her soft, peachy warmth. But then I remember that, like everyone else in school, she almost certainly has nits. I really don't need those on top of everything else. So instead I go downstairs and slide back into my own bed. I close my eyes and do my best to ignore the quiet rumblings below, the slow, growing hum of the city as it wakes. But it is not to be.

Michael's phone rings, snatching me back from the brink of oblivion. Blearily, he reaches out, unplugging it from the charger, sitting up on his elbows and clearing his throat, composing himself briefly before answering in that deep, calm, modulated voice of his: 'Hello?'

'Michael?' the excited, if discernibly weary, voice of his special adviser (SpAd) Henry Cook says. 'Michael, guess what?'

'We've won!'

And so began the strangest, maddest and, without a doubt, most surreal time of my life. If I thought that the months of uncertainty and anxiety beforehand would be resolved by polling day itself, I was about to find out that it was merely the start of it.

'Gosh,' says Michael to Henry, juggling the phone to put on his glasses. 'I suppose I had better get up.'

When really major things happen in life, it can feel like a curious mixture of the momentous and the mundane.

There you are in your pyjamas in your 1930s two-up, two-down on the No 7 bus route in North Kensington (not, as everyone always assumed, a Palladian mansion in Ladbroke Grove – that was always George Osborne) with its slightly rubbishy loft conversion and garden laid with plastic grass and dog turds – and suddenly the whole world is staring at your front door.

A sense of eerie calm descends, there's a sense of time slowing down. It's as though you were observing yourself from the outside, as though all these things were happening to someone else.

Life takes on a kind of cinematic quality, and even years later that morning still plays over and over in my head on a relentless video loop, thoughts and images crowding in from a thousand different camera angles.

My father Roger watching the tumbling markets in his office at home in Turin, the sun coming up over the Italian Alps, the first of innumerable black espressos at his elbow. My brother Ben in his flat in Madrid, raging at Michael, frenetic with worry about what it all means for him and his Spanish family.

I picture Michael's adoptive parents, Ernest and Christine, waking up in their toasty-warm bungalow in Aberdeen, sitting on their blue velvet sofas with cups of milky tea, turning on the telly to discover that their son, that peculiar, bookish boy they had adopted when he was just four months old, has helped bring about a revolution that no one believed possible.

I think of Michael's team, tired but elated – and more than a little incredulous at the victory they have pulled off against all the odds – frantically debating what to do next. Friends, colleagues and supporters, bruised and battered by the viciousness of the campaign, shell shocked – but vindicated at last.

I think also of the millions of ordinary voters who, undeterred by apocalyptic tales of death and destruction, turned out to vote and voted to leave – and who are, this morning, waking up and, to their astonishment and trepidation, discovering that for once in their lives they are actually on the winning side.

I wonder too about the others – the losers – no doubt just as shell shocked but for different reasons. Old friends, good friends on the other side of the debate, and in particular my friend, Samantha Cameron, no doubt doing her best as always to maintain a modicum of normality in the family's flat at No 11 Downing Street, making tea and getting the children ready for school, all the while knowing full well that, for her and Dave, everything had changed. That for us all, that gang of mates who had been all but inseparable over the course of more than a decade, life will never be the same again.

We had been up early the previous day, the 23rd. I had intended to cast my vote on my own later that day, but at the last minute Michael and his adviser Henry Newman decided we should go together. With hindsight this was a bit of a mistake, not because I didn't want to accompany him, just because I wasn't ready for it.

For some reason it really didn't cross my mind that anyone might take a picture of us, and I wasn't prepared. I remember clearly standing in the hallway, having just tied my hair back and shoved on a bit of lipstick, asking Henry whether I looked okay, and him not looking entirely convinced but, through politeness and sympathy and maybe just a little bit of desperation, saying, 'Absolutely fine.'

I didn't. Look absolutely fine, that is. Not by any stretch of the imagination. In fact, I looked truly dreadful.

Let us just savour the horror, shall we? Picture a catastrophically see-through Marks & Spencer leopard-print top, paired with a jacket that was at least three sizes too small for me, a pair of three-quarter-length jersey palazzo pants and some very unflattering boots, which only served to highlight my ghostly and very possibly hairy white ankles.

Quite why I chose this ensemble for what was arguably the photocall of my life, I will never know. All I can say in my defence is that I wasn't really thinking about it in those terms; in fact, I wasn't really thinking ahead at all. Either way: I looked like I had not only got dressed in the dark, but out of a skip. Or my daughter's dressing-up box.

It is, of course, absurdly narcissistic to dwell on it. But there is something about that image – along with so many of the paparazzi snaps that were taken of me during the period in the run-up to the vote – that just remind me of the unease, uncertainty and unhappiness of those weeks.

That picture in particular has come back to haunt me countless times since, online and in print, a reminder not only that I have a very good face for radio but also of the craziness of those weeks and days. Google me, and it's the first to pop up. It literally follows me around the internet like a particularly tenacious troll. I hate it so much that I have made both my children promise that, when I die, they will make sure that picture is nowhere near my funeral programme. Otherwise they'll get nothing.

I know you'll be dying to see it, so go on: google it.

See what I mean? Absolute horror.

If I look a little demented, grinning maniacally at the camera, a rabbit caught in the headlights, it's because I am. My stress levels were off the scale. I was eating and drinking too much just to keep going, and sleeping far too little.

I was in bits emotionally. None of my friends were speaking to me. My family was furious with me. One of my uncles became so abusive on Facebook I actually had to block him, and I'd had a terrible fight with my brother. Newspapers and social media were awash with horrible stories about us, and the trolls were out in full force.

I wasn't really in control, either of myself or the situation. All I could do was take it one day at a time, and I made so many stupid mistakes; my judgement impaired not only by my emotions but also, if I'm honest, by fear and worry and a nagging sense that perhaps – just perhaps – none of this was quite right.

I was in a uniquely conflicted position, genuinely pulled in opposing directions. For a start, I am a journalist – always have been. It's not a profession that mixes easily with politics. The two are like oil and water, and in the years since Michael swapped the newsdesk for the dispatch box there had been moments of real tension between us. But nothing quite so intense or dramatic as those past few months.

Michael had been flat-out campaigning for Leave while at the same time running the Ministry for Justice and attending cabinet. His days were packed with meetings from dawn to midnight. The kids and I had seen virtually nothing of him, and when we did, he was monosyllabic with exhaustion.

But we still felt very keenly the effects of the campaign. And even if I had wanted to stay out of it, I couldn't. My job as a writer and columnist on the *Daily Mail* brought me into regular contact with Paul Dacre – my editor, a man of commanding stature, uncompromising principles and steely determination – who was absolutely determined to make the case for Leave. In practice, my own feelings about Leave aside, this meant I had little choice but to join the public debate around the referendum, which in turn exposed me, not unfairly it must be said, to even more scrutiny.

Everyone who ever worked for Dacre found themselves at some point pushed to the very brink, and I was no exception. It was simply the nature of the beast. It was the secret of his success; what made the *Mail* the very best newspaper it could be, what infuriated his rivals and saw the sales figures soar. Working for him was a great privilege and an education; but on a personal level it could also be very demanding.

The *Mail* was staunchly Leave. The *Mail on Sunday*, its sister paper was, by contrast, fiercely Remain. This familial tension fed quite well into the mood at home where, my own mixed feelings aside, I was obviously fiercely loyal to Michael (what wife wouldn't be?).

But there were other people, equally important, equally vital pillars to my existence, who took the opposite view.

My family was the first. My parents had emigrated to Rome in 1974, when I was 5 and my brother was still a baby. We swapped Stourbridge for Frascati, leaving behind a suburban semi-detached, power cuts and the three-day week for a tiny tumbledown villa in the village of Grottaferrata, surrounded by fig trees and olives and what felt like endless summer.

I was enrolled in the local primary school, a sturdy milk-white English girl surrounded by tiny dark-eyed Italians. As I didn't speak the language, they put me in the kindergarten to begin with, so I spent my days at the back of the class, wedged into a desk that was far too small, not having a clue what was going on.

But it wasn't long before I picked up the lingo, and within months my Italian was as good as – if not better – than my

English. Even today, almost 50 years on, I remain bilingual. But of the four of us, I'm the only one to have returned to make a life in the UK. My brother married a Spaniard, has a Spanish son and lives in Madrid; my parents remain in Italy. Their lives are and always will be in Europe: for them, coming back is not an option they are willing to contemplate.

It was because of them – and more besides – that I understood, on a deeply visceral level, the impetus to Remain. And a large part of me shared it. But then a part of me also shared my husband's deep dislike of Brussels as a political and bureaucratic institution. I felt I was being asked to make an impossible choice, one which, whichever way I went, would inevitably mean me upsetting someone. And I'm just not that good at upsetting people close to me.

It was in this topsy-turvy frame of mind that I woke that Friday morning. For Michael it was rather different: this was what he had wanted, what he had fought for all along – he just hadn't expected it. It was what his parents and family back home believed in; it was what all those around him had been striving towards.

Although he was genuinely taken aback that Leave had won, there was no doubt in his mind that the British people had made the right choice.

Unlike me, he had very sensibly gone to bed at 10:30 p.m., just after the polls had closed, and had slept soundly until woken.

My journalistic colleague Tim Shipman has described this as 'one of the more remarkable acts of intellectual detachment of our times' but it was far more prosaic than that. A veteran of innumerable election nights, Michael knew there was nothing to be gained from staying up late – it would not change the result but would make the following day very tiring, and he was already worn out. Not for him, the noble art of powering through on Modafinil or Red Bull. In times of real crisis Michael is nothing if not deeply pragmatic.

I, on the other hand, had stayed up, wound up by the excitement of the day and overtired from the events of the previous few weeks, to watch some of the first results roll in.

Earlier, our friend and chef Henry Dimbleby and I had cooked a delicious hunk of roast beef, sliced wafer thin by Henry, for a small group of our close friends: Henry D and his writer wife Mima, the TV presenter Kirstie Allsopp, the writer John Preston and his wife Susanna Gross, former literary editor of the *Mail on Sunday*, now a professional bridge player.

Alongside them were the usual suspects: one of Michael's many Henries, Henry Newman (it was always a bit of a joke that every time Michael acquired a new SpAd they always seemed to be called Henry), Neil Mendoza, the Provost of Oriel College, and Steve Hilton, an old friend and David Cameron's former adviser.

Although Steve then left to do a television interview, and Henry felt he should go to the Vote Leave headquarters at Westminster Tower to join one of the other Henries, Henry Cook, a few of the others stuck around after Michael said goodnight.

Ever the consummate host, Michael's last act before sloping off was to open a Jeroboam of claret, cueing some inevitable wry laughter about the need to maintain good trade relations with the vineyards of the Continent.

It seems hard to imagine now, given the subsequent radioactive fallout, but despite the fact that half of these friends were committed Remainers, it was a very good-natured evening, perhaps partly because the Remainers were still confident of winning.

It was the same for other friends of mine that night: one friend told me that she and her husband (she was a Remainer, her husband a Leaver) went to a party quite near to us, in Queen's Park, where there was quite the mix of both. Her husband had his nose rubbed in it for most of the night by Remainers, incredulous that anyone with a brain could vote Leave, but he stuck it out with good will, and stayed to watch the results start to come through on their enormous TV.

At about 12.30 a.m., Mark Gallagher, a famously right-wing political pundit and lobbyist, who had also been defending his Brexit stance that night, sidled up to my friend's husband. 'Anthony, I would advise you to leave,' he said quietly. 'I've just had news that indicates that Vote Leave will win … I'm actually off to Westminster Tower now to, er, celebrate … but I think the mood here might turn quite nasty.'

My friend said that they snuck out only minutes later, actually feeling nervous about a Leave victory and what it might mean for their friendships.

Although Michael made it clear that night that he did not think Leave would actually win, he certainly felt that, for all the ups and downs, he had fought a good campaign and been true to himself. He was hoping for a respectable Leave turn-out, after which he could set about mending some fences.

Earlier that day he had had lunch with Nick Boles, one of our greatest friends and another committed Remainer, in a tapas restaurant opposite the Wallace Collection. Nick told me later that there was a 'strange, almost elegiac atmosphere' at the lunch, with Michael acknowledging that Leave was close, but not winning, and how keen he was to pull things back together among both MP colleagues and with his friends.

Although there was never any doubt in his mind about the argument for leaving the EU, I think that, like me, a big part of him just wanted the whole damn thing to be over, for life to start getting back to normal.

In fact, much of the conversation around the table that night was about how much everyone was looking forward to repairing the friendships that had been fractured during the course of what had turned into a very vicious and divisive campaign.

One person in particular played heavily on my mind that evening: Michael's very old friend and sparring partner Chris Lockwood, who had in recent days become very angry, both in public and privately. Chris was as passionate a Remainer as Michael was a Leaver, and he had just stopped being deputy head of the prime minister's Policy Unit at No 10.

Before that, since 2006, he had been the US editor of *The Economist*, a role for which he'd cut his teeth by being the magazine's Asia editor since 2000. Even in the 1990s, when he was working his way up through the ranks at the *Daily Telegraph*, he'd always had an overseas, 'global' slant and simply couldn't understand a pro-Britain stance.

In an early example of what we later came to call 'Brexit Derangement Syndrome', Chris had been posting increasingly hysterical tweets about Michael, as well as sending both of us really nasty private messages. His wife Venetia and I, meanwhile, had been exchanging increasingly exasperated messages, trying desperately to find a way for the boys to stop arguing. I had also been texting him directly, imploring him to turn it down a few notches. After all, Chris and Michael were proper friends. They used to go to the opera together, their second boy was (is) Michael's godson, we had shared countless dinners and holidays. It broke my heart to see the way politics was ripping the heart out of their friendship.

Theirs wasn't the only relationship being shredded, either. Our close-knit group of friends – many stretching back to university days – was being slowly but surely pulled apart. Godparents were at war with each other, children who had grown up in each other's houses were suddenly on non-speakers as the adults took sides. Politics had infected every aspect of our lives, and it was causing untold damage.

So much of my life – my identity – had been built on these relationships, and now the whole landscape of my existence was fracturing. Huge fault-lines had begun to appear that I could never have previously even imagined. Looking back, it truly was the beginning of the end of almost everything. Including my marriage.

All I really wanted now was for the whole thing to just stop. So although part of me was furious at the way Michael had been treated – at the way the Remain campaign had cast anyone who wanted to leave the EU as racist, regressive, knuckle-dragging Neanderthals undeserving of a democratic vote – even though I was torn inexorably between loyalty to my husband and my family and friends on the opposite side of the debate, I was, in my heart of hearts, willing to accept whatever outcome would most likely restore my sanity. I was ready to accept the status quo.

* * *

Just before 10 p.m., we turned on the telly to watch the results come in. The BBC were predicting a victory for Remain by 52 to 48, while an IPSOS Mori poll had the advantage at 54 per cent. They were still running the social media post from a man who had been on the DLR with Boris earlier, as Johnson raced to get his vote cast in time (he finally did so with just half an hour to spare), to whom Boris had apparently conceded he'd lost anyway.

A few minutes later Nigel Farage popped up looking downcast and defeated. Apparently, he had been called on his mobile by a Sky News reporter while Nigel was shaving … 'Looks like Remain will edge it' he told the reporter. Nothing like trying to own the defeat, as well as the campaign, I thought crossly. Shortly after, Michael said goodnight. I remember feeling a mixture of disappointment, sadness – but also a pinch of relief. It really did feel like it was game over. Tomorrow things would go back to normal, and it would be like Bobby Ewing emerging from the shower: all just a bad dream.

Those of us who stuck around a bit longer, drinking wine and speculating, were exhausted but too tired to throw in the towel. There was still no question in any of our minds that Remain would win, not least because of the tragic murder of the Labour MP Jo Cox just a few days earlier.

We had all been shocked to the core by this utterly sense-less and brutal act. And although the killer – a far-right sympathiser by the name of Thomas Mair – was not in any way connected to the Leave campaign, there was nevertheless a sense that the strength of emotion generated by the debate (and the fact that Cox was in favour of Remain) would mean that sympathy for her poor husband and children, combined with perceived notions about racism among Brexit supporters, would open up the advantage. No one was willing to admit that in public, of course; but it was nevertheless the case.

The other side clearly believed it too. News had already reached me via mutual friends still in touch with Dave that the Remain campaign had all but declared victory. I had a friendly exchange of text messages with Kate Fall, Dave's chief of staff. She, like me, was looking forward to it all being over.

I spoke to my dad, a foreign exchange dealer (now retired), who was his customary blunt self: 'I hope to God the polls are right, S,' he said. 'Otherwise we're in for a right horror show.' Searching for some kind of certainty I texted Dom Cummings, shortly after the first result from Newcastle-upon-Tyne. They had voted to remain – but only just. The margin was much smaller than anticipated, and Dom – always the king of data – thought it highly significant. 'Sunderland will be decisive,' he said.

He was right. Less than half an hour later, Sunderland declared, a stonking yes to Brexit, 61 per cent to 39. That was the moment everything changed.

The pound, which had soared earlier in the night, wobbled. My dad rang, 'It's carnage out here, S, absolute carnage.' The markets were going crazy – according to one friend some of the banks had commissioned secret polling showing a Leave victory. But still no one knew for certain.

The evening, which had started out in an atmosphere of quiet relief and resigned exhaustion, suddenly became electric. I, by contrast, felt like all the air had been sucked out of me. It was beginning to look like the country might have voted to leave the European Union after all, and I was in no way ready for what that meant. Exhaustion hit me like a freight train. I decided to call it a day. I left my friends to it, asked them to turn out the lights when they left – and climbed the stairs to bed.

CHAPTER TWO

BECOMING A WESTMINSTER WAG

'The woman approached us at lunch in Oxford. "Sorry to bother you," she said politely. "I just wanted to say well done for all your education stuff." Everyone beamed. The woman's companion joined us. "Look, dear," she said. "It's that nice Michael Goat."'

Sarah Vine, *The Times*

You think you've married a journalist, then, horrors, he becomes a politician.

LESSON ONE IN HOW NOT TO BE A POLITICAL WIFE:
becoming one in the first place.

When I met Michael Gove, sometime towards the end of the last millennium, politics was an unknown country to me. Westminster was just another stop on the District Line in the other direction to Tower Hill, which is where I got off the Tube on my way to work at *The Times* in Wapping. He was comment editor, I had just been put in charge of the arts desk by the editor at the time, Peter Stothard.

It had been a somewhat unexpected elevation. I had no inkling whatsoever that Peter – a legendary *Times* editor with a towering reputation as an intellectual – was even aware of my existence.

When he summoned me to his office one Friday afternoon, I assumed it was for a firing (in newspapers, such things always happen on a Friday afternoon, it just makes it easier). But even that seemed odd, since I was a mere jobbing editor on one of the supplements – why wouldn't he just get a minion to do it?

But as I ventured nervously into his dark, book-lined office, he was all smiles, inviting me to sit down, offering a cup of tea. In classic Stothardian fashion, he asked me if I had seen the new production of the *Oresteia* and whether I thought there was scope for the Classics in the modern world. I stammered some sort of half-arsed reply, and then he asked me about Caitlin Moran, who at the time was a rising star critic on the paper. I said I thought she was rather brilliant and very funny, and suggested she could do more for us.

He pondered this notion for a few seconds, and then said that sounded like a good idea, although he couldn't really be sure since pop culture wasn't terribly his thing. And then, almost as an afterthought, he asked whether I would like to be arts editor.

I was completely blindsided. Arts editor? For *The Times*? How? Why? He didn't elaborate. 'Let's just say I hear good things about you,' he said. I accepted on the spot.

I went home that night as elated as I was incredulous. Being arts editor anywhere was my dream job – being arts editor on *The Times*, overseeing a team of highly respected critics, was like being handed a golden ticket to the chocolate factory.

Especially since it had been a tough few years for me. I had been at the paper for barely a couple of years following an unhappy stint at *Tatler* magazine under the editorship of Jane Procter (of which more later). That was followed (not for the first time) by heartbreak, and the acrimonious end of a relationship which had left me bruised and deeply saddened. As a way of taking my mind off it, I had thrown myself into work. And now, here I was, in charge of one of the most long-standing sections of the paper (*The Times* began, back in 1784, as the *Daily Universal Register*, for the most part an arts and entertainment listings).

My path to journalism had not been a straightforward one. It was certainly not a career that ever crossed my mind growing up. Mine was a household where no one read a paper, save for my maternal grandmother Ruth, who used to take the *Daily Telegraph* and the *Daily Express*. The newsagent was under strict instructions to secrete the latter inside the former, which she would hand to my grandfather before immersing herself in deliciously forbidden tabloid gossip. My parents were wholly uninterested in current affairs and, in any case since we lived in Italy, British newspapers were not an option. They had a subscription to *Time* magazine (mainly, I think, for the free gifts), and that was about that.

At university I studied modern languages, more out of convenience than any real passion for the subject: I spoke fluent Italian, and could acquit myself fairly well in French, having studied it at school in Italy. My joint honours at UCL in French and Italian left me plenty of time for extra-curricular activities, namely having a job since, being resident outside the UK, I wasn't eligible for a grant. I managed to secure part-time employment at The Body Shop, in the so-called 'flagship' store just around the corner from campus in Oxford Street.

I must confess, I found working there considerably more stimulating than most of my lectures. I was never very academic at school, and university didn't interest me half as much as the real world. My job at The Body Shop was a window to all that, and I loved interacting with customers, advising them on what to buy, lining up all the little bottles of lotions and potions on the shop floor, organising the stock-room.

One of my favourite tasks was making gift baskets; selecting the products, arranging them for maximum effect before shrink-wrapping the lot in clingfilm with a repurposed hair dryer (we were nothing if not resourceful in those days). When Barbara Daly's make-up range hit the store, I would spend ages giving impromptu make-overs to customers, something I love doing to this day. There's just something so incredibly joyful about making a woman feel beautiful. I still inveigle friends on their way to a party, who haven't got a clue about how to make themselves look good despite being in their fifties, to let me do their make-up.

Another advantage was the 50 per cent staff discount – which made me very popular with girlfriends. I'll be honest,

I wasn't the most engaged of university students; during my so-called year abroad, when I was supposed to spend time at French and Italian universities, I first buggered off to the South of France for a few months and then took a job in the Italian Alps for the winter ski season. Not for the first time, the authorities were unimpressed.

Nevertheless, I managed a 2:1, thanks in large part to the fact that in those days all that really counted were your finals. Since I'm one of those people whose brain only ever seems to engage under pressure, this played to my advantage. I think this is also why I love newspapers: I thrive on deadlines. There's genuinely nothing I love more than having to think on my feet, with people breathing down my neck. The downside is it makes me a terrible procrastinator.

After university, I felt shiftless and lost. I had no real idea of what I wanted to do with my life and, despite a decent degree, there weren't many options around for someone with no contacts or connections. It was the tail end of the Eighties and the UK was a pretty grim place. Interest rates were touching 15 per cent, people were losing their homes. There was no money, no enterprise, no hope. Britain felt altogether rather bleak.

For a while I worked at the head office of Hobbs, as their 'customer services officer'. Ostensibly my job was to deal with faulty returns and refunds but, in reality, that meant finding excuses not to give customers their money back. When I was not fobbing people off (which I hated), I was using my language skills to reprimand suppliers in Italy, which was where most of the stuff was made back then. My distaste showed, and the management took note. Still, I was cheaper than a translator, so they kept me on.

One gloomy Sunday, my old roommate from university, Lucy, asked me along to a birthday party. The venue was The Stag in Fleet Street, known in hack circles as The Stab in the Back, well frequented by *Daily Mirror* hacks, whose offices were located around the corner. Until they moved out in 1994 (after which the building was demolished), the *Mirror* was written and printed there, so the pub hosted both the journalists and the printers. Never the twain shall meet – there was an unspoken 'them and us' system whereby the printers stuck to the saloon bar while the journalists and subs lorded it in the lounge bar at the front; but there were industrial levels of drinking in both.

I spent the afternoon chatting to yellow-fingered, beer-soaked elderly gents with tall tales of Fleet Street shenanigans. One thing led to another, and by the end of the night I had somehow managed to blag myself a shift on the newly formed *Daily Mirror*'s TV listings desk, largely by convincing them I could use an Apple Mac computer.

As it happens, I could, having taken a short course – but not to any great extent. Still. I was a lot more proficient than the old guard, most of whom, despite being skilled journalists, were really struggling. 'Pissed old hacks baffled by new technology' was how *Private Eye* summarised the so-called 'advances' revolutionising the newspaper industry, but I felt for them. They had more experience in their little fingers than I had in my entire being, and yet here they were, being told what to do by cocky little upstarts and hapless newbies such as myself.

For me, though, it was an unmissable opportunity to break into a world that otherwise would have been entirely closed off to me. All I really had to do was show up, use a mouse, be able to spell – and not make a complete fool of myself. Again, one shift led to another – and suddenly I was on the rota. I took all the work I was offered (mostly at weekends, since I was still at Hobbs Monday to Friday) and at £50 a shift – an unimaginable fortune – I couldn't believe my luck.

My job was to regionalise the TV listings, typing them in from the *Radio Times*, writing little blurbs for whichever programmes I fancied. To me it was the most exciting thing ever – to the 'proper' journalists elsewhere on the paper, we were a joke, the very lowest of the low. So much so that once, when there was an IRA bomb scare just up the road in High Holborn, they evacuated the entire building except for us, since they'd apparently forgotten that we even existed. We all laughed it off, of course. Nonetheless, it was a little disconcerting.

My greatest excitement was to deliver proofs to the main building over the road, to the compositors' room. Here was where I got my first whiff of newsprint (and whisky) and the excitement of putting a paper to bed – walking through the big news hall, loving the pall of smoke over the whole room, the sleeves-rolled-up concentration of so many people hunched over screens as big and thick as fridges, marvelling at the skill and pace and sheer craftsmanship of the whole operation.

All I wanted was to get there, to be a 'real' journalist, hammering out my own stories on the chunky keyboards click-clacking all around me. I had no training, no official journalistic qualifications, I didn't know the difference between an 'n' dash and an 'm', but I knew I never wanted to do anything else. I got myself a copy of *The Simple Subs*

Book by Leslie Sellers, first published in 1968 and still the bible for sub-editors (which is what I was, albeit only a TV-listings one) and learned it off by heart. I chucked in my day job at Hobbs (a moment of great satisfaction: my boss's parting shot was to tell me I had an attitude problem and would never get anywhere in life) and signed up for as many shifts as I could get.

But then, in the autumn of 1991, Robert Maxwell, the infamous owner of the Mirror Group, fell (or jumped) off a yacht and died. And we all got fired. It seemed like my Fleet Street career was to be, indeed, fleeting.

But I was lucky. I scrabbled around among my new friends and managed to get some shifts on the *Sunday People*. It was quite an eye-opener. One of my jobs was subbing 'Dr Vernon Coleman's Casebook', the hilariously no-holds-barred 'agony uncle' column (he was the merciless uncle, the agony was all yours) written by the eponymous medic. It was brilliant training. Having to edit and sub a piece entitled 'My penis is a strange shape – is this why I don't have a girlfriend?' doesn't half teach a girl a thing or two.

By hanging around and making a nuisance of myself, I gradually picked up more and more shifts here and there, inching up the ladder from the *Guardian* to the *Mail on Sunday* and eventually making the transition from sub-editor to commissioning editor at the *Sunday Express* by becoming deputy editor on the 'Espresso' supplement (see what they did there?). By the mid-Nineties, I had landed what should have been a plum position: features editor at *Tatler*, the ultimate high society magazine. A golden future of parties, freebies, handsome aristocratic boyfriends, and friends called Biffy and Bunty surely awaited me.

How wrong I was. In the Nineties, Condé Nast was a vipers' nest. It was hands-down the bitchiest, most back-stabby and generally unpleasant place I have ever worked. Chief 'Viperess' was *Tatler*'s celebrated editor, Procter, the trickiest woman I have ever bumped up against in the swill and slurry of magazine media. 'What do you mean, you can't find five dukes who own poodles and each have a villa in Mustique?' might be her opening line of a Monday morning. 'Try harder!'

Her editing style consisted of plucking an outrageous concept out of the ether – usually involving some unreacha-ble member of the royal family, or some impossible A-lister – and then raging when, inevitably, it didn't happen. If ever we did succeed at one of her infernal tasks, she would gaslight us – decades before we knew that term existed – and tell us that a chimpanzee locked up with a typewriter for long enough could have done the same. 'You!' she would bark, jabbing her reading glasses at me. 'You may not know anyone with a title or a helicopter but you've worked in Fleet Street, so the least you should know is how to write bloody copy.'

I wasn't the only one who got it in the neck. She was at least an equal opportunities tormentor. Under Procter, nice society girls of all shapes and sizes came and went, arriving with bright eyes and bushy tails, leaving in a vale of tears. She trumpets now about being the *Tatler* editor who tripled the circulation of the magazine and wrote the road map for its ongoing success, but there was quite the body count along the way. My friend's mum was head of HR for Condé Nast and she joked that she should have had a revolving door into and out of her office, so great was the turnover of nubile *Tatler* girls. For the record, she denies all this and even wrote an article for the *Daily Mail* explaining to the readers why I was such a hopeless employee.

But I stuck it out, and ended up being almost grateful to her: forged in that crucible of fire, I have seldom been fazed by social situations since. Thanks to the cachet of *Tatler*, I was on at least nodding terms with the brightest of that bright era all on my own wicket – something which is often forgotten by my political critics. I was no Cinderella, being scooped up by the Great Gove like a magician's assistant, and hanging onto his coat tails as he climbed the greasy pole of Cameron's Camelot: I had quite the little black book of my own.

Eventually, I was rescued from *Tatler* by a friend at *The Times*, the gorgeous Jayne Dowle, an old mucker from my *Sunday People* days, who was looking for a commissioning editor on the new Saturday supplement then called *Metro*. I was back in the main current again, swimming more strongly than ever before. Editor jobs on beauty and fashion desks followed, which I loved, until one day I hit the top note: arts editor of the Newspaper of Record.

But not everyone was delighted with my appointment. A few days into my new job, the editor received a stinging letter from Garsington Opera denouncing me as a lightweight whose elevation to the role would surely signal a catastrophic drop in standards. Later, when I met Caitlin for lunch to introduce myself, she said afterwards – with some consternation – 'You're not at all what I expected. For a start, everyone said you were bald.'

So when, just a few weeks before I was to take up my new role, I got a call from my friend Topaz Amoore, saying that someone had dropped out of a skiing holiday that was being organised by her old friend Robert Hardman (now an esteemed royal journalist and author), I decided a short break would be a good idea. It was to prove a pivotal decision.

A few days before we were due to depart I discovered Michael Gove – *the* legendary Michael Gove – was also on the holiday. My heart sank. I had never even spoken to Michael – as comment editor he was far too grand for the likes of me – but I knew he was close to Stothard and something of an intellectual powerhouse. Former President of the Oxford Union, a regular contributor to Radio 4's *The Moral Maze*, writer of robust columns in the comment pages, he had recently published a book, *Michael Portillo: The Future of the Right?* Okay, it was perhaps an early example of his not exactly stellar political judgement but it was nonetheless an impressive achievement.

What had promised to be a jolly week in Méribel (a.k.a. Merry Hell) now looked to be shaping up as a rather awkward works outing. Worse, I was terrified that Michael would realise I wasn't nearly as clever as I had been pretending to be. 'He wrote leaders and knew all about politics,' I wrote in 2004. 'I liked movies and knew about handbags. Damn, I thought. I've come all this way to let my hair down (i.e. get pissed); now I'll have to stay sober and pretend to understand the long-term situation in the Balkans.' Maybe he would quiz me on Greek theatre, and realise I knew next to nothing about it – and report back to Stothard, who would then take the advice of the good folk at Garsington and bin me.

I confided in one of my colleagues, 'Uncle' Brian MacArthur. Brian may have gone down in history as the *Sunday Times* deputy editor who bought the fake Hitler diaries in 1983, but to me he was one of the real greats – a man with the strongest moral core, a respect for 'proper' reporting and a hatred for the scummy shortcuts pursued by ever more media lizards in the name of journalism.

I'd had lunch with him a few days before going skiing and told him that I was slightly quaking at the thought of sharing a chalet with Michael Gove, among others, because despite both of us working at *The Times*, we hadn't met; and he was always so bright and outspoken in our morning conference with the editors in his role as comment editor, while I was still a little shy in my new arts editor role.

'Don't worry about Michael,' said Brian. 'He's one of the good ones. Gay obviously, but collegiate and fun.'

We all met at Victoria Station, ready to catch the infamous 'Snow Train' to France. The line-up – except for our actual host Robert Hardman, who was a Cambridge alum – was wall-to-wall ex-Oxford friends. Michael's ex-girlfriend Simone and her husband Alex, Chris Lockwood and his girl-friend, later wife, Venetia Butterfield, Ed Vaizey, Topaz, Randal Dunluce, Bob's sister Harriet, Bob and Michael. For a moment I quailed, wondering how on earth I was actually going to enjoy myself. But what I hadn't then worked out was that, aside from Topaz, I was the only single girl there – and all the men on that trip had already tried and failed with the dazzling Topaz years before, at university, including Michael who – despite Uncle Brian's assurances – didn't give the impression of being at all gay.

'You had us all at your feet,' joked Michael, when I asked him for his memories of that trip. 'Eddie was flirting with you, Randal was flirting with you, I was flirting with you. You were Queen Bee!'

He paints a flattering picture of me as femme fatale but I remember only that miraculous feeling that in among all these super-bright Oxford graduates, I was the only one (apart from Bob, who is an excellent skier, having spent much of his youth chasing Prince Charles across the slopes in search of royal exclusives) who seemed even vaguely competent on skis (a misspent youth in the Italian Alps). Michael, it turned out, had never been skiing before. Nonetheless, he turned up looking very much the part in a Prada ski jacket, and each morning would shell out 60 francs for a private ski instructor who became so enraged by his hopelessness that she eventually fired him.

Far from being dismayed by this turn of events, Michael seemed delighted. It meant he could spend his days drinking hot chocolate and reading, which was what he secretly much preferred to do. He also regaled us with hilarious anecdotes about his sporting ineptitude. When the aforementioned skiing instructor had finally conceded defeat, Michael enquired: 'Am I the worst pupil you've ever had?' There was a pause, apparently, and then the instructor replied. 'Non. I 'ad one once 'oo was worse; but he was – ow do you say? – 'andicapped.'

It was this self-depreciating, good-natured sense of humour that made me like him so much. He was so unlike the rather Presbyterian persona I had imagined from his columns in *The Times*. I couldn't believe how much fun it was being with him – here was a man so funny, clever, naughty, full of mischief, who – most importantly – was the first man I'd ever met who could truly laugh at himself. It was a potent combination and a breath of fresh air after all the toxic masculinity of Fleet Street.

Most people are first impressed with someone's looks, their physical prowess, their ability to dance. I fell for Michael's modesty, the fact that his physical bumbling was in such contrast to his razor-sharp brain, and his wit: there is no funnier person in a room, and a chalet-full of bright minds for him to bounce off showed him off to his best advantage.

I was also intrigued by how different he was to any other man I'd met: he would have hour-long baths in the chalet, reading *Paradise Lost* and emerging, pink and smiling, in his pastel lavender Hackett dressing gown and matching pyjamas, smelling of Clarins Blue Bath. The confidence of the man was astounding. He was camp but definitely not gay, assiduously gentlemanly but not a sap, adept at crossing swords in debate, but the first man I'd ever met who really listened to what I had to say and asked me questions and, even more incredibly, questions about me. That week, the Kylie Minogue hit 'Can't Get You Out of My Head' was being blasted all over the ski slopes. I knew how she felt.

On the last day of the trip, as we both stood outside in the snow, waiting to catch the train back, Vaizey asked me what I thought of Michael. I blushed, and said I quite liked him, and would probably see him again in London.

Back in London, Michael asked me out for a drink at the newly fashionable Claridge's bar. Somehow Vaizey, who had not quite given up, got wind of Michael's intentions and crashed it with another journalist and Vaizey musketeer, Tom Baldwin (now Keir Starmer's official biographer and leading light of the Islington dinner party set). Both being assiduous party-types, what had started out as a more sophisticated romantic date quickly turned into something rather more raucous, ending up – if I remember rightly – at a late-night Lebanese restaurant with Ivan Massow, where politics soon replaced any putative romance as the chief topic of conversation. Given that all of them – and Ivan in particular – were raucously fascinating, I didn't exactly mind.

Round two – our first proper date – was dinner at The River Cafe. I thought it was a bit of an odd choice because, although fabulous, it closed at 9:30 p.m. and also because it was completely the other side of town to Wapping. Given both our work commitments (in those days the paper still went off stone at around half-seven, eight, in the evening), it seemed somewhat impractical – and indeed it turned out to be. There was a breaking story in the office – as so often is the case in newspapers – and Michael ended up being over an hour late.

You might have thought that would be a red flag; but I had my eye on the lamb chops. Greed overcame my embarrassment; I waited – and the evening went off with a bang. I would like to say his lateness was a one-off, but I'm afraid punctuality and Michael remained strangers. In any case, the large bunch of Moyses Stevens flowers that arrived the next day made up for it.

As the millennium hurtled to a close, Michael and I hurtled into a relationship. An old friend of his tells me that one of his previous girlfriends – not Simone, who quickly became a great friend of mine (and remains so to this day) – had boasted to all and sundry how she and Michael were 'London's foremost media couple'. There was an even better story about the same friend seeing an entry in that girlfriend's diary for 'RMT' and joking with her about her apparent links to the rail union with the same acronym. The girlfriend replied quite sharply that this stood for 'Relationship Management Time', which she had to book into his diary and hers because otherwise Michael was too busy to see her on his own. In retrospect I perhaps should have paid more attention to this.

But at the time none of that mattered to me. For the first time, I was in a relationship of equals: we were equally busy, equally social, equally go-getting. Michael was sharing a flat with Ivan Massow (later director of the ICA and London mayoral candidate) and Nicholas Boles (truculent former Conservative and quite honestly one of my favourite people in the whole world) – both impossibly glamorous Tory A-gays-about-town – in Mayfair (where else?). I suspect this contributed in no small part to the rumours about Michael's sexuality which persist to this day. It seemed incredible to me then, and it seems even more so today, that people could jump to such lazy conclusions – but I suppose Michael's fondness for the perfumeries and the finer things of Jermyn Street, combined with his tendency to surround himself (and even share flats) with extremely handsome gay men like Nick Boles, Marcus Kiggell and Ivan Massow (a penchant that extended to the majority of his SpAds in government) might have fostered that impression.

In fact, Michael was always drawn to glamorous people and locations. For a boy from Aberdeen, he has always enjoyed the finer things in life. He was also drawn to clever people, and they to him. People like Ben Elliot, who turned being an It Boy into a profitable career as the founder of Quintessentially, the ultimate little black book of the aristocracy turned concierge to the uber-rich; Ben's first cousin, Tom Parker-Bowles, the son of Prince Charles's one-day wife and our now Queen, Camilla; Zac Goldsmith, son of billionaire businessman and financier Sir James Goldsmith and a good gambling wingman. But also less well-known names (back then, anyway): David Cameron, George Osborne, Steve Hilton, Rachel Whetstone (who worked for Michael Howard), Dominic Cummings, Anthony Frieze, Andrew Roberts, Simon Sebag Montefiore, Boris Johnson, Dean Godson, Eddie Vaizey – a seemingly endless stream of super-bright, super-connected people the likes of whom I had only ever read about in the pages of *Private Eye* or *Tatler*, and certainly never imagined I would ever even meet, let alone get to know.

Michael brought with him a world of excitement and fun, a never-ending round of animated dinner parties and week-ends away. I had never experienced anything like it, or these people, and I loved it, even if some of it was a little peculiar. Not long after we became an item, Michael asked if a friend of his, Douglas Smith, might stay in my spare room for a while, since he was between accommodations. Of course, I said yes – not realising that his side-hustle was organising what effectively amounted to posh orgies, known as 'Fever' parties. I never went to one, being of a fairly shy and prudish persuasion, but I do remember feeling a bit alarmed by the whole idea. Douglas is now, of course, a major player in the backroom politics of the Conservative Party.

Away from the social whirl, we had time together on more holidays: a magical one to Cuba (where, bizarrely, we bumped into Jeremy Hunt on his way to a ballroom dancing convention, as you do) and even a whole two-week trip in late 2000, to Vietnam. It was on this one that I decided it was time Michael and I had 'The Talk'.

I could see us gallivanting deliciously onwards without a care in the world, but time was marching on. I was never one of those women who desperately craved having children, but I knew I wanted them and, at 33, I also knew the clock was ticking. So, one night, over a spicy, sweaty supper in Danang, I laid my cards on the table. I said I completely understood if marriage and family weren't part of his plan, but they were part of mine. I just wanted to know if he was in the same ballpark. Because if not, that was absolutely fine but I did want to have children so couldn't shilly-shally. He nodded and beamed, chiming in with his characteristic 'hmm's, but it wasn't until well after the holiday that he proposed – on 16 April 2001, my 34th birthday, at the Connaught. Better late than never.

My parents, it's safe to say, were nonplussed by Michael. Unsuccessfully hiding their amazement that anyone had proposed to me, let alone someone as obviously clever and ambitious as Michael, they were equally as baffled by the sheer Goveness of him in the flesh, by the fact that they just couldn't put him into one of their pigeonholes. He wasn't posh but he was pure Oxbridge; he wasn't as rich as they had wished for me, but he had a taste for the high life that bettered even their own; he was clearly clever but the opposite of street smart; he was charming to my mother and affable to my father but gave no sign of being impressed by them, which was the only currency they could understand.

'Roger was like the Eye of Sauron back then,' Michael reminded me, when I asked him for his memories of those early years together. 'When his eye fell on you, you were meant to fall back in awe, in admiration, in supplication. So he couldn't understand it when I did none of those things. I am famously conflict-averse but I'm also very stubborn. Your father couldn't place me, but he sensed early on that he couldn't bully me and it drove him wild.'

Sometimes, this tacit wrestling match between my fiancé and my father led to some surreal developments. There was one memorable evening in the run-up to the wedding, when we were staying with my parents at their place in Monte Carlo and were out for dinner at Château Saint-Martin, the planned venue for our wedding that September. It was a hot night and probably only the third time they had met Michael but the unspoken strain that fencing with my father was having on him suddenly demonstrated itself halfway through the main course when Michael fainted facedown into his mushroom fricassée.

He lurched straight up again, mumbled 'I'm absolutely fine,' and promptly collapsed again. Sitting with him in the back of the ambulance on the way to Nice, I wondered how I was going to explain this to my parents but the distraction, once we got there, of listening to a Marseillaise rent boy in the cubicle next door having a glass milk bottle removed from his bottom, gave us enough anecdotal material to brush over the whys and wherefores of the actual fainting. Later my father, in his characteristically caring way, said: 'Are you sure you want to marry him, S? He seems a bit faulty to me.'

Undeterred, my mother threw herself into the wedding preparations – she always loved a party, and this was as much their celebration as it was ours. Since this was a moment when my father's finances were in a boom not bust phase of the usual cycle, our wedding in September 2001 was a blast. Over a hundred people flew out to the South of

France for a weekend of Riviera razzmatazz. My mother had planned everything to the last rose petal, even down to including half bottles of Nebbiolo, the wonderful wine from where we lived in Italy, in every room, complete with specially made labels. There were – surprisingly – quite a few of these left over but not for long: my father, being my father, drank them all.

We all had lunch the day before the wedding at the enchanting Colombe d'Or, the hotel in Saint-Paul-de-Vence in the hills above Nice, where artists like Picasso, Miró, Chagall and the like had paid their way with paintings since the 1920s, when it was the humbler Chez Robinson. By the 1950s it was the hotspot for the Côte d'Azur coterie, and Yves Montand and Simone Signoret, both iconic French actors and global superstars, had married there in 1951. Fifty years later, we couldn't follow in footsteps that glittering but our own wedding, up the road from the Colombe d'Or, at Château Saint-Martin, a stunning Knights Templar castle with its own chapel, views to die for and enough rooms for most of our guests, was enough of a fairy-tale setting for me.

The actual wedding was to be in the church of Vence itself. But owing to the complexities of the French bureaucratic system, we had officially got married the previous Tuesday, at Chelsea Register Office. I left our flat in Queensgate alone that morning wearing a trouser-suit and wedges, stopped off at Moyses Stevens in Sloane Street to pick up a small bouquet ('And what does madam require the flowers for?' 'Oh, I'm getting married this morning,' I replied, all cool and nonchalant), then caught the bus down the King's Road to the Register Office.

It was a very low-key affair, with just a few close friends as witnesses – and afterwards we repaired for a slap-up lunch in a small private room at Mark's Club, Robin Birley's private members' establishment in Mayfair. It was, quite simply, a fabulous day.

Afterwards, we were booked to spend our first night of married life at The Connaught Hotel, where Michael had proposed. We had a gorgeous room, fluffy bathrobes, complimentary slippers, bowls of free fruit, exciting bathroom miniatures – the full works. But during dinner in the restaurant, Michael suddenly announced that he was feeling unwell. Fearing another mushroom fricassée episode (which, after extensive tests, doctors had decided was something called a vasovagal fit, also coincidentally the same thing that George Bush had once suffered from, an association which Michael, being something of a fan, rather relished) we abandoned supper and repaired to the honeymoon suite. The hotel doctor was called, Michael was examined – and the verdict pronounced. Nervous exhaustion. Clearly being married to me was already taking its toll. We thanked the medic for his advice, gave him his 60 guineas and ordered room service. Not for the last time at key moments in our life together, Michael retired early.

That Thursday, I flew to Nice for our 'real' wedding. October was the off season, which is why the Château Saint Martin – the sister hotel of the Hotel du Cap – was available. My father had negotiated special room rates for the guests, and the festivities were on him. There was to be the ceremony itself in the local church in Vence, followed by drinks, then dinner, then dancing, with lunch the following day. Even now, post-divorce and over two decades on, people still remember it as quite the weekend.

Anyone looking at the guest list for our wedding could have seen the way the wind was going to blow. As well as dear friends from before my Michael days, plus of course relatives and several of my parents' old friends, there were the Camerons, the Osbornes, as well as Nick Boles, Ed Vaizey, many of whom later became MPs, plus Sebastian James, future captain of industry, and stars in the making like Tom Parker-Bowles and Imogen Edwards-Jones. It was like a checklist of every establishment figure who would later put Britain on the map – studded by some vivid exceptions: such as my Russian friend Igor (an 'art dealer') and his mysterious friend, who gatecrashed, bringing with them fist-fuls of dollars and white lilies.

But it wasn't all shiny-faced Tory boys and girls. Labour stalwart Baldwin and his wife Rebecca were there, together with *The Observer* columnist Barbara Ellen (who managed, somehow, to drink my father under the table, something that to my knowledge no one has ever done before or since). Sean Macaulay, brother of Sarah Macaulay, wife of the then Chancellor of the Exchequer Gordon Brown, was also there. I had known Sean since my days as a sub-editor on the *Mail on Sunday*. Now a successful scriptwriter in Hollywood, he had flown in especially.

Poor Sean got rather more than he bargained for. A naughty friend had been given some ecstasy by a fellow guest, which she had slipped into her glass of Champagne, intending to sip it slowly. But Boles, who had been working his mojo hard on the dancefloor, suddenly found himself rather thirsty. Pausing momentarily to catch his breath, he grabbed her drink from her hand and knocked it back in one, not realising the full contents. She was left gasping – but not as much as poor Sean. Before long, the effects had taken hold, and Nick was suddenly seized with fervent amorous intentions towards Sean (who was, and remains, a happily married man). He spent the evening pursuing his quarry vigorously around the dancefloor, at one point, Sean recalls, whispering hoarsely into his ear, 'Before the night is out, I will turn you.'

Poor Nick. The previous evening, at a small pre-celebration dinner, he had sat next to my father who, as the generous father-of-the bride, was in full show-off mode. Nick complimented him on his choice of hotel, and said how well-appointed his accommodation in one of the newly built bastides within the grounds was. 'Oh, you're staying there, are you?' said my father. 'You wanna watch out: that's where they put all the pillow-biters, you know, so they can bugger each other senseless without bothering the other guests.'

There was a sharp intake of breath. We all looked at Nick, and I began to stammer an apology. My mother flashed my dad a furious look: Roger always liked to sail close to the wind, but even by his standards that was a deeply offensive thing to say. But Nick just laughed and said, 'Is that so, Roger? I'll be sure to give you a wide berth then.'

I've always loved Nick, but at that moment I loved him more than ever. Rarely has anyone been so witty or gracious in the face of such bigotry. My father, of course, thought he was being hilarious. He also hadn't clocked that Nick was gay.

I don't recount that anecdote lightly. I know it casts my father in a terrible light, and of course he wasn't like that all the time. But the truth is he was often cavalier and cruel, and I've included it because it helps illustrate what kind of a man my father was in those days, and how he had often behaved while I was growing up. It's hard to really explain quite how cutting he could be at times, or how sharp he could be when on the attack. I've never met a man who could more accurately pinpoint a person's weakness and then exploit it, entirely ruthlessly, often sadistically. It's probably what made him such a success in business; but, sadly, it did not make him a universal success as a parent.

But as obnoxious as he could be, he was also possessed of a kind of devilish charisma which fascinated and intrigued people, even as it shocked them. He was completely unfiltered, a trait that I have inherited and which has, on more than one occasion, got me into seriously hot water.

He had a strange kind of vulnerability too. On the day itself, as we drove together in the car to the church, I suddenly realised my father was in a cold sweat. 'I'm not feeling too good, S,' he confessed, as we wound down towards Vence. 'What's wrong?' I asked, attributing his nerves to the prodigious amount of alcohol imbibed the evening before. There was, if truth be told, a slight aroma of whisky rising off him.

'I don't think I can do this,' he replied. A small part of me smiled – wasn't that supposed to be my line? I patted his hand in daughterly fashion. 'I'm sure you'll be fine,' I said. 'All you have to do is get to the altar without falling over.'

'That's just the problem, S,' he said. 'I don't think I can do that.' He continued. 'I've been a very bad man, S, a very bad man. I haven't been to church since I was a child. I don't know what will happen.' I realised at that point that some part of him genuinely thought that if he walked into the house of God he might burst into flames.

In the event, he made it up the aisle – just about, leaning heavily on my arm before collapsing, relieved, into a pew alongside my mother.

They always say you marry your father. I thought I was doing the precise opposite but, a few years later, I was reminded of that moment when Michael had a similar religious epiphany. It was not long after the 2010 election, in his first months as Secretary of State for Education; Pope Ratzinger was on an official visit, and as Secretary of State, Michael was part of a delegation due to greet him as he addressed a teacher-training college in Twickenham.

But the night before another old friend and flatmate, Marcus Kiggell, who lived just a few doors down from us, came over for supper, bringing with him a particularly nice bottle of single malt as a present. Whisky is not really my thing, so after supper I left them to it. They must have reminisced about old times well into the night, because when I woke up the following morning to do the school run, Michael was sound asleep in a cloud of peaty fumes, and the bottle had just a wee dram left in it.

I took him a cup of tea. 'Aren't you supposed to be meeting the Pope this morning?' I said breezily, albeit with a slightly panicked wifely undertone. There was a momentary pause as Michael's whisky-sodden synapses registered this information, and then he shot out of bed like a scalded cat.

One scalding hot shower, hurried shave and several Alka-Seltzer later, he clattered down the stairs and out the front door into the waiting car. But pretty soon it occurred to him that he was apocalyptically hungover. 'Food,' he thought to himself, 'what I need is food – and coffee.' A strong cappuccino and an almond croissant were duly procured and consumed, and the car sped on towards Twickenham.

By the time Michael got to the school, the combination of alcohol, milky coffee and almond paste had begun to take effect. As he stood in the receiving line, sweating through a pounding headache and swaying ever so slightly, it dawned on him that he now felt alarmingly sick. Clutching Vince Cable's arm for support, he focused his eyes on the floor. Visions of him throwing up on the papal moccasins swam before his eyes, together with the next day's headlines: 'Gove Vomits on Pontiff'; 'Possessed Tory in Papal Assault'. 'Are you alright, Michael?' said Vince. He didn't dare open his mouth to reply.

And then it happened. After what seemed like an eternity, the red papal shoes finally came to a halt in front of him. Benedict XVI clasped Michael's trembling palms in his and uttered a quiet greeting. Michael looked up and, in that very moment, his hangover simply evaporated. The instant his flesh made contact with the papery skin of the Pontiff, he was cured. Verily, it was a miracle.

Anyway, back to the wedding. Afterwards, at the dinner, clearly in high spirits having avoided the wrath of God, Roger spoke hilariously, if rather unnervingly, about his great importance as a shadowy figure of both wealth and influence (others tell me that he even hinted that he was a leading arms dealer, but I missed that – something about the exchange rate between guns and drugs in the Strait of Messina). I looked out over the roomful of laughing, confident men and women that surrounded us and marvelled at how far I had come that these were my actual friends. It was only later that people pointed out that my father, in his entire father-of-the-bride speech, had failed to mention me once. But even that – and my friends' insistence that my mother, in a skin-tight navy and red leather skirt suit, followed by a red, floor-length La Perla sheath, seemed to have done her level best to upstage me – couldn't taint the memory of a day whose events are seen only through a rosy-tinted lens of happiness and pink champagne.

For our honeymoon, we chose Mexico. Again, the connection to politics seemed inescapable. We kicked off in Cancùn, where we spent a few nights at the wildly luxurious Maroma Hotel. A few months previously Tony and Cherie Blair had also spent a brief sojourn there, something the hotel manager was very proud of. Keen for us, as journalists, to experience a sense of the hospitality they had enjoyed, he insisted on introducing us to the same Temazcal ceremony Cherie had experienced. She had reportedly enjoyed it so much the first time, she did it again, insisting that her husband, the prime minister, join her.

It took place in a yurt near the hotel. As we followed our shaman across the sand dunes in bathing costumes, not knowing quite what to expect, I couldn't help wondering what the prime ministerial security detail must have made of the somewhat peculiar arrangement. Inside the tent, a fire was burning, heating a pile of lava rocks over which herb-infused water was thrown, in order to create a 'cleansing sweat' and help balance our energy.

We were told to close our eyes and meditate as Mayan prayers to the four winds were said. I felt utterly absurd, and half opened one eye to peer at Michael in the gloom, whose cheeky wink in return indicated he clearly felt the same.

More water was thrown on the rocks, raising the temperature even further. We were invited to visualise animals in the steam. 'A swan?' I ventured, as a long whisper spiralled up to the ceiling. Apparently, this signified beauty and fertility. 'A bull?' said Michael. This seemed to delight our shaman. 'The bull is a symbol of male virility, power and strength,' she intoned, to which Michael added, 'Yes, I can see more bull, plenty of bull, nothing but bull!'

I shot him a hard stare and tried not to laugh.

The final part of the ritual involved us smearing ourselves in local fruit, including watermelon and papaya, and mud. Then we had to make a wish and scream out loud at the top of our lungs, before walking together into the sea to be cleansed. The whole thing was joyously absurd.

The rest of the honeymoon passed more traditionally. Michael tried (and failed) to get me interested in playing bridge, and there was a spot of bother with Hurricane Michelle, but other than that we had a lovely time.

The honeymoon over, it was back to work for both of us at *The Times*. Michael was on track for greatness there – or at least he was until he inadvertently blotted his copybook during one of those off-site corporate bonding weekends with the big boss, Rupert Murdoch.

I can't remember exactly where it took place (somewhere in America, I think), but after a long day of networking, Michael had decided to have a bath before dinner. He set the water running, then lay down on the bed to relax with a book for a few moments. Next thing he knew, the phone was ringing. It was the reception clerk. Apparently, a fellow guest (whose name may or may not have been Rupert) was incandescent with rage because 'some bloody fool in the room above' had flooded his. Oops.

About six months after our wedding, we moved into our first marital home (up until then, we had been outstaying our welcome at my parents' place in Queensgate) to Barlby Road in what is now called North Kensington, but was then called the North Pole, in part because of its proximity to the actual North Pole Road, but also because it was at the outer reaches of where was considered socially acceptable to live. Indeed, it always made me laugh when we were later described by over-enthusiastic commentators as living in a 'mansion' in Notting Hill. Our cosy 1930s redbrick could not have been more unlike the stucco-fronted villas made famous by Hugh Grant and Julia Roberts in Richard Curtis's eponymous movie. No dreamy garden squares here, or elegant balustrades. It's true that we had a garage that led out onto a cul-de-sac (later very useful for giving my colleagues in the press the slip), but that was mainly used by the local drug dealers and hookers. I once came out the back door with the kids in tow only to walk straight into a young woman entertaining a client in the front seat of his car; on another occasion a small explosive device went off. Later, when the 7/7 bombers were arrested, they were found to be living just behind us.

Another time our car, a K-reg Skoda complete with roof box and Camberley Town bumper sticker, was stolen from outside the house, later recovered burnt out in Wormwood Scrubs. The police were very apologetic, but they never found the culprits. Just joy-riders, apparently.

Personally, I thought this was a bit lame of them. As I wrote at the time, the glove box contained my husband's prized 28-CD collection of Dostoevsky's *The Brothers Karamazov* (unabridged), the collected speeches of Ronald Reagan, *Sigh No More* by Mumford & Sons, Wagner's *Parsifal* and a *Best of The Smiths* collection, all of which appeared to be missing from the wreck. How many Dostoevsky-addicted, Reagan-loving hoodies could there be living in White City?

Don't get me wrong – some of my happiest years were spent at Barlby Road; but a mansion it most certainly was not. Indeed, as Michael's political career progressed, and donors and party grandees started coming to the house on a regular basis, I always enjoyed seeing the slight look of horror on their faces as they would alight from their Bentleys and Jaguars onto the pavement, in between the bookmakers and the No 7 bus stop.

But we made it our own, and the place was soon overflowing with books and friends. Nick very generously bought us our first sofa, as a wedding present, and we entertained around my grandmother's mid-century table with the plates and glasses other guests had given us from our wedding list, from the now defunct General Trading Company in Chelsea. We imagined ourselves very grown up and middle class, to the point that Michael even paid to have an 0207 landline telephone number rather than the 0208 number that Barlby Road had ordinarily (one of those skeweringly accurate descriptions of snobbery that is now as anachronistic as Norman bringing out the fish knives).

This didn't stop my parents being horrified at our new address. The proximity to Wormwood Scrubs didn't help, and neither did the fact that our bid for independence represented something of an inconvenience for them.

Once engaged, Michael and I had lived together in their rather glamorous apartment in Queensgate, which they had bought for a song at the height (depth?) of the early Nineties housing crash. On one level, this certainly ticked all the boxes – an easy commute to Wapping, a swanky postcode to impress those we wanted to impress and on the doorstep of all cultural London: the concerts at the Albert Hall; the parties in the museums of the V&A, Natural History and even the Science Museum; the dinner parties of Notting Hill.

But on a personal level, it was problematic. Bluntly, Michael was very respectful of my parents, but he didn't want to have anything to do with them, and he certainly didn't want to be beholden to them financially. He understood – more perhaps than I did at that time – that my father was neither financially nor emotionally stable, and in particular that he used money as a way to control people in his life.

Knowing that we wanted our own place but couldn't have afforded to buy it from them outright, my parents – who really didn't come to London all that often – proposed a deal. They suggested we buy half of it off them, on the understanding that they would retain the option to come and stay whenever they wanted, along with exclusive use of the master bedroom.

I was keen; but Michael, whose relationship with my father had deteriorated considerably since the wedding, was dead set against it. It wasn't just that he didn't trust Roger, he reasoned that being beholden to him for the very roof over our heads would be a disaster for both of us, but especially for him: that it would, effectively, emasculate him in the eyes of my father. He also judged, rightly, that psychologically I needed to move on.

Not for the last time in my marriage, I felt very torn. I had not yet learned to stand up to my father, and I didn't want to stand up to my new husband. When I look back now, I realise of course that this – my tendency to cave into the demands of the men in my life – has always been one of my greatest flaws; arguably the cause of so many of my many mistakes, the one remnant of my difficult childhood that I've never managed to overcome. Not so much through weakness – few people who know me would say I am weak – more as a result of a certain emotional hardwiring which I have never succeeded in short-circuiting. My father instilled in me at a young age an unshakable sense of inferiority and worthlessness; in many ways it's what drives me. But it also is the source of a great deal of pain and regret, not just for me but for those around me.

In the end, Michael won. I felt a sense of betrayal but also a huge sense of relief at the fact that my father no longer had any agency in my life. Owning our own place gave me a warm glow of both independence and shared enterprise that I could hardly have imagined before I'd met Michael. It was the Goves vs the World, and it felt good. For the first time in my life, I felt like I had someone on my side.

Towards the end of 2002, this sense of belonging became even more relevant when I discovered I was pregnant. I think we were both rather surprised it had happened so soon. In many ways, we didn't feel remotely grown up enough. Michael didn't even drive, for heaven's sake, a shortcoming that came home to roost when I went into labour. I ended up being driven to hospital by Eddie Vaizey, in a bizarre echo of our first official date, when Ed was setting himself up as a positive fall-back from Michael.

My mother always used to say to me that if anyone thought for more than five minutes about what having a baby actually entails, the human race would have been extinct long ago. I think she was right about that. Pregnancy was a whole new world of strangeness and surprise, not so much from a physical point of view (I had a very easy time of it by most measures), more from a cultural standpoint. At the time, most of our friends who were on the baby train were paying to go private. But at £5,000 a pop minimum that just wasn't an option for us. Besides, Queen Charlotte's was just a few stops away on the No 70 bus, and it had a great reputation, not least because it was the professional home of Sir Robert Winston, a.k.a. TV's favourite baby doctor. I've always been a sucker for a TV doctor.

It was my first real experience of the NHS, and quite the eye opener. For a start, I seemed to be the only expectant mother with a job. I would arrive efficiently on time for my appointments, having booked a morning off from the office, only to end up being held up for hours. The idea that I might need to be in and out within a certain timeframe on account of work commitments was treated with a kind of bemused condescension. At times, I would even say I felt unwelcome, as though the staff somehow felt that as a middle-class working mother-to-be, I should be having my baby elsewhere, ideally nowhere near the NHS. One time, having been kept waiting for over an hour and a half because the woman ahead of me had requested a translator and none could be found, I dared to question why she even needed a translator, given that she was there with one of her children, who clearly spoke English. I never made that mistake again.

The ante-natal classes were no different. At the 'geriatric' age of 34, I was almost always the oldest in the group, sometimes older even than the prospective grandmothers-to-be attending with their teenage daughters. Most of the fathers seemed little more than babies themselves, and in many cases unprepared for the responsibilities of fatherhood. Again, I felt like a cuckoo in the nest, as though as one of the few active taxpayers in the room I had no right to be accessing the services to which I was contributing. Some midwives were obviously personally charming but it was as if the politicised and, frankly, fascistic approach of the culture required anyone with intelligence or an enquiring mind to leave such skills at the door and sign up to unthinking obedience. Pain relief in labour was not necessary, we were told, because birthing was a natural thing; the implication being that even asking about it was an admission of failure, that we were doing something to subvert the natural joy of childbirth. I remember being shown slides in which a Native American woman squatted to give birth in a picturesque nature setting and thinking, 'All well and good, but how is this relevant to me?!'

Giving birth did not, it turns out, come naturally to me, so by the midwives' exacting standards, I failed at the first. My beloved daughter Beatrice, contrary before she even drew her first breath, had decided that her debut into the world would be a posterior presentation. That is to say, head down but the wrong way up – also known as 'sunny-side up'. In obstetrics terms, a bit of a cul-de-sac.

Not that I knew any of this nor, apparently, did any of the midwives who came and went, rummaging around inside me, tut-tutting at my inability to dilate effectively. Their solution was to pump me full of Oxytocin to speed up my contractions, which worked but did not have the desired result. After 23 hours of doing everything I was told, I was only a measly 5cm dilated and barely able to catch my breath between excruciating contractions.

Michael meanwhile, not for the first time in a crisis and assuredly not the last, was nose deep in a book, only coming up for air occasionally to complain about how uncomfortable the chairs were. As I wrote afterwards, 'when I was attempting (rather ineptly) to expel our first child, my husband read all of volume three of Robert Caro's biography of Lyndon B. Johnson in the birthing suite: more than 1,000 pages about a dead American president in 23 hours. As far as I recall, he complained only once, and that was to request a proper chair 'instead of this silly beanbag'.

Somewhere around 10 a.m. the duty obstetrician came on her rounds, took one look at me, made a call and before I knew it I was off to theatre for an emergency C-section. Having spent hours being treated at best indifferently, at worst unkindly, by the midwives, I suddenly found myself in the hands of the medics. The difference was remarkable. They were kind, calm, ruthlessly efficient; worlds apart from the amateurish arrogance of the labour ward. Beatrice was duly extracted, bruised and battered but otherwise unscathed, a healthy 8lb 8oz.

That first night with her was both surreal and magical. Dosed up on morphine, I slipped in and out of consciousness, this strange, new little creature cradled in the crook of my arm. Like most new mothers, I was ill prepared for the flood of emotions that accompanied her arrival. You can read all the books, talk to as many people as you like – but until you actually have your own baby, you can't even begin to understand what it feels like. I was transformed.

Like many new fathers, I think Michael struggled to understand the depth of my new obsession. Matters weren't helped by the fact that the day after Beatrice was born he got a call from the new editor at *The Times*, Robert Thomson, offering him a promotion with a vastly increased workload. Our own Caesar was rising through the ranks.

As much as I loved my new baby, I found being a mother absolutely terrifying. My own mother paid a fleeting visit with my father to inspect the new arrival – but then left me to my own devices, not quite ready, I suspect, to assume the role of grandmother. I had read Gina Ford's *The Contented Little Baby Book* – the fashionable manual for new parents at the time – cover to cover but was singularly incapable of following any of her instructions. It was all just a blur of bewilderment, accompanied by a growing feeling that I was wholly unsuited to the role of mother. For the first time in a long time, I felt like a total failure. Judging by what seemed to be Beatrice's perpetual state of rage, she agreed. With Michael busier than ever, I missed him and, if I'm honest, I missed my old life. Looking after a baby was far more taxing than any job I had ever done.

Even in the early years of this century, we all knew about post-natal depression. I would have caught its emergence in someone else – and have done so since, with friends – but it's harder to detect when you're suffering from it yourself; and once you're in the spiral, it needs someone else to throw you a lifeline and pull you out. I've always been so capable, so competent in others' eyes that no one – except for me –

imagined that I would be so frail as to succumb to depression and uncertainty and, with a mother far away in Italy, an unobservant brother in Spain and an increasingly distracted husband, I flailed. And then, as ever, I realised that I was going to be the only one who could dig myself out of this trough ... so I did. Back to work full-time when Bea was five months old, *The Times* was my lifeline.

Unfortunately, I was so busy pulling myself hand-over-hand back to life that I failed to notice that *The Times* was no longer Michael's lifeline. When Bea was three months old we went on holiday to Portugal with what was now our 'gang': Sam and Dave Cameron, Chris and Venetia Lockwood, Eddie Vaizey and Rachel Whetstone. Dave, a long-time friend from Oxford days, was now an MP, as was Eddie (and George Osborne, a more fringe friend through Ed from their St Paul's schooldays) and the talk around the pool was politics, politics, politics. This was no surprise. In our relationship, in our social life, on every sun lounger on every holiday, at every dinner table, in every restaurant, we had always talked politics in the abstract: what I was oblivious to was that for Michael politics was gradually becoming personal.

Back home, Michael and I were fine – within eight months of Bea's birth, I was pregnant again – but I didn't notice that his air of distracted remove had become endemic and that the constant discussion of politics, from the General Election of 2001 onwards, but intensifying through the winter of 2003 and into 2004, had pivoted into an intense campaign by Michael's political friends to bring him over. Stop being a pundit, start being a participant, you know you want to, was how I now imagine the whispering went – not just from the 'gang' but in particular from Steve Hilton, who was working hard behind the scenes with Dave at 'detoxifying' the Tory brand, but also from Michael's great if unofficial mentor, political grandee Michael Howard, who, Michael told me long afterwards, had sat him down and told him firmly that the long-serving Labour Government was going to be taken down and that Michael needed to be part of this. 'We are all going to do this together.'

Juggling full-time work, a baby and another pregnancy, I had no idea what Michael was going to say when he sat me down in the summer of 2004 and gave me his intense, Govean 'stare of import'.

'I know I said, when we got married, that I would never actually try to become an MP. But how would you feel if I did?'

What would have happened if I had said no? I've often asked myself that question. Our lives would have been so different. He would have risen through the ranks of journalism; I probably would never have become a columnist at the *Daily Mail*; we might even still be married.

Instead, I laughed, and told him to go for it. I could see that it was all he wanted to do, and all his friends were doing it too. There was a sense that together, as a big, happy political gang, they might change the world. It seemed to me they had the right ideas, the right motives. There was an energy to it all that was undeniable. Who was I to say he couldn't be part of that?

Besides, I knew it wouldn't happen straight away. First, he would have to get on the candidates list; then it would take ages to secure a safe seat (that was my only caveat: we just didn't have the time or resources for him to fight a marginal).

How wrong I was. Within weeks he was in the running for Surrey Heath, up against another unknown, one Jacob Rees-Mogg. Before the year was out, I had become a Westminster WAG.

CHAPTER THREE

FAKING IT

'The only solution sometimes is to understand that occasionally there is no-one in the entire world who gets it. This is the human state, and there is no pill for it. It is part of the deal ... You can take it. It's life, Jim, just exactly as we know it.'

Sarah Vine & Tania Kindersley, *Backwards in High Heels: The Impossible Art of Being Female* (Fourth Estate, 2009)

LESSON TWO IN HOW NOT TO BE A POLITICAL WIFE: stay trapped in an out-of-body experience, where you constantly look around incredulously and think, 'How. The. Hell. Did. I. Get. Here?'

This was the default description for how I felt from the moment Michael went into politics to the minute when I reluctantly left him – and politics – behind. Even when I was having fun, larking around by the pool in Ibiza with Sam Cameron or mixing cocktails at Chequers, or in those grander moments of front-row incredulity, like having supper with the King and Queen at Clarence House, or going to one of Rupert Murdoch's weddings, there would always be a moment when the fat, awkward child within me would rear her large head and whisper in my ear, 'You're a fake. You don't belong here.'

I was, after all, painfully experienced at feeling like an imposter, right from the moment of my birth. Because, let's remember, I should never have been born. That's what my father told me in his angriest, unkindest and usually drunkest moments, that I was the unwanted product of a summer romance and, if I'd been conceived just six months later, when abortion was legalised in the UK, that might well have been my fate (indeed, it might also have been Michael's fate – he was born in the August of 1967, and given up for adoption by his birth mother).

When it came to their romance in 1966, my father should have been the imposter: the homegrown Welsh boy from Mumbles, still living at home as a Swansea University student, punching far above his weight with my mother, the delicately gorgeous English colonel's daughter heading to university after a summer on the 'Welsh Riviera'. But this was a man who, in his prime, looked like a clever version of George Best: bright-eyed, shaggy-haired, virile and with enough swagger to bottle and sell.

History does not relate the exact time and location of my

parents' first encounter, but I do recall my father telling me that her presence behind the bar at the Langland Bay Hotel that summer caused quite a stir. He once told my son that the reason he stayed so close to home for university was because, after 'extensive' research into which further education establishments had the 'best birds', he concluded that Swansea was top for talent.

According to my godfather, my mother was a 'sensation', inundated with offers of drinks from enthusiastic punters which she accepted gracefully and sent them the way of my father. She was the diamond of the season – and she was his. It might have been the perfect fleeting summer romance. But then I came along and ruined everything. Not, some might say, for the last time.

We've all seen this rom-com. Local handsome boy sweeps beautiful but shy incomer off her feet in summer romance, blind to all differences between them, obstacles knocked flat before the rush of sun and sex and summer fun. Trouble is, this was Wales in the Sixties, and rather more your kitchen-sink drama.

She and Roger were barely 20. Rosemary, bright and promising, was due to go to university that autumn. Roger was only in his second year at the University of Swansea, still living at home in his parents' tiny terraced home, paying rent to his father, a few streets back from the seafront of Mumbles, one of the houses still with an outside loo, hardly a penny to his name.

But my father has never allowed circumstances to hold him back, an attitude nurtured in him by his father Bernard, a bank clerk with a dream of higher horizons for his clever, grammar-school-boy youngest son. Under the hard eye of

Bernard – or Niggin, as I later knew him – Roger had always been schooled for great things.

It was Bernard/Niggin who insisted he learn to play the violin, on a three-quarter-sized instrument brought back from Germany after the War. Bernard – and Gwen, my grand-mother – had a deep love of classical music and in particular the violin, which stemmed in part from an incident during the War. On a precious night off, the rest of his platoon went to the cinema; Bernard had declined, preferring to attend a violin recital instead. When he emerged from his concert, his companions were gone; killed by a German bomb that had flattened their cinema. He'd made the better choice.

It may well have been an apocryphal story (so many were when it came to my father's side of the family), but it never-theless served as a motivating force. My father's older brother John had been born before the War, and had not made it to grammar school. Bernard was not taking any risks with young Roger going the same way. He seems to have come back from war with an urgent desire to produce a child prod-igy. I think if he had been less hard and demanding with my father, or a tad more forgiving, he might well have succeeded in nurturing Roger's many talents. Instead, I fear, he created someone who, while brilliant in many ways, was also very damaged.

According to my father's own account, Bernard drilled Roger for hours at chess, all as part of an all-round quest for excellence, and regularly threatened to break his fingers if he failed to hit the right note on the violin. Such was my father's ability that he was offered a place at the Royal Academy of Music – but his father made him turn it down on the grounds that unless he was good enough to become a top soloist, being a musician would be a poverty-stricken existence, taking hard to please to new summits.

But perhaps the most significant moment in my father's young life came around the age of 16 when he reached the semi-finals at Junior Wimbledon (he really was quite gifted at tennis). After the quarter-final match, he had broken his racquet during practice and, in a moment of meanness, Bernard refused to buy him a new one. So my father played in the semi-final with the broken racquet, and duly lost in straight sets. 'I promised myself then,' he told me many years later, when we were having one of our many conversations about his undeniably avaricious nature, 'that I would never find myself in the position where I could not buy my own racquet.'

Again, how true these stories are is hard to tell. I remember Niggin as a benign, endlessly patient grandfather who would make me Ready Brek laced with condensed milk while all the other adults were sleeping, sipping strong tea from the saucer while enjoying his first fag of the day. But given my own father's subsequent behaviour towards me, they don't seem entirely implausible. During his own ill-fated attempts to teach me the violin, which more often than not would end with me in tears and him raging about what a total and utter 'retard' I was, he would tell me that Paganini's father broke his son's little finger in order to achieve the necessary reach. In vain, I would stretch my own deficient digits as far as I could: my hands were most emphatically not those of a musician. Broad palms, stubby, rather thick fingers, more suited to manual work than the arts.

Nor, sadly, was I 'shaped for sportive tricks' (like many grammar school boys of his generation my father had – and still has – a Shakespeare quote for every occasion). Not quite the misshapen hunchback of Richard III, I was nevertheless encumbered by my extreme myopia which, as well as compelling me to wear unflattering bottle-bottom glasses which made my eyes look 'like piss-holes in the snow', impeded my ability to play games, and in particular tennis, yet another source of my father's un-concealed disappointment.

But back to 1966. Fair to say, then, that both sets of grandparents-to-be were less than delighted by the news of my impending arrival. My uncle Tim – my mother's brother – remembers his parents being very disappointed with Rosemary's choice.

'I didn't go to the wedding,' he recalled, when I asked him about those days. 'I know Ruth and Arthur (my maternal grandparents) were very disappointed with her choice! I think they'd hoped for a posh match for their beautiful daughter. I may be putting my own take on it, but I think Arthur especially struggled with it. Roger was often very rude to him, and he wanted to like whoever his darling Rosemary was with, but he really struggled.

'Honestly, one of my early impressions of Roger was arrogance,' he adds. 'I do remember him lecturing my father about his beliefs and politics – whilst sitting at his table.

'I think he forgot – or perhaps never knew – that Arthur also came from working-class Welsh roots: his father had been a boiler-maker. Unlike Roger, there wasn't access to university, or he'd probably also have gone, and become an engineer. He loved cars, and nature. As a boy he used to ride his cycle off into the hills, and he loved watching otters. Instead at 22, about the same age that Roger was delivering his lectures, he was trudging his arse towards Dunkirk.'

The War was incredibly traumatic for many young couples like my grandparents. Commissioned around 1939, Arthur was in his early twenties, a strapping six foot two, and strikingly handsome. The War took him from France to Dunkirk, Crete, Tobruk, North Africa, India and Burma. After a few months in the Burmese jungle, where he fought as a Chindit, he emerged, he told my uncle, 'weighing under 8 stone and riddled with every tropical disease you can think of'. Tim still has the sword of the Japanese officer who came at him intending to take his head off. Arthur shot him from just feet away, but he always said he 'came at me every night for years'.

There were other things too, even worse things that would make him tremble, made him wake up sweating and screaming, but seldom talk about. One time he did unburden himself was with my uncle when Tim was 19 or 20, not much younger than Arthur was at the beginning of the War. They were watching a docudrama on TV about the Chindits and Arthur suddenly said, 'Hang on, I knew him,' pointing at a face pictured on the TV screen, 'I served with him!'

For the next four hours, sometimes struggling to keep his composure, he opened up. There were heartbreaking tales of young friends and revered superiors being killed beside him in the bloody campaigns of Dunkirk, Crete and Tobruk, but it was when talking about Burma that he started to stumble and stammer. In common with so many others from that terrible campaign, Arthur, it turned out, had had to do the worst thing an officer ever has to do behind enemy lines: he had killed some of his own men, as an act of kindness, because they were too sick or wounded to carry on and no one wanted to end up in the hands of the Japanese. 'I did some things you shouldn't have to do,' he said haltingly to Tim. 'Nobody else can understand.' He drank hard to silence the memories, and eventually drank himself to death.

Ruth, Arthur's wife and my maternal grandmother, was one of six – three girls, Esther, Ruth and Mary, and three boys. The girls all married; one of the brothers emigrated to Australia, another to South Africa; the third stayed behind and became the local ne'er-do-well: Mary's husband used to bail him out from time to time. Ruth's family were tenant farmers in Norfolk, but she always harboured grander ambitions, always dreamed of going up in the world – and never really lost the fear that her humble background might come out.

By the time I knew her, she and my grandfather were living in a tidy little two-bedroom terrace in Bickley, Kent, with a Ford Cortina in the garage and the railway at the bottom of the garden. She kept an immaculate house, like most Army wives, and was very particular about her appearance. She used to love catching the train to London to spend the day at Harrods or Harvey Nichols, impeccably turned out, browsing the racks of clothes she couldn't possibly afford, making careful little purchases to squirrel home with her, persuading the sales assistants to give her samples of this or that perfume or face cream. For the journey, she would make mouth-watering sandwiches, bread sliced wafer thin, butter thick and salty, filled with cucumber or chicken, and a flask of perfumed Earl Grey tea. Preparation would entail a lengthy session in front of her dressing table, still in her bed jacket, 'putting on' her face, as she used to call it. I was fascinated by her process, struck by her ability to make C&A look like Chanel. She had a few simple rules: always invest in a good coat and shoes, accessorise with care, look after things. She would spend hours sitting in front of the telly, plucking her jumpers to remove the pilling, repairing hems. She was the personification of 'make do and mend'. But she also had an innate sense of style that no amount of money can ever buy.

At the outbreak of war she was pregnant with my aunt, Susan. She moved back to Norfolk, where she may or may not have made friends with a few American airmen. By the time my grandfather came back from the War, physically wrecked, deeply scarred and with the seeds of the raging alcoholism that was eventually to kill him already firmly implanted in his psyche, they were total strangers. She really had no concept of Arthur's war, and I'm not sure he ever told her about it. My mother was born the following year, and he absolutely adored her. Having been absent for the first five years of Susan's life, he hardly knew her; but Rosemary was the apple of his eye.

Having remained in the Army after the War (he rose to the rank of Lieutenant Colonel in the Royal Electrical and Mechanical Engineers), Arthur was posted to Singapore and Malaysia. Ruth and the girls went out to join him (both sisters were later sent back to school in the UK at a heartbreakingly young age). The story goes that Ruth – who was always rather glamorous, just like my own mother – met a wealthy planter on the way to Sri Lanka, who wanted her to get off (the boat) with him. She declined, and she and Arthur lived in the Far East for a number of years before tragedy struck: Ruth gave birth to a stillborn baby, delivered by a drunk Army doctor.

Arthur was devastated and furious; Ruth, not surprisingly, had a breakdown. Later, after my uncle was born in 1956, she suffered from terrible post-natal depression. The children, including the infant Tim, were sent to live with her sister Mary and her husband Reg (two of the kindest people I ever set eyes on), and she was sent to a psychiatric institution, where they gave her electric shock treatment, against her will. By the time she was released, Tim was three. What must she have gone through, having her baby and two young daughters taken away from her, then locked away and subjected to that?

The fact that either of them managed to live even a half normal life after all that strikes me as a miracle by today's standards; but then they weren't the only ones whose lives had been irrevocably altered by the War. Half the population was in the same boat, battle scarred and weary, brutalised by the things they had seen and done, traumatised by the loss of loved ones. They just got on with it: they had no choice. But you can understand why the callow attitude of a young man such as the 20-year-old Roger got thoroughly up Arthur's nose.

'Roger hated the Germans,' Tim remembers. 'My father, despite having fought both them and the Japanese, hated neither. He knew bad things happened, and there were bad people – but he had seen too much suffering during the war for yet more hatred. Interestingly, Roger didn't hate the Germans because of the slaughter, or the Holocaust. I remember this very clearly: he hated them because they made Britain poorer with the cost of the war, and that made *him* poorer. I remember even then being astounded at his even making the war about *him*. And then, of course, having taken a free education and post-grad, as soon as he was able, he left the country before he might have to pay some taxes.'

Nonetheless there was a wedding for Roger and Rosemary – for which Arthur wore his ceremonial sword, his regimental moustache twitching as he fingered his weapon threateningly throughout the proceedings. I was born the following April, an enormous, unsightly 10lb 4oz, two weeks overdue, covered in dark hair and with remarkably large feet.

Having almost killed my mother and myself in the process of exiting the womb, I was kept in an incubator for two weeks. The doctors assured my poor mother that I would almost certainly present as brain damaged in one way or another, and perhaps they were not wrong. I was certainly not what you might call 'neurotypical' at school. I have always had a very poor memory, I struggle with numbers – and I have always suffered from acute levels of anxiety, even as a child. Decades later, I had a brain scan as part of a health piece I was writing for the newspaper. The right side of my brain appeared to have perfectly normal function, the lines of neural activity neat and consistent; the other side looked like a child's crayon drawing, just one giant, random scribble. The specialist wanted to know if I had ever sustained a serious brain injury. It certainly might explain a few things.

Little surprise, then, that I always felt painfully different to everyone else and never more painfully was this in evidence than when Michael introduced me formally to constituency politics. Michael insists that I have a faulty memory about this period. In my head, spinning anyway with the twin shock of having one child under one and another one on the way, I remember not actually thinking about it all that much – just being along for the ride from the moment all those cosy, rambunctious dinner-table chats about the Big Society, education, self-responsibility and so on, suddenly coalesced into two words: Surrey Heath.

I had never even heard of Surrey Heath, much less been there, unless unwittingly while speeding down the M3 on the way to the West Country. Comprising Lightwater, Camberley and Frimley Green, it was the epitome of a certain type of English suburbia, what might once have been termed Betjeman country. Miss J. Hunter Dunn, Aldershot sun, the six o'clock news and a lime juice and gin, dancing at the golf club, nine o'clock Camberley heavy with bells: you know the famous poem. The reality was rather more prosaic, a somewhat soulless tangle of grey roundabouts, shopping centres and cul-de-sacs. Everything was perfectly neat and tidy, and the people were (for the most part) lovely; but there was just a soullessness to it. Despite having some great expanses of greenery – at one point the highest concentration of forest in the UK – it had none of the blousy charm of the Surrey Hills, none of the prim elegance of Farnham or Guildford, none of the gin 'n' jag swagger of Ascot. Even Bagshot, home to Bagshot Park, the official residence of the Duke and Duchess of Edinburgh, was strangely nondescript as a town. Chobham and Windlesham were nice, but boy did they – and their inhabitants – know it. Home to a thousand Hyacinth Bouquets.

I knew nothing of this, of course, when Michael announced he was in the running there. We had been told time and again by friends who had been through the process that it could take many attempts to be put forward for selection, and then even longer to actually win a candidacy. But, for whatever reason, he'd got his foot in the door quicker than expected. I was by no means prepared – and neither, I don't think, was he.

Truth is, becoming an MP or, in my case, a Westminster WAG is not something you can really comprehend until it happens to you. In that sense it's a bit like childbirth: you can read all the books, speak to your friends, do all the pelvic floor and breathing exercises, but until you actually push a small human out of your vagina, you've no concept of what you're letting yourself in for.

And besides, people only tell you the good bits about politics. It's like when friends move to an edgy new area of town. They never mention the crackheads or the local hooligans, they just wax lyrical about the splendid architecture and that wonderful new artisanal cafe that's opened up between the dodgy phone repair shop and the bookies, hoping you'll move there too.

It was a bit like that with the Tory Party. At that stage, with Tony Blair's Labour riding high and the Tories very much in the doldrums, becoming a Conservative MP felt a bit like moving to W10 before it became gentrified. Which was also, as it happened, precisely what Dave and Sam had done.

I remember countless cosy, twinkly evenings at their gorgeous house just off Oxford Gardens, which they had bought for a relative song at the end of the Nineties, when prices were low and when anywhere north of the Westway was considered cowboy country. Sam had her mother Lady Annabel's keen eye for interior design, and a clean, almost utilitarian aesthetic which was reflected in her art school paintings, dotted around the place. The result was a stylish combination of ancient and modern, the stainless-steel kitchen countertops contrasting with the vintage furniture, along with the occasional OKA prototype which Annabel had rejected or was simply testing out.

Sam was the personification of effortless chic while most of us were still struggling, metaphorically, to hold a knife and fork. She was cool, younger than Dave, and into music and fashion but also focused and functional. But she was also incredibly kind, and very welcoming – the absolute opposite of a snob, which some of Michael's Oxford circle had a slight tendency to be (then again, she studied at Bristol and, famously, had hung out with the likes of trip-hop legend Tricky, a far cry from the Bullingdon Club, which Dave had belonged to). She seemed to have endless equally cool step-brothers and sisters, including her own sister from her mother's first marriage to Reggie Sheffield, Emily, who worked at *Vogue* and later went on to become the editor of the *Evening Standard*. They were like opposite sides of the same coin, Sam endlessly upbeat and generous, Emily rather spikier and, I was later to discover, quite spiteful.

Dave had been elected as the Member of Parliament for Witney in 2001, the summer before Michael and I got married. I have a gorgeous picture of them together at the wedding looking absurdly young, Dave cherubic, Sam still blonde.

Those were the happiest of days, a whirlwind of invitations and social excursions. Earlier, towards the end of summer, we had been invited to stay with Sam's mother and stepfather, William Astor, at Annabel's fabulous house on the Scottish island of Jura. Not having grown up in that set, and never having studied at Oxford, it was my first real experience of that icon of British upper-class life – the windswept, highly impractical yet utterly charming ancestral pile.

Sam's father, the effusive Reggie, had the magnificent if somewhat bleak Sutton Park in Yorkshire; the rather more bohemian William and Annabel had a bothy on Jura, which she had transformed from three buildings into one house, creating an oasis of rustic style. I remember lots of scrubbed wood and stone, a warm, cosy kitchen, deep, inviting sofas and a well-stocked cellar. The entire place was lit by gaslight, roaring fires in every room and there was a huge bath full of peaty water into which to sink after a day amid the mist and midges. William and Annabel were the most generous of hosts. It was magical.

It was also not easy to get to. Indeed, George Orwell, who wrote the novel *Nineteen Eighty-Four* on Jura, once described the island as 'an extremely un-getable place'. Having flown to Glasgow the plan was to get a ferry to the island from Oban. But the bad weather followed us, and by the time we got there we had missed the last ferry. Undeterred, Dave – never a man to be put off by a bit of bad weather – knew a man with a rib further down the coast prepared to take us, and we bundled aboard.

Michael is not a happy sailor at the best of times, perhaps because, having been adopted by a family of fishermen in Aberdeen, he is acutely aware of the dangers of the ocean. That part of the world is also famous for the Corryvreckan Whirlpool, the world's third largest, which forms at certain tides, in the narrow straits between Jura and Scarba – and which we had to pass in order to reach our destination. He was understandably apprehensive. I, not having any real sense of the danger, was characteristically gung-ho, like Dave.

We decided to go for it. I shall never forget that crossing: the grey sea, the huge swells, the sound of the engine, the boat rising up at every wave then slamming back down into the water with a jolt. It was as exhilarating as it was terrifying – and probably very reckless. I remember sitting at the back with Sam, clinging on for dear life, laughing nervously as we sped through the water, skirting the dreaded whirlpool, while Michael sat low in the hull, somewhat ashen faced. Dave, characteristically, was upfront next to the skipper, seemingly fearless, face to the wind and spray, clearly enjoying the ride.

By the time we arrived we were sodden and freezing. The house stood alone on the shore like something out of *Robinson Crusoe*, with the Paps of Jura behind. William came down to the bay to greet us in his waders, grinning from ear to ear, laughing at our wet luggage, especially mine. Not having anticipated such close proximity to the elements, I had foolishly brought along a rather chic leather weekend backpack that had been a present from Michael, and which was now soaked in brine. 'Schoolgirl error,' observed William cheerfully, as we picked our way over the rocks onto dry land and restorative tea and cake.

The rest of that trip opened my eyes to a world I had read about in books and novels, but never actually experienced first-hand. A world of faithful, elderly retainers and wise old ghillies, of deer stalking and fishing, early morning swims in the freezing sea (Dave being a particularly enthusiastic proponent, emerging ruddy and glistening from the waves, steam rising gently off him in the freezing air), smoking fish over hot coals and boozy, rowdy dinners in front of a roaring fire. I was struck by the way everyone just said exactly what they thought, boldly, unapologetically. I realised then that that's the real difference between the British upper classes and the rest of the world: that innate confidence, that effortless self-assurance that comes with generations of wealth and status. It was intoxicating.

Dave may have been a new bug in the House of Commons, but it was clear from the start that he was in it to win it. By the time the notion of running for parliament had begun to solidify in Michael's mind, Dave was already some way up the greasy pole of politics, a mover and shaker in the re-emerging Conservative Party under Michael Howard.

Surrey Heath was a very different prospect to Dave's seat, Witney. Both were true blue at that time, but while Witney was more gentleman farmers and fox hunting, Surrey Heath was aspirational lower-to-middle-class professionals. As one of that tribe himself, this suited Michael down to the ground.

The Association agent, Alan Cleverley, was larger than life, a man of generous spirit and tastes who embraced his role with gusto. In many ways, Alan personified your average consituent, an aspirational self-starter and bon viveur with a finger in many pies. He was a leading light of something called the Strangers' Gallery Club, which would host glittering fundraisers for the good burghers of Surrey Heath at The Dorchester each year, always with a guest speaker. One year we had Carol Vorderman, when she was in her pro-Tory phase (as opposed to her sucking up to Labour phase): rarely have I encountered such a heavily cantilevered bosom; another time we had Julian Fellowes, creator of *Downton Abbey*, who regaled us all with tales of Hollywood; Roger Lewis, the writer, brought the house down with his unique brand of wry humour. Always Alan would preside over events with a mixture of pride and panic, forever fretting (unnecessarily) about the arrangements. He was a great one for a gavel, and loved to make important announcements in his booming baritone. Things were never quite the same after he passed away in 2016 from cancer.

Being pregnant with our son William, while looking after our 1-year-old Beatrice and having gone back to work at *The Times* full-time, I didn't have much to do with the early stages of Michael's selection. I was vaguely aware of debates and hustings, most of which took place in the evenings or weekends, but otherwise really didn't pay that much attention. Besides, I don't think either of us expected him to get down to the final list.

But he did. The night of the final speeches, we drove to the Lakeside Hotel in Frimley Park (also, as it happens, the home of International Darts) and sat in the car park beforehand, rehearsing his arguments and waiting for the proceedings to start. I remember spotting a pair of magpies and thinking that was a good omen: I had a strong sense that his dream was about to come true.

It seems faintly ludicrous, but I had been barred from the room for this final stage on the grounds that my pregnancy might give Michael an unfair advantage over the other candidates, who were so far childless (the irony: one of them was Jacob Rees-Mogg, now procreator extraordinaire).

This suited me just fine. I don't think my presence would have helped Michael's nerves, and in any case at this stage I still very much saw this as a 'him' project, not an 'us'.

So, me and my ostentatiously fertile womb were banished out of sight to another part of the hotel, where I sat in the bar sipping mineral water and twiddling my thumbs (those were the days before smartphones) while waiting for events to unfold.

A few minutes in, and my eyes alighted on another guest, who looked remarkably familiar. I looked again, and realised it was none other than Jim Davidson, host of *The Generation Game* and everyone's favourite sexist comedian. We got chatting, as you do. I expected him to be a bit of an oaf; instead I found him utterly charming, if a little rough around the edges. I told him what I was doing there, and he wished Michael luck, and raised a glass to us. 'Rather you than me, darlin',' he said. It was an early lesson in the way fame can distort someone's true persona. Years later, after he founded his veterans' charity, Care After Combat, it was a privilege to sit next to him at a fundraiser. Altogether, a much-maligned man who has ended up doing more good in the world than plenty of others who tick more PC boxes.

Sometime around 9 p.m., a jubilant Alan burst into the bar, followed by a flushed-looking Michael and various other leading members of the Surrey Heath Conservative Association. He had won! By over 50 per cent of the vote! There followed an evening of celebration, fuelled by copious amounts of red wine.

5 July 2004: the night I became a Westminster WAG.

There was no time to lose. The election was the following May, and although it was a 'safe' seat, the Conservatives' standing in the constituency had taken a bit of a beating after Michael's predecessor had stepped down under a cloud. There was much pressing of doorbells – not to mention flesh – to be done.

There was also the small matter of money. Michael had – rightly – promised that if he were selected to fight the seat, he would step down from his role as Saturday editor of *The Times*. I was back working, but on a much smaller salary than him – and besides, most of mine went on childcare. Not for the first time in the history of working mothers, I found myself effectively paying for the privilege of going to the office every day.

The Times were very understanding, allowing Michael to take up a position as a columnist which, together with his eventual MP's salary, would avoid a catastrophic drop in earnings. But I don't think either of us had quite factored in the additional costs of running for office, from basic things like train tickets to extra childcare and the big one: setting up a base in the constituency. Neither of us were in a position to ask our parents for help (Michael's didn't have any spare cash, and mine would have certainly said no), so we were on our own. We decided to rent out our house in Barlby Road and move full-time to Camberley.

With hindsight, this was not a wise decision. But at the time, not only did I think it was the right thing to do, I also thought it was the best way of ensuring Michael embraced his new role without bankrupting us.

The last trimester of my pregnancy was a blur of packing, unpacking and a growing sense of astonishment that my husband, whom I thought I knew, had suddenly become something of a stranger to me. Michael threw himself into the selection with a man-of-the-people gusto and focus that, I think, surprised even him.

Nonsense, says Michael, when I share this memory with him. For a start, he insists that it was actually my words that opened the floodgates of politics for him. Apparently, at lunch with the Camerons in Oxfordshire, I looked at him after the usual blandishments and coaxing flattery from Dave and Sam about how it was time for Michael to flex his political muscles and said, 'Oh yes, why don't you?'

He also says it was my idea to move lock, stock and smoking barrel to the countryside. 'You have always oscillated between liking the hustle, bustle and friendships of London and yearning for the space and seclusion of the country – and it was you who pointed out that we would save money while you weren't earning your usual wedge during maternity leave by renting out the house in Barlby Road. You genuinely gave the impression that you welcomed the switchback element of the rollercoaster ride that our lives had become.'

I don't doubt that I did indeed give that impression. But then I have always had a pervasive desire to please the people in my life. If I think someone I love really wants or needs something, I will adopt a blanket can-do attitude. Or at least I did back then. These days, I'm a recalcitrant old cow.

But in truth the real reason I failed to voice any misgivings was because, really, I didn't have any. I had no sense of what we were really getting ourselves into. I was just swept up in the excitement of it all, and the idea of being part of something with friends. And the model I had – the effortless Dave and Sam – made it all look so easy. Naively – arrogantly, you might even say – I thought it would be the same for us.

Ever the persuasive influencer, Michael even claims that I embraced the life of a candidate's wife with the vim and vigour of the new convert; pointing to the fact that I set up a Surrey Heath Conservatives' patrons' club called Vines, with me as president, as inescapable evidence.

Oddly, I have no recollection whatsoever of this, although I wouldn't necessarily dispute it. Michael had two affectionate nicknames for me. The first was Mrs Blurt, based on my uncanny ability to say precisely the wrong thing at the wrong time in any given social setting (a skill I retain to this day and one that is crucial to not being a good political wife); the second was Amnesiac Squirrel, for my tendency to forget important dates and items of significance, coupled with my ability to be distracted by the smallest thing, especially if the matter at hand was in any way tedious or time consuming.

Both nicknames, if I'm honest, were entirely fair and justified. Several of my friends have, over the years, wondered aloud whether I might not, in fact, have raging ADHD. One of my closest friends, who is an expert on these things, says I'm the most ADHD person she's ever met. I have never sought a diagnosis and since middle-aged women with ADHD seem to be all the rage these days, I probably won't, since I've never liked to be a cliché; all I know is that it has taken me a lifetime of serious self-discipline to develop what most people would consider a fairly rudimentary level of organisational skills. I remain forgetful, impulsive and I am a terrible interrupter. On the plus side, I'm generally not dull.

Either way: the moral of the story is never make any major life decisions/promises when your body is awash with lovely fuzzy pregnancy hormones. You will inevitably agree to things that, were you in your right mind and not under the influence of nature's most powerful happy chemicals, you wouldn't dream of doing.

I have always been a creature of strong passions – while they last. But even if I did sail off into the Surrey heathland with a determination to turn the rather 1950s image of a political spouse into a modern Technicolour banner image of a triumphant galvanising partner, effortlessly juggling work and children with our new joint venture, then disillusionment set in quick. It only took a few dinners with some of the more antediluvian grandees of the SH Conservative Association to push me off course. I was heavily pregnant and it was Michael they had come to see; who was I kidding that I had any skin in this game?

William was born in November 2004, just a few months after Michael was selected to be the official Tory candidate. He arrived a week early by elective caesarean at Frimley Park Hospital, his birth as calm and well-ordered as his sister's had been fraught and chaotic. That difference seemed to be reflected in their personalities: where Beatrice was a spiky, feisty little thing, he was the easiest of babies, a snuggly little Boule de Suif, the human equivalent of a Labrador puppy who loved his food and his naps.

It's always the easy ones who lull you into a false sense of security. At three months old, while on a family break in France with friends, I noticed something wasn't quite right. My hitherto perfect baby began to fuss all the time, crying incessantly, never settling, never happy, hardly feeding. I put it down to teething pains, but on the flight home he was hysterical, his cries indicative of something more.

Before leaving, I had noticed that one of his ears seemed a bit sore, and had asked the nurse midwife at the baby clinic if he perhaps needed antibiotics for an infection. Nonsense, she told me, in that annoying way that nurse midwives have, it was just a bit of baby eczema and, besides, antibiotics were the Devil's work. I protested, explaining that ear infections run in my family (I spent much of my childhood with otitis, which can be extremely painful) and I recognised the signs.

Still, she refused (midwife mantra: mother *never* knows best), telling me I was just being an 'over-anxious mum'.

A couple of days after we returned home from holiday, after a particularly fractious night, I lay him down on the bed after feeding him and suddenly noticed something very odd. His ear, the sore one, appeared to have moved, sticking out at an odd angle, and it was oozing some sort of brown goo. I knew that something was very wrong.

I rang the clinic, but they had no free appointments. I protested, and eventually the receptionist relented and said I could come at the end of surgery and wait to see if the doctor could fit me in. After waiting for what seemed like forever, I was eventually ushered in. The doctor examined him, and an expression of surprise and disbelief crossed his face. He took a book down from his shelf, checked something, checked William again and then turned to me. 'I've never actually seen this before,' he said. 'In fact, I'm not sure they even still teach it in medical school. But if I'm not mistaken, your son has mastoiditis – an inflammation of the mastoid bone behind the ear. It used to be a common childhood disease before antibiotics – but it's virtually unheard of these days. He needs to go straight to hospital. I'll ring ahead and tell them to expect you.'

At Frimley Park they admitted us and put him straight on intravenous antibiotics. A scan revealed a large abscess behind the mastoid bone, which was what had caused the ear tissue to move. 'But you can fix it, right?' I asked the consultant. He was hopeful, he said, but it wasn't guaranteed. He explained that the infection was quite advanced, and that the antibiotics might not work. The problem, he explained, was that the mastoid bone is essentially like a honeycomb, full of air holes (for sound amplification) and low on blood supply, making it hard for intravenous drugs to reach. In a child that small, the problem was compounded. They would give it a try – but if it didn't work he would need an operation to drain the swelling.

What he didn't say, but which I quickly realised after some basic research, was that mastoiditis used to be a leading cause of child mortality – before the advent of antibiotics, etc. It's also a complication of otitis. I spent the night in hospital kicking myself and pacing desperately.

The next day, William was no better – indeed, if anything he was worse, drowsy and unresponsive. The antibiotics were not doing their job: a mastoidectomy – in which a portion of the bone is removed and the infection drained – was the next step. But the problem was his age: Frimley did not have the expertise or the paediatric staff to perform the procedure, so the decision was made to transfer him to St George's, Tooting, in London, where a specialist team was being assembled.

I'll never forget that awful ambulance ride, speeding along the A3 with our tiny, very sick son in his car seat, both of us in stunned silence. It felt very frightening to think that we might lose him over something as trivial as an ear infection. Once again, I cursed myself for not being firmer with the nurse.

At St George's we were met by the surgeon and the paediatric anaesthetist (a precise skill, I now realise), and within a few short hours Will was in theatre. Thanks to their incredible skill the abscess was drained, the site packed with antibiotics and my son was returned to me; trussed up like a turkey and bristling with tubes, but alive. Now we just had to wait and see.

It was a sobering, exhausting and deeply humbling experience. Indeed, over the course of the next two weeks I came to realise how truly lucky I was, not only to have one healthy child at home (albeit furious that I had 'abandoned' her, something she still brings up on a regular basis) but to have a baby son who, ultimately, was on the mend, thanks to being in the care of experts. There were plenty of parents alongside me in that draughty paediatric ward whose children were seriously, sometimes terminally ill. We would shuffle in and out of the shared parental kitchen, making endless cups of tea and talking in hushed tones, the bags under our eyes and general dishevelment testimony to the grenades that had gone off in our hearts.

I thought also of Ivan, Sam and Dave's first child, who was seriously ill with Ohtahara Syndrome, a condition which left him prey to constant epileptic fits, and his poor parents in a permanent state of exhaustion. He needed round-the-clock care, and they had been told he would never live a conventional life. I remember visiting them at their home in Oxfordshire a few months after his diagnosis, and seeing the deep sadness in their eyes as they cradled their tiny, very sick baby. It was nothing short of heartbreaking. I finally had a tiny inkling of what they had been going through, and it was very humbling. My admiration for them both only increased.

These were the thoughts running through my head, up there in my mother and baby room, the lights of London twinkling beneath me at night, nothing but Radio 4 to keep me company. Michael brought Beatrice to visit once or twice, then sped off, back to work, leaving her in the care of a hastily arranged live-in nanny, recommended by some friends of ours. But what else could he do? By this time, he was in his own hamster wheel of getting up early, commuting to London by train from Woking and working as a speechwriter for Howard, tasked with taking the Conservatives into the 2005 election.

He was at the frontline and couldn't have been happier; I, by contrast, was in a slightly different place.

CHAPTER FOUR

THE NAKED CAR CHASE

> *'How Not To Go Mad, Part Three: Never try to change a man. You know this, but sometimes it is necessary to be reminded. You can polish him up a little, buy him a sharp suit, make gentle hints about getting rid of that fringe. But you can never change him in any fundamental way. Love him just the way he is, otherwise you are setting yourself up for the heartbreak of dashed expectations.'*
>
> Sarah Vine & Tania Kindersley, *Backwards in High Heels: The Impossible Art of Being Female*
> (Fourth Estate, 2009)

Will's illness had been a real shock to the system. I blamed myself, of course – but I also saw it as an extension of my general inability to get parenting right.

I hated the feeling of being cut off from any friends I could appeal to for support or advice. I was so exhausted, so bone-crushingly tired, that I couldn't do my usual trick of reasoning my way out of the maze. Despite endless breast-feeding, I was failing to lose any baby-weight. The feeding really took it out of me, left me feeling exhausted and greedy in the evenings when, alone in front of the TV, I would console myself with bars of Green & Black's almond choco-late. Not even the hungriest baby needed that many calories. I was also, yet again, losing my hair so I was becoming bald – balder it seemed than the last few times it had all fallen out. My self-hatred plumbed new depths.

If I'm honest, this next period is all a bit of a blur. I remem-ber returning home with William, and the endless post-operative check-ups. The doctors seemed very worried about his immune system – in addition to the mastoiditis he had terrible eczema, which would sometimes become infected. I tried endless solutions – the mildest washing powders, restricting my diet, covering him in 50/50 cream – but always it would come back. No one seemed to know what was causing it or what to do about it.

At one point one of the specialists asked me, somewhat sheepishly, if there was any chance that Michael and I could be blood relatives. I laughed and said not that I was aware, but that it was theoretically possible, since Michael was adopted and did not know his birth parents. A tiny part of me, that still had the ability to laugh at myself, marvelled at the headlines that would be ours if we did turn out to be related, like a bad plot line in a Barbara Taylor Bradford saga.

Slowly, gradually, Will recovered, the only long-term effect of his illness a mild heart murmur. I returned to work at

Wapping. My commute was brutal. The trains from Woking were unreliable, overcrowded and often cancelled; by car an hour and a half minimum across central London, each way (this was in the days before congestion charging and hard cycle lanes: I imagine now it would be twice that).

Driven by necessity, Michael finally passed his driving test – on the seventh attempt. He bought himself a Skoda Fabia, and promptly wrote it off by somehow drifting into a ditch on the A3. Another time, I had only just finished battling my way to the office when I got a panicked call from Michael: could I come and rescue him? He was in Camberley and had got stuck in a multi-storey car park. I drove all the way back to find Michael in a humiliated puddle of embarrassment at being so stuck, flushed pink from repeatedly and politely refusing offers of help until I got there. It turned out he hadn't been turning the wheel the right way.

Driving and Michael never really got on. Later, when he was at Education, he used to sometimes drive himself to the Department, which had one of those car parks operated by a car lift. While manoeuvring in, he managed to get the car stuck half in and half out. He tried to dislodge himself but the lift doors slammed shut, neatly bisecting the car. It looked as though it had been attacked by a giant pair of pliers. Worst of all, someone, somewhere, has some very embarrassing CCTV footage.

When I wrote this story up in *The Times* (later reprinted gleefully in the *Daily Mail* under the headline 'Is there ANYTHING Sarah Vine won't disclose about life with Britain's Education Secretary?'), I concluded, 'my husband is the worst driver in England, possibly the Western world. I love him dearly, but it's true. It has taken him seven attempts to pass his test, and even then I'm sure the examiner caved in only because he wanted to get out of the car as quickly as possible.'

These remarks, along with other observations about my husband, were not intended as put-downs, as some critics seemed to think, rather affectionate odes to Michael's quirkiness, a trait which I adored in him and which grew, over time and under the battering of politics, less and less pronounced. This notion that politicians must somehow be infallible, that they must never under any circumstances admit to the slightest human weakness or error of judgement, has always struck me as one of the biggest problems with this world. It's just so stupid and reductive and above all restrictive – after all, who has not at some point in their life made a cock-up, large or small? To err is to be human, and politicians must above all else be human, otherwise how can they possibly be any good at representing their fellow humans?

I also think that in some ways these musings of mine were a way of trying to preserve his identity, his fantastic personality, this complex, sensitive, funny, kind man I had married. Part of me could already see that the Westminster machine was sucking the joy out of him, making mincemeat of his unique character, replacing it with an 'on message' public persona I just didn't recognise. Maybe I thought that if I wrote it down, it would show not just him but the real world out there how much I loved him, the real Michael, the old Michael – *my* Michael. Then maybe he – we – would stand a better chance.

But the truth was, car parks aside, Michael was out most evenings and gone at sparrow's fart, leaving me to take over from the nanny the second I walked through the door. So writing about him ended up being the time I was closest to him. I was always running, always late, never quite up to speed with anything, either at work or at home.

My only slight relief was that an absent Michael couldn't see how badly I was juggling the plates. This hadn't always been the case. Back when he'd still been at *The Times*, just after I returned to work after Bea was born, when he was comment editor, I had written a leader for him. I was just about to head home, when he called me in. I was annoyed: I couldn't be late to pick Bea up from the childminder. As I walked into his office he waved the piece in my face, curtly informing me that, frankly, it wasn't good enough and told me to re-write it. I stared at him in astonishment: 'But I'm your wife!' 'I know,' he replied. 'That's no excuse for bad copy.'

With hindsight, that tiny episode foreshadowed a long-standing theme in our marriage: Michael's stern Presbyterian work ethic trumped everything else in our lives. It was that severe critic who, as we sailed deeper and deeper into political waters, began to gain the upper hand.

One day, I took Will to his doctor's appointment and, after he'd checked him over, the doctor made the terrible mistake of asking me how I was doing. I just burst into tears. Handing me tissue after tissue, he listened patiently (he really was a very kind man) as I did my best to express how wretched I felt and how much I loathed myself, but also how guilty and ungrateful I felt about feeling like that because I knew how lucky I was to have two beautiful little children, and how angry and upset I was with myself for being so utterly useless.

He let me blow myself out and then, very calmly and gently, he said he thought I ought to go and see someone.

I was apprehensive. This was 2005; mental illness was still heavily stigmatised. Indeed, a few months previously, when I had taken out life insurance in case one or both of us popped our clogs and the kids needed taking care of, the question 'Have you ever suffered from depression or other mental health issues?' had carried some serious weight.

This wasn't, you see, the first time that I had wrestled with the black dog of panic and depression. The first time was in my teens, when the relationship between me and my father had collapsed to the point of what I imagined was no return.

When we moved to Italy, I was almost 6 years old, already twice as tall and as wide as my Italian school peers, bursting out of my grembiule – the smocks with giant bows on the front that was what every school kid wore then. As I spoke no Italian, they put me in the class below, sat at the back and squished into a tiny desk. I was like a giant, milk-white cuckoo squatting fatly in a nest of quick-winged swallows. What made it worse was that no one had yet worked out that I was catastrophically short-sighted which (I, of course, knew no different), from my place of exile at the back of the class, meant that even if I had been able to understand the words on the board, I wouldn't have been able to physically see them. Both teachers and classmates concluded that as well as being foreign, I was also somewhat retarded.

My parents, by contrast, were living their best life, true followers of La Dolce Vita, in this exciting new playground. Broke, but still in their twenties and both fabulously charismatic and good looking, they got by on their wit and charm, adored and feted by their new Italian mates.

My own memories of their glittering social lives were of falling asleep on benches in noisy, smoke-filled trattorie, or of waking up late at night to find the house empty, my parents having sneaked out for a quick bite and a spot of revelry (childcare was not something that would have ever crossed their mind). No doubt they thought no harm would come to us for just a few hours – and they were probably right: Grottaferrata in those days was a peaceful little village, where everyone knew everyone else.

But when you're 7 or 8 you don't see that; you lie in bed listening to the cicadas in the garden, to the sound of figs ripening in the summer heat, the gentle 'plop, plop' as they fall to the ground, straining your ears for the sound of the adults returning, unable to get back to sleep until they do. I remember at one point being terrified that there was some-thing living underneath my bed – I was sure I could hear it moving at night. And, indeed, there was: I eventually discov-ered that it was my baby brother Ben who, clearly feeling just as scared as me, had developed a habit of crawling under-neath my bed with his blanket and teddy for comfort.

Despite the five-year age gap, our experiences as young children in that slightly unhinged environment brought us close together as siblings. I always felt very protective of Ben, and did my best to stick up for him whenever he was in trou-ble.

But when we became teenagers and adults, the madness we lived in had the odd effect of pushing us apart. The older we got, the more emotionally abusive my father became, as his drinking and wild lifestyle became ever more toxic. We each responded in different ways to his extreme behaviour; Ben turning in on himself while I looked to get away as fast as I could. When I eventually left Italy to return to England aged 15, I was no longer there to share the burden of my father's outbursts, and Ben was suddenly in the firing line. One minute he was the golden child – handsome, charming, fitted the bill as an appropriate son for these two to have – but before long, expectations would turn to disappointment and somehow my father would find a way to divert his own frustrations into rage with his son. With hindsight, I feel terrible for abandoning him. But by then I really felt I had no other choice. It was for me a question of self-preservation.

The main effect of all this was a kind of intangible anxiety which has accompanied me all my life. Rightly or wrongly, and I'm sure that was never their intention, my parents instilled in me the notion that I was both inconvenient and unimportant. As a result, where others – like Frances Osborne, or Sam – somehow managed to shelter from the slings and arrows of politics in the bosom of their family, I never had that option.

Somehow, I always managed to ruin things. I remember once going on holiday and getting a very painful ear infection: it was my fault for spoiling the holiday; or there was the time I saved up my pocket money to buy a toy that I had my heart set on: I got into trouble because my mother had earmarked it as a Christmas present, and now I had ruined her surprise; another time my father brought back a pretty necklace from a trip abroad – but it was too small for my neck and he made his disappointment clear.

Once, while on holiday, my brother slipped and fell on some glass, cutting himself badly. My father was just tucking into a plate of fresh prawns. Ben had to wait for him to finish before Dad, extremely reluctantly, took him to the *pronto soccorso*. There were countless incidents like that, small and large, but all significant in the way that unimportant things can be, all seemingly engineered as a reminder of how far down the pecking order we were – like the time he gave me and Ben each a signed photo of himself as a birthday present – and they all added up in my head to a sense of myself as a colossal waste of space. I just wanted to disappear, to '*togliere il disturbo*', as the Italians say.

As I got older, and we moved around, from Rome, to Milan, to Turin, always changing schools, having to start all over again, under my anxiety was a deeper fear: that I was the rotten apple in my parents' lives, who was beginning to sour their happiness. The bigger and clumsier I became, the more my father would shout at me and then at all of us.

My mother's brother Tim puts it very well, if a little baldly. 'Roger and Rosemary were these two beautiful creatures who were meant to produce an Elle Macpherson of a daughter and what they got was an ugly duckling.' He did then go on to tell me that he reckons I'm a swan now, if only for my paddle-paddle work ethic alone, but you get the picture.

I had no violin skills like my father, was hopeless at tennis; first I was clumsy and blind, then I had bottle-bottom glasses; and, as I veered unhappily into puberty, I started to eat my feelings and get not just lumpy but plumpy.

This was the last straw for him; Roger despised fat women – fat was laziness, weakness, repugnant. He also seemed mortified at the prospect of having an unattractive daughter, as though that would somehow reflect poorly on him. A firm believer in the mantra 'Non c'e niente piu brutta che una donna brutta' ('there is nothing uglier than an ugly woman'), he would remind me of this at every opportunity.

He referenced my weight constantly, to the point where mealtimes became miserable, every mouthful an opportunity for jibes and reprimands. I learned to curb my appetite in front of him, but ate instead in secret, sometimes even stealing food. I remember clearly one Christmas, I was caught eating a Mars Bar I had pinched from the cupboard in my room. My father was so furious, I was barred from Christmas lunch.

Just to add fuel to fire, my hair started to fall out. 'Your parting is so wide – oh wow, you're going bald!' said a boy at school. Could I become any more repugnant?

It took me years to work out that I was on a hiding to nothing with my dad. But I loved my mother, so where was she in this?

I realise now that she was struggling with Roger just as much as I was, albeit of course in a different way. It's really hard to explain quite how impossible he was to live with – it almost had to be seen to be believed. Sometimes he could be utterly charming and hugely affectionate; but he could also be dangerously unhinged – and for an intelligent man, he had a tendency to do some really stupid stuff.

There is, however, one incident that in many ways encapsulates the way he was.

I was around the age of 12 or 13. We were living in Turin, in a rather lovely rented house out in the hills towards Revigliasco. It was at the very top of a long, steep windy road, with a big terrace and garden.

It was summer, and there had been a party, my father barbecuing fat Tuscan sausages outside and making bruschetta, The Rolling Stones and Tina Turner blaring on the stereo, people dancing, my mother handing around her famous potato salad, everyone smoking like chimneys. Most of their friends belonged to the local tennis club; a fast, fairly louche set, plenty of old Turin money and new drugs. I remember watching my mother from the kitchen, utterly radiant in some Jerry Hall-style halterneck, her auburn hair thick and luscious (unlike mine), her lips a glossy shade of rust red, her bright blue eyes dancing in the candlelight. It seemed as though the whole gathering revolved around her. I could not imagine a creature more captivating – and neither could the men in the room.

One of them, Teresio, a respected local architect who worked for the *comune*, the local authority, was besotted, and in truth he made no secret of it, even with me. Driving me back from the tennis club one afternoon, slipping me illicit cigarettes as he swung his Fiat around the tricky bends up to our house, he put The Beatles' 'Taxman' on the stereo, adding his own words. 'Amo la MAMMA!' he bellowed, at the top of his voice. Even I could divine that he was trying to tell me something.

Later that night, then, I was woken by the sound of my parents arguing – not unfamiliar, but there was an urgency to this particular altercation. I turned over, trying to ignore it, hoping that if I could just get back to sleep it would all go away. But it didn't. The guests had all left, but the party was far from over. I ventured out of my room into the corridor and saw my father, sweating and swaying with drink, my mother throwing things into a suitcase. I retreated.

The front door slammed. There was a brief silence, and then the sound of my mother's little Fiat starting up in the driveway. The door of my bedroom burst open: it was my father, stark naked save for a glass in one hand and a bottle in the other. 'Quick!' he stammered, his voice breaking with emotion. 'You have to stop her.' I found my specs, and followed him down the steps of the house in my nightie, I guess not knowing what else to do.

His car was in the driveway, a Ford Cosworth; he climbed into the driver's seat, I into the passenger side, and he fired up the engine. Queen burst forth from the speakers, insects danced in the headlights as we set off in pursuit, tyres screeching as we rounded the bends in the road down, Freddie Mercury at full blast. Ahead, the tail lights of my mother's car, heading towards town. He revved the engine, shifting gears as he pursued her, tailgating like a man possessed. I gripped the leather of the seat, not knowing what to do or say, terrified. I turned my head and saw him, out of his mind with drink, both terrifying and faintly ludicrous in his nakedness.

She didn't get very far. We reached a straight stretch of road, and he put his foot down, overtaking my mother's car and blocking her progress, executing a screeching U-turn so that the lights of his car shone directly at her. He got out, ran around the front, dropped to his knees, burst into tears and begged her to come home. She looked at him kneeling there, starkers, exposed in the headlights. She was exhausted, exasperated, her face a mixture of anger and pity. Her hands dropped from the steering wheel and she shrugged her shoulders in a gesture of defeat. We drove back to the house in silence, and he helped her up the stairs with her suitcase. I went back to bed.

I tell that story not to humiliate or embarrass Roger, simply to illustrate the degree to which he would push things sometimes, especially when fuelled by drink. What I hadn't realised then was that both my parents were slightly out of control. At some point in their marriage (I suspect fairly early on) one of them had strayed, and after that it was a series of tit-for-tat flirtations and lovers. The notion of me being integral to persuading her to stay was part of their trauma bond: years before, when my father had first walked out, to live with his Italian teacher, Mara, Ben had been a babe in arms. My mother had taken him with her when she knocked on Mara's door. Roger came home.

Both of them seemed to be chasing something that they could never find in the other – and yet, somehow, they were always drawn back together like magnets. My father's insecurity led him to seek sexual validation elsewhere; my mother's frustration with his drinking and general boorishness meant she was forever seeking intellectual stimulation. He could never understand this: he just wanted to eat, drink and, if possible, fuck. Despite his talents, he rarely played the violin or chess – although he loved tennis, and for a while could still beat men half his age with relatively little effort. But again, it was all bravado: he would rock up to the tennis court, gin and tonic in one hand, cigar in the other, deliver a few killer backhands, mock his earnest Italian opponents and head off early for a two-bottle lunch.

His drinking was prodigious. He would start with a beer at around 11 a.m., then a gin and tonic before lunch, then wine, then a beer or two in the afternoon, then another gin and tonic, then more wine, then whisky. Blessed with an iron constitution, he seemed determined to push it to the absolute limit. As for rules, they were for fools. He drove everywhere, never sober, always with a stogie in one hand, often with a beer in the other, his seatbelt stubbornly unplugged.

My mother could not have been more different. She loved art and fashion, and gravitated towards those worlds. Teresio, the architect, became her constant companion, and it drove my father mad. He responded by having an affair with Teresio's girlfriend. It was all incredibly complicated and extremely toxic, and – to us kids – very confusing.

When at home, my father was restless and bored. He took to taking it out on me: picking holes in my appearance, my performance at school, my weight. It was as if my very existence was an irritant. The tiniest thing – just being in the wrong place, or some minor misdemeanour – would set him off, and the result would often be a prolonged, escalating rant which would end up in a kind of emotional evisceration. These were the times when he would tell me I had ruined his marriage, that I was a hopeless disappointment, that he couldn't understand how he – the ultimate alpha – had produced such a dud. Later, he always said that he was trying to help me, that it was supposed to be character building. At the time, though, it felt very bleak.

When I tell people I grew up in Italy, they always exclaim, 'How lovely!' But the truth is, I couldn't wait to leave. Italy for me was chaos, confusion, failure; I desperately wanted to come home, to Britain, with its neat, tidy houses, Radio 4, rules and regulations, away from the madness. One day, shortly after I had finished Italian middle school, and after yet another bruising Sarah-bashing session, I decided I had had enough. I told my mother I was either going to run away or they could send me back to England. To my amazement and relief, they agreed to let me go.

It was obviously daft, though, to think that all my troubles were over. I swapped the bullying of my father for the bullying of English schoolchildren who couldn't believe their luck in having such an alien land on their plate. It was 1981 and everyone else was in shiny pastels, with short hair flicked to the side and ra-ra skirts. I had long hair, parted old-fashionedly in the middle, I spoke Italian, wore thick glasses and was painfully reserved. Fresh meat! Within my first term, the Anti Sarah Vine Association had been formed, complete with printed badges. At St Bede's, a strange, new, mixed-sex boarding school set up in a rambling Sussex house that had previously belonged to satanist and WWI profiteer Sir Horatio Bottomley, to house all the reprobates expelled from other South-East private schools and the precocious children of African dictators, this was what passed for entertainment.

I'd like to say I didn't care. There were, after all, so many reasons for celebration. I had escaped the corrosive acid attacks by my father, fleeing into the brisk but warm embrace of my grandmother Ruth, who was my appointed guardian for weekends away, and whom I adored. I knew nothing about her own troubles – my grandfather's war, his drinking, her stillborn baby, her post-natal depression. To me she was just Granny Ruth, her neat, regimented home my haven. I still dream of that little terraced house in Bickley, with the tiny study that doubled as my bedroom, the galley kitchen where she would make me Angel Delight, the pink bathroom suite. It was there that I felt safe and loved, free from the responsibilities of failure. It was there I was able to switch off my flight mechanism, and just be myself. Whoever that was.

'Evolve or die' became my motto for this new life, one which I have often returned to, despite my more natural desire to swim against the tide. I came up with a plan for living that embraced all these factors. To stop being bullied,

I would have to become like the people bullying me: short-haired, with gas-permeable contacts so I could ditch the glasses, obsessed with boys and sex, and, above all, thin. This was the ultimate control – simply stopping eating – and it was easy when faced with English food, and boarding school food at that.

I told myself that only weak people needed to eat; that, by stopping eating, I had transcended all who mocked me and challenged myself to have as little intake as possible: I felt high with triumph when I lasted a whole day on only an apple. And it worked so beautifully: I starved myself into the ranks of the St Bede's mean girls, all of whom had names ending in 'ie', like Buggie and Flicksie, and started to dissolve everything that was me into the starchy gelatine of English life. I discovered the joy of lying on my stomach and feeling my hipbones jutting into the ground. I hallucinated on three tiny Wheat Crunchies per meal – and medicated myself against such giddiness by taking iron supplements. I wore drainpipes from Topshop. In a size 6.

That sense of triumph soared when I went back to Italy for the Christmas holidays. My father couldn't believe my trans-formation and excitedly took me shopping to Benetton, where he kitted me out with all the striped, collar-turned-up shirts, crisp cigarette trousers and candy-coloured sweaters that my new English friends were falling over themselves to buy back in England. Dolled up in my new togs, he sent me into a restaurant to 'wiggle for a table'; right off the bat, he was working my new sexualisation for his own ends.

I didn't understand this at the time, of course, but that brief period hard-wired something into my brain: to be thin was to be loved. I don't think that notion will ever desert me.

It was the magic wand that made everything alright. By being thin, I had made my father proud. Now he showed me off instead of berating me; now it didn't matter that I couldn't play tennis or chess: my new appearance was a credit to him, and that was enough.

This is something that has stayed with me all my life, and it's why my lifelong battle with my weight, forged in that crucible of misery, has been such an endless source of self-loathing. Put simply, I hate myself when I put on weight, and it leads to a dark place and very dark thoughts. Fat, I become unworthy of love, unloveable, a failure and a source of revulsion, not least to myself. I am someone who has stood in front of the mirror, punching themselves in the stomach, pinching the excess flesh until it bruises, fantasising about slicing it off. Even now, when I'm at an age when none of this really matters, I still can't live happily in my body – and I doubt I ever will.

My periods stopped when I was 15 but I didn't care because I was so much more woman now that I was thin, as evidenced by the fact that I had attracted the attention of one of the older boys, one of a number of Nigerian students at the school. Despite my new-found bravado, I really had no idea about boys, or what they were interested in. When he came to visit me one late afternoon in the gym, where I was practising the saxophone, I had no idea what was about to happen, and he certainly had no hesitation in obtaining what he wanted. Nothing could have been further from my mind – I had never even really kissed a boy and, if I'm honest, I didn't really understand what was going on. Afterwards, back in the dorm which I shared with three other girls, I kept quiet. So, strangely, did he, although later on, after I had left

St Bede's, I briefly dated one of his distant cousins, who was at Harrow.

By then I was living in London with one of the few people who had actually been quite kind to me, Alexi, and renting a room in her parents' house. Alexi was the coolest girl in school, not to mention stunning, and we had a few wild months, aged 16 and 17, hanging out in clubs and generally making nuisances of ourselves. I was like Alexi's little puppy: I followed her everywhere, wide-eyed in admiration, copying her every move: the way she smoked, the way she dressed, the way she spoke, the music she liked. She was a bit like my mother in the sense that all the men (well, in our case, boys) in any given room were instantly besotted with her. With a bit of makeup and a lot of attitude, we both looked older than our years, and had no trouble getting into nightclubs, where we would smoke Sobranie cocktail cigarettes, sip vodka and pretend to be very sophisticated. It was a lot of fun. But it was short lived: her parents clamped down on the naughtiness, and I was given my marching orders.

I went home in mild disgrace. My parents didn't seem all that worried by the underage drinking and clubbing, they were more shocked by the news that I had a black boyfriend. In any case, they needn't have worried too much: the boy's parents weren't too keen on the relationship either, for similar reasons, and after a brief correspondence we never saw each other again. That was the way it was in those days.

It was decided that I should return to England to finish my A-levels, only this time the destination was Brighton, not London. Here, aged 17, I lived on my own in a one-bedroom flat in Charlotte Street, next to a B&B run by a delightful gay couple and with an old Irish woman in the basement who was convinced I was a prostitute. Every day I would take the train to Lewes, where I attended the technical college and met my first 'proper' boyfriend. He was the son of the biology teacher, one of four brothers, all of whom had been raised in a staunch socialist household. His father was a lecturer at Sussex University; his mother, Anne, was one of the kindest women I ever knew, and a lifeline to me at that point.

I think she understood instinctively how lost I was, and how lonely. These were the days before mobile phones, when international calls were expensive. I would go for weeks without speaking to my parents. All I really had were my friends and the nice gay couple next door.

It was Anne who let me stay in her house, who gave me a glimpse of what a real family could be. Her boys were classic Doc Marten and grandad collar types, and I think the older ones took a dim view of me. But I think she quite liked having another girl around the place, and I still remember happy evenings on the sofa, watching *The Young Ones* or *The Tube*, feeling very snug in my newfound rug.

It was Anne who encouraged me to apply for university. Without her gentle guidance and patience, I'm not sure I would have bothered: I had a part-time job in town, that seemed like a decent enough prospect. Otherwise I just assumed I would go back to Italy and be miserable there. But Anne was having none of it. It was she who helped me fill in my UCCA forms, she who helped me decide which universities to go for.

I was amazed and delighted when I got a couple of interviews (in those days, all universities interviewed prospective candidates). I travelled to London, feeling very grown up, to meet the panel at UCL. I babbled away in Italian, spoke a bit of French – and a few weeks later an unconditional offer landed on the doormat. Which was lucky, because I didn't exactly cover myself in glory with the A-levels: A, D, D. Oh, and an E for biology.

The boyfriend and I split up soon after we arrived at university, as is often the case. But I remain eternally grateful to Anne for what she did. She changed the course of my entire life. She taught me that anything is possible, provided you put in the time and the effort, and that a little kindness can go a very long way.

So, when it came to being a floundering political wife and a post-natally depressed mother, I genuinely believed I had no reason – no right – to be feeling this way. I kept telling myself I should just jolly well snap out of it, again, if I just put in the time and the effort. It had always worked before. But for some reason this time I just couldn't.

I was referred to a professor at The Priory in Woking. I sat in his office on a rather gloomy afternoon and answered all his questions honestly and openly, at times swept away by a self-generated vale of tears. At the end of the session, he said that he was in no doubt that I was suffering from post-natal depression. He added that he thought it was probably quite severe, and that had I not been who I was (i.e. the wife of the local MP), he might well have recommended I be temporarily separated from the children for their own safety.

This shocked me to my absolute core: I was a danger to my children? The only person I ever felt like harming in my moments of doubt and pain was myself, this loathsome, useless lump that I had become. Did he really mean that? I don't know. But it was enough to make me sit up and notice.

How much Michael noticed, I can't say. He was certainly aware that I wasn't exactly thriving. Weekends, which should have been precious quality family time together, were often fraught. We were both tired after working all week, yet had two energetic young children to entertain – a conundrum that all working parents will recognise.

Just getting out of bed in the mornings felt like climbing Mount Kilimanjaro. My body and brain ached; the joy that I should have felt at having a happy, fulfilled husband and two beautiful, bright babies was tainted by bone-crushing exhaustion. I was fractious, tense, moody. I remember one Sunday, on a shopping trip to Farnham, I couldn't get the double buggy to open. The kids were both crying in the car, Michael was on a work call in the passenger seat; something in me suddenly snapped, and I started smashing the wretched thing on the tarmac like a woman demented. For a few brief moments, that poor buggy became the object of all my anger and frustration. By the time Michael emerged from the car it was, to coin a phrase, an ex-buggy.

Michael reacted to my increasing neurosis in the way many men do when their previously normal wives apparently go mad: he retreated into his work, spending more and more time in London, especially in the evenings. And who could blame him, frankly? I wasn't much fun to come home to, and any social life we had in Camberley was politics-related, and therefore not really conducive to proper friendship. People were nice enough – but I always felt like a bit of a fish out of water: as ever, I suspected that they were the normal ones, I was the freak.

Meanwhile, my hair got thinner as my waist got thicker, and eventually blood tests revealed that my thyroid had basically gone kaput. The symptoms? Exhaustion, slow metabolism, joint pain, muscle aches, mood swings: check, check, check, check and double check. That, at least, explained some of it. But the mental malaise that I felt lingered.

I went back to see the professor, and he told me – not for the last time in my life – that something had to give. Work, kids, commute: one of them had to go. The solution was obvious: move back to London and plug back into my support network of friends: Sam and Dave, the Lockwoods, Rachel and Steve Hilton, the Osbornes, my old mucker Imogen Edwards-Jones, Nick Boles and others: I missed them all so much.

By now Michael had been elected, with a stonking majority, and his association seemed pretty pleased with their new MP's evident rising star. Still, they made it very clear that they wanted him – us – to live in the constituency, to really embrace life in Surrey. I think at the heart of it was also a slight bewilderment that I would want to carry on working now that I was the wife of a Conservative MP. The feeling – never actually expressed directly but always implied in a myriad of tiny ways – was that my main role now should be supporting Michael.

Truth is, that was never going to happen. Work was, and always has been, my great refuge. Journalism – and writing – is the one thing I am actually fairly decent at, and thoroughly enjoy. As to motherhood, I adore my children and wholeheartedly enjoy their company now that they are interesting, vibrant young adults – but I found the baby and toddler stage incredibly dull and repetitive, physically and mentally challenging in a way I just didn't terribly relish.

Like so many working mothers, I *wanted* to keep working, not just because, like most families these days, we needed the money, but also because it was, quite frankly, my sanity; the one place where I wasn't just someone's wife or mother but *me*, valued for my ability alone.

Motherhood made me feel trapped in a way I had never anticipated; but it's one thing to be trapped in the same boat as all your friends; quite another to be adrift in foreign waters, where none of the local flora and fauna seem to understand you. The professor was right: something had to give, and that something was Surrey Heath. I needed to be back among my own tribe.

I think Michael thought I was weak for not giving it more of a go; I wanted to fight back by asking what was the point of representing a completely safe seat if one couldn't play the advantage of not having to kowtow to the tyranny of constituency life at every turn, but I never quite found the courage to say it. Luckily, over New Year 2005–2006, we had had our old friends Topaz and her husband Christian Fraser to stay.

'Listen to Sarah or lose her,' she told him. He finally paid attention. For the sake of my sanity and our marriage, we agreed that we would reclaim our London home as our main residence, and use the parliamentary second home allowance to keep a weekend place in the constituency. Little did we know how that decision would come back to haunt us.

Going back to Barlby Road felt like surfacing from a deep nightmare. I felt re-energised, started going to yoga and Pilates classes, began hosting suppers with friends and colleagues. The children saw much more of Michael – sometimes he even had time to come home for bedtime before going back to Westminster to vote. If he wasn't around I could invite a girlfriend over for a glass of wine and a chinwag. My friend Imogen and I, who lived just around the corner and whose own husband, a successful TV producer, was often out on the town pressing the flesh of an evening, started a tradition which continues to this day. We would position ourselves, shoes off, at either end of the sofa, crack open a bottle of wine and set the world to rights until the men finally came home. We still ring each other up and say, 'Fancy a bit of sofa?'

In short, I was back in my element, within striking distance of everyone and everything I loved. Those years were some of the happiest of my life: everything seemed suddenly possible again and our star was in the ascendant. Dave, with Howard's stewardship and blessing, had become leader of the party almost as soon as the votes were counted from the 2005 Election, giving a speech at the 2005 autumn party conference that saw hitherto frontrunner David Davis boxed and coxed into second place, and Dave the new leader, at only 38 years old.

Funnily enough, and with more than a shard of crystal ball in his figurative fist, unlike Cameron's other friends, who were all very gung-ho, Michael had urged Dave to think very carefully about running for the leadership, calling him at his Oxfordshire home one weekend, saying that he was genuinely worried about the effect on Dave, on Sam and on the family, and 'pleading' with him not to do it.

I say crystal ball through slightly twisted lips, because if I had to choose one man to take the rap for the mess this country found itself in for the next 20-plus years, I would put Dave Cameron into pole position – so if Michael could have dissuaded him from standing as leader in 2005, who knows where we might be now? Ten years later, when Dave wrote *For the Record*, he had taken a similarly revisionist view on that conversation, commenting, 'For all the subsequent dramas in our relationship, I think he had nothing but the best of intentions in making the call.' Nice touch of acid in that little 'I think' interjection – especially since Michael then went on to do a fair bit on Dave's leadership bid, including writing speeches and articles for him.

Mind you, if David Davis was the only alternative, Dave always had it in the bag. I was rightly reported in *The Times* as being furious on Michael's behalf when he was flagged down in the corridor of the 2005 conference by some Davis flunkey, warned intimidatingly that he was a new boy and should know his place, and that his place was to vote for Davis. Bit thick of that underling not to know the connections between Dave and Michael, thought I, and of course, when it came down to it, Michael did vote for Dave, whereupon he trounced Davis by an astonishing margin of two to one.

Suddenly our dinner party chats had become discussion points at a national political level; friendships had matured into political alliances. Michael was part of the inner circle, a leading voice in the spirited and youthful opposition to an ailing Labour regime; now that we were back in W10, no matter how ordinary our actual house, we were – for better or for worse – considered part of the 'Notting Hill Set', not just by friends, but by the nation's newspaper readers.

Nor was this confined to Michael. At some point, without noticing, always assuming that it would only ever be Michael who attracted attention as a public persona, I had become associated with him and his beliefs in the eye of the public. For the first time, therefore, my home life and my work life were presenting potential conflicts of interest. This national focus on 'the Goves' had all crept up on me while I had been gaze-down on baby sick and potty training, avoiding the petty scuffles of constituency power plays and worrying about money; leaving me a little unprepared for what came next.

LESSON THREE IN HOW NOT TO BE A POLITICAL WIFE:
allow yourself to be hijacked into a life for which you are woefully unprepared.

At the time, of course, I was so relieved to be back in London that I threw myself into this most recent twist and turn of the rollercoaster. I was also so relieved that Sam and I were now neighbours; both working mothers, both with tiny children, in this together. And for her, I could recapture that elusive feeling, so precious to me, of being useful: I could cook dinner parties, pick up the slack on school runs, organise our holidays.

The reason for this, of course, was because she had Ivan, beside whose challenges my tiny motherhood quibbles were as nothing.

Never have I known a child more loved – and more secure in that love – than Ivan Cameron. He couldn't speak but anyone could see the delight he took in his life – and the joy he brought both his parents. Never once did I hear either of them express any sadness or self-pity about the freight train that had cannoned through their safe orderly lives when he was born with Ohtahara syndrome. Ivan brought out the very best in Dave: he was so kind and patient with him, resilient and tireless in his efforts to make his son more comfortable. His passionate commitment to the NHS, for example, could not be questioned after the praise he constantly gave to his son's carers and medical team. And Sam! She was always impressive, always competent, and I had always admired and liked her. But when I saw her with Ivan, I'm not embarrassed to admit to some hero worship. She was unfailingly gentle and patient, light-hearted and natural, never anything less than loving without being indulgent and cosseting.

When he died, in February 2009, not long before Dave became prime minister, it was devastating. He had been rushed to hospital in the night with violent seizures; the medics had fought for almost an hour to save his life. I had been due to drop by that morning; instead I drove my two to school in shocked silence, and then went on to the office. There was a terrible, cruel photograph of Sam and Dave returning home from the hospital; pain etched on Sam's face, Dave's eyes downcast. I felt so angry on their behalf, that the world had intruded on their raw grief in that way.

Considering the many and varied shitshows that were to follow, without question the most brutal roasting we had as a couple was the expenses scandal, for the simple reason that it was the first punishment beating we received as a result of politics. As Rod Stewart famously sang, the first cut is the deepest.

The expenses scandal couldn't have come at a worse time for me. For some reason my immune system had decided to desert me; I caught swine flu, then tonsillitis, double pneumonia and even a quinsy (which you may remember from *Chitty Chitty Bang Bang*), feeling like a Dickensian tragic victim as I doubled up coughing in the street, wrangling with the post-viral fatigue and the toxic after-effects of troll-strength antibiotics. One of the necessary pillars of being a political wife is to be just that – a pillar of strength. In 2008–2009 I couldn't even manage that.

What, to the outside world, looked like just another duck-house-owning fat cat Tory exploiting the system for his own red-trousered ends was, of course, the sorry tale of my failure as a political wife. I had tried to make Surrey Heath my home. And I had failed; William's sickness, my own post-natal depression and my desperate need to be back in London had dictated a reversal of our living arrangements, leading us to reclaim Barlby Road as our primary residence, making the new house in Elsted now designated as our second home and therefore eligible for support from the Additional Costs Allowance (ACA) to which Michael was entitled as an MP. For us it was lifesaving support: Michael was able to claim for moving costs and the expense of having to furnish two houses. Frankly, that was about the extent of my working knowledge of the ACA: that it was one of the few perks of the job.

Of course, to the outside world this would be taken, not as the flailing of a young family trying to work things out in a life split between two places, but as a cynical 'flipping' of properties to suck on the teat of taxpayers' money and get them to pay for – as the *Telegraph* reported with glee and relish – upscale interior design items from OKA, co-founded by Sam Cameron's mother. I could almost hear the fist-bumping between writer and editors over in *Telegraph*

HQ in Victoria: an ex-competitor-turned-MP, who could be tarred with the same brush as the undoubted excesses of those claiming phantom mortgages, installing duck houses and moats, and with a whiff of cronyism thrown in – bingo!

On the page, the *Telegraph* ran a deliberately cat-and-mouse campaign, leaking MPs' names they were targeting bit by bit, toying with a public that became hungrier and hungrier for salacious incriminating detail. Off the page, in the real world, for us it was pure torture.

We were on a family holiday in Wales, pootling around Dolgellau and Portmeirion with the children, when news reached Michael that something bad was brewing. The Labour Government had been battling against the disclosure of MPs' expenses for years and in 2008 had lost in the High Court, cueing a succession of spats over issues like the 'John Lewis list' which put a value on household items that could be claimed. In March 2009, the chairman of the Committee on Standards in Public Life announced an inquiry into MPs' expenses, to report after the 2010 election – but the *Daily Telegraph* trumped all that by obtaining leaked computer discs, and from May started to publish details of particular MPs' claims.

Michael had been getting calls about the *Telegraph* coverage and it gradually became clear that we were being edged into the firing line. The holiday was ruined, so we returned to London. Michael was shattered, asking me and the kids, strapped into their car seats, why he was being treated like a crook. 'Am I a crook?' he demanded of 6-year-old Bea. She looked at him witheringly. 'Dur. You're Daddy. Can I have some more raisins please?'

He wasn't a crook. Later, an investigation entirely vindicated Michael and found no fault in the expenses claimed, but this was all lost in the noise of the cumulative scandal, the revelations of which led to public outrage, resignations and a re-evaluation of the expenses system.

Once alerted that the story was going to run, Michael had only five hours in which to respond. He did so robustly in an email to the *Telegraph*, refuting the allegations. He went on to describe straightforwardly and in great detail the process by which we had rented out Barlby Road and rented, then bought, in Surrey; thereby incurring legitimate expenses, after which we realised that London had to be our home after all. He did not explain the personal circumstance around that decision – my post-natal depressions and so on – but even if he had I'm not sure it would have made any difference. The die was cast, and Will Lewis, the editor of the *Telegraph* at the time, was going to get his scalp. He ignored every single word of that email. The story ran, Michael's face plastered across the front page as 'expenses cheat', details of our supposed venality gleefully listed.

It was our Five Pentacles moment, cast out from the Court of Cameron. In Kate Fall's memoir *The Gatekeeper*, she confirms the approach taken by the leadership to the expenses scandal. I find it interesting how cold-blooded she sounds when talking about how Cameron and his private office tackled the scandal: there was no sense of pulling together or sorting out the reasonable turning over of stones from more misguided, politically motivated attacks. It was crystal clear from the top, she says, that everyone had to fall on their sword, no matter how they protested their innocence. It certainly felt that way at the time: that sense that we were all being herded into a pen for an abattoir mass slaughter, no matter the individual merits of our case.

Andy Coulson – Dave's head of communications, former editor of the *News of the World* who was later sentenced to 18 months in jail for his role in the phone-hacking scandal – insisted that Michael had to do an apology in front of the cameras. Dave told him to go and explain himself to the constituency. Michael felt so traumatised that, never the most confident driver, he had to be driven there and back by Dominic Cummings, who took a characteristically bracing line, telling him to just take it, take it, take it. In the end, the 400 constituents packed into a church hall in Camberley were very understanding – but the public were by now baying for blood.

So Michael apologised for our armchair, our table, our cupboard, our £35 cot mattress (which did fall foul, not being deemed an allowable claim, leaving me to wonder whether the public expected William to sleep in a drawer ...) and our elephant lamps, even our moving costs. 'The events of the last week – in which I myself have been caught up – require us as a political class, as a political party and as individuals to show contrition,' he said. 'I am sorry for the mistakes I made, but words are cheap.'

It's a masterclass in sorry, not sorry because no reason to be sorry, but it didn't stop us being cancelled, which was a strange new experience. Witnessing the public taking on twisted facts from the papers, ignoring how little MPs are paid, then the extended press collating each story into a catastrophised whole, soon made me feel like the world was running at us with pitchforks. I wanted to fight back somehow but Michael would not let me. 'When an armed mob is running towards you, you don't fight – you run,' he said.

It was also heartbreaking to see how destroyed Michael was by the fallout. 'Lawmakers can't be law-breakers,' I remember him saying to a friend, 'but this is ridiculous, vengeful.' I remember him coming back from that church hall meeting in Camberley, trembling with emotion and just necking three-quarters of a bottle of whisky in 20 minutes, as if it was Coca-Cola. I think it stripped away his sense of who he was and what he was trying to do to improve things for every person in the country, that it cheapened his decision to exchange the big bucks of Fleet Street for the small beer of being an MP.

It also impacted seriously on his mental health – and on that of other MPs caught up in it. A few even tried to kill themselves. After the worst of it was over, we went up to Scotland, to Colonsay – our happy place – to try to re-set and recover. But even there, the agony seemed to follow him. I remember him saying to me in one of his darker moments, that the thought of throwing himself off the ferry back from Colonsay to Oban had crossed his mind. He said he thought we would all be better off without him, which frightened me but also filled me with an unspeakable rage at the injustice of it all. It awoke the tiger wife in me, and I had to resist hard the urge to speak out. Plus, I was astonished at how distant and unsupportive Sam and Dave were about it all. With hindsight, I suppose this should have been a big red flag. But I guess I did not yet want to believe that politics already mattered to them – or to Dave at least – more than friendship.

Truth is, Michael being an MP only ever cost us money: his pay went down by a half and our living costs, with two houses to maintain, doubled. Meanwhile, I was essentially paying to go to work as, after childcare and commuting costs, my salary evaporated.

This was, of course, our choice: I had been told by the psychiatrist at The Priory that I had to go back to work and move back to London for my mental health; Michael obviously chose to be an MP. And I am not naive: I knew that the abuse of public funds made for good indignant copy, but even the hack in me has always considered whether the person or people I am criticising or mocking actually deserves the takedown: and, even wearing my journalist hat, I don't think we did.

From this point on, I became obsessed with convincing people to see Michael as the kind, serious, intellectual public-spirited campaigner that I knew him to be, battling against the tall poppy syndrome the more successful he became. A foolish quest.

This came back to bite me when I made the decision to appear on television, on *This Week* with Andrew Neil and Michael Portillo in 2015. The expenses scandal was just part of it, of course, but there was an undercurrent of nastiness during the interview that I felt had its roots in 2009 and they eviscerated me; calling me bitchy, spiteful and abusive for a mischievous piece I had written about the Milibands' kitchen.

I was blindsided, made to look like a Pollyanna-ish twerp with my bleating talk of integrity, injustice and the importance of having good policymakers. I made the point repeatedly that being mocked was part of the reality of the political world, like it or love it, and that it wasn't just the media that indulged in poking fun, but the general public, through the new social media platforms.

The blokes on the sofa opposite, with their pale pink shirts, shuttered faces, crossed arms and splayed legs, were having none of it; I should have had standards and been nice to poor Mrs Miliband, they said, because I was a political wife too. I wanted to ask when was the last time anyone had sprung to *my* defence, not that I was asking them to. I did invite them to look at all the death threats and vitriol hurled at me on my Twitter feed, but they weren't listening and I didn't want to stoop to asking for their sympathy. It was a terrible mistake and I will never speak to Portillo again.

Back in 2009, notably lacking in any chivalrous defenders like Portillo was for Mrs Miliband, both of us were in a terrible state for weeks after our skewering, not helped by me being hospitalised with acute appendicitis. They say that psychological trauma often plays out in the form of physical illness, and this certainly felt like the case for me. Michael paid back over half what we had claimed, as decreed by his leader; had to give up – by party order – any future journalism fees for articles; and grew a carapace, telling me that we just had to 'suck it up'. But I remained soft-bellied, vulnerable to attack in just this one more way, and I needed to toughen up.

And I was angry, very angry. I remember going to a party at Andrew Feldman's house the week the directive about shadow ministers not being allowed to earn extra income had gone out. Michael's income as a columnist for *The Times* had been a vital lifeline for us; now it was severed. I genuinely had no idea how I was going to fill that hole. A couple of glasses down, I remonstrated with George (Osborne), who I always found easy to talk to, and who I sensed even occasionally actually appreciated what I had to say. He just laughed. 'Can't you just ask your dad for some money?' he said, and moved on. 'That may be how it works for you,' I thought to myself, biting my lip. 'But that's not how it goes in my world.'

Expenses broke something in Michael, but it awoke something in me. It felt like I had yet again failed another lesson in how to be a political wife. I was meant to smile and wave, take it all on the chin and silently stand by my man, comforting him behind the scenes and not allowing myself to be affected by it. Instead, I was beginning to find my own voice, my own anger, and this may have influenced a slight tilting in my own course: from editor to writer, from critic to commentator and, eventually, from *The Times*' cosy embrace to the rollercoaster ride of the *Daily Mail*.

Being a successful journalist had always been my armour against the world but now I was suddenly on the other side of the fence, going from being just another hackette to being the target of my fellow hacks. This dominoed into my own relationships at *The Times*. I started to get the feeling that old colleagues – people I had worked with for years – now saw me in a different light. They eyed me with a strange new kind of distrust, as though I was no longer one of them – again, that cuckoo in the nest. The final straw came a few years later when Will Lewis, who had been the *Daily Telegraph* editor leading the charge on the exposés, came to work on News at *The Times*. I knew then it was over for me there. I hated knowing he was in the building; how could I work for the same organisation as the man who had deliberately tried to ruin our lives?

LESSON FOUR IN HOW NOT TO BE A POLITICAL WIFE:
thinking fairness is still a word that has any function in your vocabulary.

It was a baptism of fire into a process of brutalisation that I simply hadn't anticipated. I very quickly realised that going into politics takes you into a world where people no longer see you as a person but as an object owned by them and, even worse, *known* by them. From the relative public anonymity of newspapers (who really takes note of a byline, unless you are pushed to do so by a photo and a controversial clickbait headline?) suddenly we were being seen and judged through the radioactive X-ray goggles of asses making assumptions.

It starts off as distant noise but then you will have a conversation at a party or at the school gate and you will suddenly see that this person thinks they have sussed you out, that they think they know what your values, your views and your motivations are – and they've built a nice snug pigeonhole for you. That's when you start to feel your sense of who you are being eroded.

I tried – and will always try – to explain through my writing that I am not a complete see-you-next-Tuesday but it's a Sisyphean struggle, always pushing the stone of public opinion uphill, ignoring the voices inside your head that suggest that maybe you are the awful person that everyone seems to think you are, staying strong because otherwise they win. That's all very fine and Nietzschean – what doesn't destroy me makes me stronger and all that, but Nietzsche doesn't pay the bills or make you sleep any better at night.

It's now 16 years since the expenses scandal but it still has the power to trigger me. The other day I was lending a table to a friend because I no longer have the room to house it. 'Watch it,' I warned, as we lugged it out of the house to her car and seeing her about to whack the gatepost, 'that table has been on front pages across the country; treat it with the respect you'd give a headliner!' It was, of course, the Loire table bought from OKA for £700. Sometimes you just have to laugh.

(I still have the elephant lamps.)

CHAPTER FIVE

LIFE INSIDE CAMELOT

'This is what we call the Notting Hill Tory set. They sit around in these curious little bistros in parts of London, drink themselves silly and wish they were doing what the rest of us are getting on with. They'll just have to be a little more patient.'

Derek Hill, MP for Old Bexley and Sidcup, 2004

The Conservatives winning the election of 2010 – albeit with a hung parliament that forced them into a Con–Lib Dem coalition – was a turning point for Project Gove. It felt like hurtling around a sharp, rain-slicked bend on a twisty country lane and coming out onto one of those magical, sun-lit, high-country vistas, through which the road ahead cuts like an arrow: straight and clearly defined. Suddenly the steep hedges, potholes and muddy puddles are behind you, sunlight ahead.

Michael had won his seat again, with a surprisingly large turnout by the Victoria sponge brigade, helped out by his son who, aged 5, had announced, in the school playground, his intention of voting for him and getting all his friends to vote for him. 'Ah, but you're too young to vote,' said a rather literal parent. Will looked up at him kindly, even a little pityingly. 'I will vote for him in my head then. That will probably be enough.'

'I know size isn't supposed to matter,' said our friend Sebastian about Michael's majority, 'but bloody hell, that's big.' My friend and fellow writer Tania Kindersley phoned from Scotland to comment on the night's 'unpredictable swinging'. I loved that my friends could turn even a general election into some kind of 1970s sex party.

For Michael, the general election as a whole meant that he was back in business after the death-by-a-thousand-cuts expenses scandal, serving in government and appointed to his dream job of Education Secretary. For me, the vista was no less sun-lit for one simple reason: it would be another few years until I had to do the nodding-dog Tory wife routine again down in Surrey.

How not to be a political wife? Just stop being one.

Of course, I didn't stop being one. Not really. Because even I could see that being a political wife had the potential to be fun, now that the 'Notting Hill Set' had been upgraded to the Cameron Court of Camelot.

Of course, we all found that moniker intensely irritating (which was the point of it). The Notting Hill Set which had formed in the years between 2005 and 2010 was, in the words of Rachel Johnson in *The Spectator*, 'more Nigella's Kitchen than Kennedy's Camelot, more clothing label

Superdry than grousemoor grandee Supermac'. Often presented in the media as a charmed, glittering clique, cheek by jowl in our West London mansions, the reality was indeed a little less magical and mythical.

From the giddy heights of the Holland Park mansion of Brunswick PR tycoon Sir Alan Parker, and the fashionable stucco of the Osbornes' townhouse off Westbourne Grove, flamboyantly furnished by his father's interiors firm, Osborne & Little, it was a swift fall to the Camerons' North Kensington terraced house within earshot of the Westway and our little end of terrace in Barlby Road, perched on what the *Evening Standard* described more accurately as, 'a rat run on the very north periphery of the set'.

Not everyone who was classified as part of the 'Set' fitted the geographic bill. Nick Boles (who always hated the description) had departed Mayfair for a chic factory conversion in up-and-coming Peckham; Simone Finn was the Queen of the North London school gate; Kate Fall was more Knightsbridge way. Even so, the gravitational pull of Dave and Sam's was irresistible.

But primarily, Ms Johnson's sneering aside, it was demonstrably – and sometimes troublingly – a close-knit gang of rambunctious friends from university days, not all of whose postcodes qualified for strictly Notting Hill appellations but, more importantly, not all of whom had necessarily been politicos on their career paths.

Cameron, I noticed from the moment I met him, was always just that little bit more obviously focused on Downing Street than the rest of them. He had cut his political teeth at Conservative Campaign Headquarters (CCHQ), rising to run the politics wing of the research department there. A young

George Osborne served under him and followed that time-honoured route of CCHQ-into-Westminster, becoming special adviser to Douglas Hogg then political secretary to William Hague before being elected, just a smidge after his 30th birthday, as the Commons youngest MP in 2001.

But others' paths into politics were, like Michael's, more meandering; Andy Feldman, who went on to become one of Dave's very closest friends and chairman of Cameron's Conservative Party, came to the group through his and Michael's shared experience in organising the Brasenose May Ball at Oxford in 1987/8. Christopher Lockwood, who went on to become Dave's director of policy, had been firmly grasping the greasy pole of media since he'd left Oxford – he and Michael knew each other well from their shared experiences at the sharp end of news journalism, Chris at *The Economist*, Michael at *The Times*.

Indeed, Chris was one of the first of Michael's circle of Oxford friends I met: he was on that fateful Robert Hardman skiing holiday, even though, having broken his leg on an earlier outing, he was not actually hitting the slopes. He was there instead to stake his claim for the very delectable Venetia Butterfield, whom he later went on to marry. They had dated previously, but it hadn't quite worked out, and he'd got wind that Vaizey had set his sights on her. So along he hobbled, just to make sure his rival didn't steal a march on him.

He needn't have worried too much: one of my abiding memories of that trip was the howl of outrage from Simone when she got up to go to the loo after dinner one night, and opened the downstairs cloakroom, which doubled as a food store, to find Ed swaying somewhat unsteadily in front of the toilet bowl. 'Oh my God, Ed! You're pissing on the bloody eggs!' she shrieked. Poor Ed. Thenceforth, that holiday became known as the one where 'Ed pissed all over breakfast'. Chris and Venetia were married not long after.

Even back then, Simone – now Baroness Finn of Swansea – was a formidable character. As I once wrote about her, 'Simone is like Samantha from *Sex and the City* but without the bashfulness Kim Cattrall brings to the role.' The state-educated daughter of a Welsh mother and Czechoslovakian father who had escaped the Communist regime, her quick mind had led her to Oxford, where she and Michael became an item, both surviving on their wits rather than their connections. Michael's affectionate nickname for her was 'Moaner', since she always – *always* – complained if she didn't get the best table in a restaurant, or the swankiest room in a hotel.

No one is more skilled at securing an upgrade than Simone – she could beat even the most recalcitrant maître d into submission. Her father, having aspiration for his clever daughter, had sent her to finishing school, in part to eradicate her Welsh accent (not entirely successfully: she still rhymes 'here' with 'year', a source of much affectionate teasing among her friends). In fact, of all that group, she was always the one who reminded me most of the Iron Lady herself: combative and fiercely ambitious on the outside, yet kind and loyal at heart. She was also instrumental in negotiating new terms with the trade unions during the coalition years; again, echoes of Thatcher, never to be underestimated.

Like Michael, I think she always felt like a bit of an outsider in that county Cameroonian set, having married Alex Finn, a corporate accountant, and settled in North London. But she was a brilliant networker, a skilled behind-the-scenes mover and shaker who helped Boris Johnson with his mayoral campaigns and went on to become a prime Whitehall fixer, both during and after Dave's premiership. If anyone knows where the bodies are buried, it's Simone.

Steve Hilton was another Oxford mate from roots even humbler than Michael's: from early days as a first-generation immigrant from Hungary, he picked up scholarships as he went, reading Philosophy, Politics and Economics at New College, worked at CCHQ and by the age of only 22 was in charge of the special relationship between the Tories and their advertising agency Saatchi's, where Maurice Saatchi said of him, 'No one reminds me as much of me when I was young as Steve.'

While at Central Office, Steve had met Rachel Whetstone, a sharp, immensely clever Bristol graduate, initially slightly chippy about her non-Oxbridge credentials but not letting those hold her back. Eating, living and breathing politics (her mother Linda was a stalwart of the local association in Sussex, as well as being a much feared and revered dressage judge in the local horse eventing scene), she pinged between the clubby frontlines of Westminster and the open-plan battlefields of corporate communications; including being a legendary assistant to Michael Howard and making a life-long ally of Tim Allan at Portland Communications.

I always liked Rachel – and Michael adored her for her gutsiness and her brains – but I found her quite hard work, at least in the beginning. She was definitely a man's woman, one of those girls who would always show up to supper in a pair of killer Gina heels, even if it was just a dull Tuesday night. She wasn't conventionally beautiful, but she was very sexy, charismatic and forthright in her opinions, and argumentative in a way that seemed to endlessly stimulate the opposite sex. She would have Dave and George and the entire lot of them hanging off her every word, leaving us wives to attend to the domestics. If and when she ever hosted herself – in the early days from her flat in Cambridge Gardens – it would be Lidgate's shepherd's pies and peas: infinitely preferable to cooking herself, which she neither enjoyed nor was especially skilled at.

She was friends with all sorts of interesting people, many of them leading New Labour figures (politics wasn't nearly as tribal back then); Tim Allan, of course, but also young guns like Ben Wegg-Prosser, a close ally and friend of Peter Mandelson. She had fingers in all sorts of pies and was famously vocal in her criticism of anyone who struck her as foolish – she seemed to relish having stand-up rows with almost everyone, regardless of seniority or rank within the party. But there was also a fragile side to her, a vulnerability that was unexpected, and often threw even the toughest of players. She could be very emotional, with a tendency to burst into tears when the conversation got too intense. I could never work out whether this was genuine or just a quick and effective tactic to change the conversation. Maybe a bit of both. Either way, it always seemed to convince the boys, even if it was met with a degree of eye rolling from us WAGs.

But she was clever, and funny too. It was she who dubbed the whole sprawling gang 'the Swarm' for the way we would descend en masse and chattering at stuffy Tory functions, irritating the hell out of MPs who considered themselves 'serious' Tories, such as David Davis and Theresa May. And I have no doubt that she would have played a key role in Dave's tenure as prime minister had it not been for an event that quite knocked the stuffing out of everyone.

She and Sam's stepfather, William Astor, had an affair.

It wasn't just some random encounter, either: it was a proper love affair, made even more extraordinary by the fact that Rachel was incredibly close to Sam and Dave. She was godmother to Ivan, and omnipresent around their dinner table; but she was also close to Sam's parents, Annabel and William Astor. She was a frequent visitor to their spectacular house in rural Oxfordshire, and the whole gang had been on many adventures together, including a riding holiday in Argentina. She and William had always got on like a house on fire: as a hereditary peer in the House of Lords, Conservative politics ran in his veins. But somehow, somewhere, their relationship had turned into something else, and it was quite the bombshell.

Their liaison came to light in the worst possible circumstances, while Rachel was holidaying with not only the Astors themselves but the Camerons as well, at the house in Jura. And it was a scoop, launched upon this unsuspecting house party, with a lead item in the inimitable Richard Kay's diary in the *Daily Mail* on 17 August 2004. 'There is, I can reveal today,' wrote Kay, 'an intriguing romantic spring in the step of Rachel Whetstone, Tory leader Michael Howard's political secretary and queen bee of the so-called Notting Hill Set of bright young Conservatives. The Benenden-educated brunette, who is one of Mr Howard's two most senior special advisers, has, I understand, formed a close friendship with a married older man who is a well-connected Tory grandee.'

The article went on to describe Rachel's close ties with Dave and underlined the connection with his stepfather-in-law William, before reminding readers that Rachel was Ivan's godmother. There was no specific mention of the affair, but the page was illustrated with a photograph of Annabel and William, with a drop-in shot of Rachel. It was a killer blow.

As it happened, Michael and I were on holiday not far from Jura, on the blissful island of Colonsay, just across the water. Bea was still just a baby and I was pregnant with Will. We were a waddling little troika: picnics in the rain, scampi and chips, and sandcastles, one of the happiest holidays we ever had. But the shockwave reverberated all the way from London, together with the news that Rachel had left Jura in disgrace. I had a mental image of her doing our journey to Jura, but in reverse and alone, being pulled into the Corryvreckan's deadly whirl, just as she had been pulled into the equally fatal whirl of patrician affairs.

I must confess I was utterly gobsmacked. I was no prude, and certainly no stranger to the idea of one's parents having affairs, my own having pursued a string of extra-marital divertissements over the years. Still, this was quite something, even by their standards. Having fled Jura, Rachel swirled out of the political waters for good – and, unsurprisingly, out of her friendship with the Camerons. Understandably, Sam viewed her actions as an unforgivable betrayal of her and Dave's trust. I think she felt partly responsible for bringing Rachel into Annabel's home – although how could she ever have known that she or William would do such a thing? As for Annabel, she was incredibly dignified about it all, but also deeply hurt. She and William had three children together, all of whom were close to their step-siblings. It was an incredibly tight-knit, supportive family, and this ripped quite a hole in the fabric of their life.

As much as I understood the sense of anger and betrayal on Sam's side, I also felt for Rachel. After all, it takes two to tango, and while it's never okay to go after a married man (or woman, for that matter), her punishment seemed harsher than his. William had his family and his title and his many palatial homes, and she was on her own in a small flat in Ladbroke Grove. Frozen out of the political circles she had been such an integral part of, she now found herself a social pariah – a situation I was to recognise many years later, after the fallout from Brexit.

But Sam never forgave her and, even when Rachel and Steve finally got together – it seemed like he had been waiting forever in the wings – she and Dave were at best cordial with each other. It was a prescient indication of the tribal nature of Clan Cameron: it was warm around the fire, but once you were out of that cosy circle, it was icy thereafter.

But that's skipping ahead. In 2010, the bonds were strong. This was no New Labour ramshackle alliance of interests but a friendship group who, though castigated in the media for being Old Boy Network and a mess of Etonians, were much better characterised by their university roots more than a decade before. They – we – had suppers together, holidayed together, partied together. And, most importantly of all, argued together: this was no echo chamber or papal enclave, far from it, as Michael and Dave's fabulous ding-dongs over foreign policy always demonstrated. Chatham House rules were at play; tempers were rarely lost.

This went for the wives and girlfriends too, most of whom were 'wives' only in the sense of being wedded to politics. One of the most joyous things about being around the Camelot table was the level playing field of men and women.

Kate Fall, who became Dave's gatekeeper, was also an Oxford friend and, despite her little girl lisp and wide-eyed baby-face, was a brilliant skewerer of bloated argument. Tempered to steel in the Welsh Valleys, Simone could hold her own in any discussion and would do so with her trademark deadpan delivery that we all loved so much. Rachel was, like her name, the sharpening tool with whom we could all hone our wits.

Finally, Frances Osborne, Sam and I were no slouches, despite our 'wife' labels. Frances had a big literary hit in 2008 with the publication of her book *The Bolter*, about her great-great-grandmother Idina Sackville. Sam was making waves at Smythson, dragging Queen Victoria's stationer into the twenty-first century. A *Spectator* article in 2010 concluded that, 'All these wives give the impression that they could run the country as well as their large households without break-ing a sweat. It's all very modern, classless and compassionate.' No doubt that last sentence came with more than just a pinch of caustic soda, but altogether this was no Boys' Club – at least, not until Boris shoehorned his way in, tipping the balance of Old Etonians from tolerable to toff-heavy.

Funnily enough, you see, Boris was never a part of this social circle of trust. He was a political loner – two years above our lot, lived in Islington, not in West London, running with a more overtly literary set and, for all his infamous wandering eye, known for being socially awkward. I remem-ber being told one story about a dinner party in Highgate, where Boris, failing to make actual conversation with the two women on either side, threw up his hands and announced to the supper table, 'Look, this isn't going too well – shall I just give a speech instead?'

At Oxford, Michael had brought himself into the political limelight through the time-honoured portals of OUCA, the Oxford University Conservative Association, but, much more tellingly, had first showed off his showman stripes in the Commons chamber in miniature that was the Oxford Union, rising to become President (like Boris, before him) in 1988. Famous pollster Frank Luntz remembers him well from those days.

'I've never seen a class of more talented people than that class of 1984–86 at the Oxford Union,' he says, 'especially Nick Robinson (of Radio 4 *Today* programme fame), Simon Stevens (Blair crony and NHS super being, now in the House of Lords) and Michael Gove: any one of those three. When they rose [in a debate] to intervene, the entire chamber shut up, there wasn't a sound.' This was, he explains, because once they were on their feet – or 'recognised', in the parlance of the Union – the previous speaker was dead on his. 'Just bring in the ambulance and take out the body, because the three of them could cut you up and show you your heart before you collapsed.'

Now that they were in government – albeit kept on their toes by the push-me, pull-you of their coalition with the Lib Dems – these formative days at the Union finally paid off in spades for Michael. I'd never seen my husband so alive. His arch fencing and cries of 'touché' both in the House and across the media as a shadow minister in opposition had just been his warm-up act. Now, in his new role as Secretary of State for Education, he meant business, had sharpened his swords and got to work, taking on the entire left-wing-rooted educational establishment – a.k.a. the Blob – in battle. Not single-handed (he obviously had a battalion of civil servants at his back, not to mention the formidable brain of one Dominic Cummings Esq.) but it might as well have been for the attacks that were unleashed upon his unsuspecting head in return.

While this played out on a political stage in a way that has been well documented since, it was the first time that politics popped our little family bubble. Up until then, I had been a political wife but not yet a political mother. Up until then, the children hadn't had the faintest clue that their father was anything other than the amiable, chatty, somewhat absent-minded fellow who appeared from time to time at mealtimes. Up until then, they had been anonymous kids in the state school system; now the teachers knew exactly who Beatrice and William Gove were.

'I thought the staff at school treated me differently because of my dyslexia,' Bea tells me now, 'which I assumed was a bad enough handicap to account for the veiled jibes. But then one day in Year 4, when I was 8, my teacher Mr W announced, "Tomorrow we won't be coming to school ... all because of Bea's dad." My classmates obviously loved that – and I do remember thinking, whoa, respect, Dad – but I can still hear the hostility in his voice.'

If you met my daughter, you'd know that this sort of snide treatment would not wash well with her. But that's now she's had a chance to grow a thick skin. Back then, she was not nearly as tough as she is now, and I will never forgive that teacher – and others – who somehow thought it was okay to take out their political grievances on a small child. What kind of a person, let alone an educator, does that sort of thing?

But then, as I was to discover further down the line, politics, and particularly tribal extreme politics, knows no boundaries.

On a family trip to New York not long before that fatal Brexit vote, the four of us were walking down Fifth Avenue just outside the famous Saks, when someone shouted, 'Oi, it's that wanker Gove!' (or words very much to that effect).

I turned to see a young blonde woman, clearly English from her accent, grinning triumphantly having got our attention. 'You're a wanker,' she shouted in our direction, illustrating her feeling with a hand gesture, keen to ram home her point. Her companion grinned and nodded his approval. We had the kids with us – they must have been about 12 and 10 at the time – and something about their shocked faces and her mocking, smug demeanour just got under my skin.

I confronted her. 'Please don't say things like that in front of our children, it's scary and upsetting,' I said. She laughed. 'I'm a teacher and your husband is a wanker,' she said, shoving her face in mine. 'If you're a teacher,' I replied, 'all the more reason not to use language like that in front of children.' Michael, who, unlike me, always handled these sorts of situations so calmly, took my arm gently. 'Come on, let's go, it's not worth it,' he said, in his best soothing voice. I acquiesced and turned to go.

'Wankers like you shouldn't be allowed to have children,' she shouted after us – at which point I'm afraid I lost it. The red mist descended, and before I knew it I had grabbed her by the rucksack she was wearing and spun her around.

'What did you just say?' I hissed, resisting the very strong urge to smash her skull repeatedly against the wall of Saks Fifth Avenue. Me, who has never hit anyone in their entire life! (Although I did throw my car keys at my brother once during an argument in a restaurant.) Her boyfriend saw my rage, I think, and they backed away.

Michael bundled us all into a cab and we went back to our accommodation. I was shaking, furious with myself for letting her get under my skin like that: so stupid, so reckless, so pointless. But to this day, whenever I think about it, I still feel a stab of rage. In that moment, she exemplified all my frustrations at the toll politics was taking on my family.

But that was further down the line at this point. William, only 5 when Cameron moved into Downing Street, was beautifully oblivious of any niggles. He had bigger fish to fry.

'One of my first memories of anything beyond the ordinary was aged 5, arriving with my nanny at Number 10 just after the 2010 election, for a playdate with Elwen,' Will tells me. 'Mostly because Candice was promptly arrested by the police at security. Her makeup pen had flagged up on the scanner as a potential weapon. I wanted to crawl under the table from embarrassment. As first memories go, it was quite a peach.'

Our family unit was very much our nanny Candice, the children and me, with Michael usually a bit part on the side; so it was a surprise for the children when he turned out to be the main attraction for everyone else beyond our gates. And not just him, but so many of these people who were by now friends with us and with our children.

Sam and I had shared a school run since about 2009, when Beatrice, Will and her daughter Nancy all started at St Mary Abbot's, a Church primary school at the corner of High Street Kensington and Kensington Church Street – a location which would later have quite the influence on my decision to jump ship from *The Times*, all the way over in Wapping, to the *Daily Mail*, less than a minute away across the road from St Mary A.

One of the reasons, I think, that Samantha and I hit it off so well was because, fundamentally, we're both quite creative, subversive people. Unlike many in our social circle, we weren't especially academic at school – and yet we had both married intellectual men. For their part, I think our husbands were drawn to our slightly chaotic minds. I always remember Dave recounting with great fondness how, when he used to visit Sam at college in Bristol, her student room was a bit like Tracey Emin's bed, the floor strewn with debris. I think he loved her free-spirited heart; the confidence with which she led her life just the way she wanted it. For him, coming from such a very serious and rather staid background, finding Sam, with her talent for painting, her love of music, her sheer enthusiasm for life, was magical.

And she had an edginess to her, a tremendous sense of adventure and a genuine curiosity for people. When Dave first became leader, there were endless slightly sneering stories about how she used to play pool with Tricky in Bristol, implying that she was some sort of spoiled little rich girl playing at being a 'real' person. But she wasn't. That was her, that was Sam, she judged people by who they were, not what they were. If she liked them she genuinely couldn't care less where they came from. She liked them and that was that.

And the thing is, to be Samantha's friend was very special. She was kind and loyal and funny and a very good dancer. She had great taste, she was a great cook, she was honest and funny and to the point. She loved a drink and a fag and a laugh, and so did I. On our holidays to Ibiza, we were on the same page: our children were there and had a great time – but so did we; we caroused and danced and drank and parcelled out the early mornings between us. Multi-tasking was second nature, as was burning candles at every end we could find.

My old editor, Paul Dacre, once wrote me a letter saying I had more 'cojones' than most men. And I guess sometimes I do, if by cojones you mean someone who can think for themselves and isn't afraid to go against the grain; but Samantha too had balls, a real courage of her convictions. It manifested itself not just in the way she would sally forth into unknown or new situations, confident of her abilities. It was there in the day-to-day decisions she made, from buying a house in the early days of her and Dave's marriage to the way she conducted herself at No 10, right from the beginning.

And, of course, it was there in the way she had risen to the immense challenge of caring for her son Ivan, for fighting tooth and nail to get him the best possible care, for knitting him so securely into all their lives that woe betide anyone who ever had the ignorance and condescension to feel sorry for any of them.

She was also, let's not forget – and with a great deal more subtlety and deprecation than Cherie Blair ever had – a very successful businesswoman in her own right. A friend of a friend used to work under her at Smythson, the luxury stationery and leather company that Sam not only put properly on the map but also essentially reinvented, and told me how no other boss she has ever had has come close to Sam. 'She was awesome,' said the friend. 'Not only insanely talented and with a great eye, but also had that fairy-dust touch of managing the team to the best of their potential – we all just wanted to do well for her. That's high-level magic!'

In opposition, Sam had always been adamant that if Dave won, she didn't want to move to No 10. The main reason, of course, was Ivan, and the special environment his care required. Having sold their first house in North Kensington, they moved to another a few streets away, and she set about making it Ivan-friendly. A wheelchair lift, space for a live-in carer, a specially equipped bedroom and wet room, a sensory garden. He was also enrolled at a specialist school for children with severe learning difficulties, Jack Tizard, just around the corner next to Loftus Road stadium.

Had Ivan lived and Dave had still become prime minister, he might well have been the first to eschew the fishbowl of No 10. But after his death in 2009 and having secured the job, it was hard to argue with the police and security services, who balked at the logistics of protecting an ordinary terraced house in a residential area of London. Also, no doubt the neighbours would have complained.

Not that Sam ever had her own protection team, a fact that I still find astonishing. Unlike America, Britain still treats prime ministers' spouses as ordinary citizens (some might say annoying inconveniences), meaning they have all of the disadvantages – constant interferences from the general public, fears for their safety, restrictions on their movements – but none of the advantages. Sam did have a driver, I recall, who was trained in evasive driving, but that was about it. In all other circumstances – at the school gate, shopping in Sainsbury's, on the way to work – she and the kids were on their own. The guys with the earpieces only showed up when Dave was in the picture.

And so, after terms were agreed with the Lib Dems – a feverish week in which Osborne's negotiating skills and Dave's patience were sorely tested – they walked through the door of No 10 on 11 May 2010. Sam had been told that morning to prepare herself for the eventuality, and had spent the day pondering suitable outfits – not easy since she was six months pregnant with Florence, who I later became godmother to (one of the greatest sadnesses of the breakdown in our friendship was losing touch with her).

Being photographed while pregnant is not the greatest of prospects at the best of times; doing so when the eyes of the world are watching was even more nerve wracking, but Sam pulled it off beautifully, in a simple blue Emilia Wickstead dress. She later joked that it was far less nerve wracking than sharing a stage with Carla Bruni, wife of the then French president, Nicolas Sarkozy. Rule 527 of being a political wife: if at all possible, try to avoid being photographed next to a supermodel.

While she waited at home for the green light, the Swarm headed to Queen's Park and the Lockwoods' house, where everyone had gathered to witness the moment the two of them walked through that famous front door. The atmosphere was electric, a mixture of excitement and incredulity, the drink flowing. It did just seem incredibly surreal, watching events unfold on TV as the governmental car pulled up outside No 10, seeing the pair of them step out, smiling and waving for the cameras, the whirr of helicopters and sound of camera shutters drowning out the commentary. We all sat there, transfixed, watching as history was made, each one of us a tiny part of it. 'It's all downhill from now on,' quipped Chris with his characteristically dry wit. I remember thinking to myself: things will never be the same again.

We partied late, but the next day it was straight to business. Michael, who had started out with the shadow housing brief before moving to education, was expected to become

Secretary of State for Education. He and Dominic Cummings had been working hard on putting together a blueprint for educational reform, and despite not being the sort of person to make assumptions, he was hopeful that he would have the chance to implement his vision.

I was excited for him: this was everything he had been working towards for the past couple of years. And after the horrible trauma of expenses, he bloody well deserved it. At some point the following afternoon, he got the call and headed off to see Dave. It turned out to be something of a bittersweet meeting.

When Michael walked through the front door later that evening, he was agitated. I handed him a glass of wine and asked him how it had gone. He explained that Dave had asked him to be Secretary of State for Education – but had vetoed Dom on the basis that he was too divisive, and a trouble maker. At the time I thought this was just Dave-speak for having a mind of his own, but looking back I realise that Dave was right about Dom. None of us knew it then, but that slightly boffinish, Professor Brainstorm demeanour masked a very nasty side. Or maybe I was just too naive back then to see it.

Either way it was, Michael said, like being offered his dream job – and then being told he could only do it if he divorced me. I blinked at that analogy then told him he just needed to persuade Dave that he could keep Dom under control – and he must have done somehow, because of course Dom did end up at Education with him. With hindsight, though, I can see it was an early indication of trouble to come.

It was also an early sign of his fierce loyalty to Dom and their close ideological bond – something that years down the line was to lead to open speculation about the precise nature of their relationship when, in 2016, the *Mail on Sunday* – then edited by Geordie Greig – ran front-page headlines, two issues in a row, alleging Dom and Michael were having an affair at the height of the frenzied EU Referendum campaign.

It would have been laughable were it not for the fact that both the kids – then at the sensitive ages of 13 and 11 – went into school the Monday after the second splash (which named the alleged lovers) and had to endure the jibes of the other kids. But Greig, despite the fact that by then I was working as a columnist on the *Mail on Sunday*'s sister paper, never let collegiate alliances get in the way of a good story.

Nor was it the last time he inflicted serious emotional and psychological damage on my family: later, during Covid, while I was actually working for him (by then he was at the helm of the *Daily Mail* itself) he ran a story that was at best inaccurate, at worst a deliberate testing of the facts, as explained to his political editor at the time, Simon Walters, by Michael himself. As a result my daughter – at the time just 15 – was cancelled online in the most brutal and traumatic of ways. I am not going to give oxygen to the story by repeating any of the details here, but I had to witness my child receiving rape threats and death threats. I remember holding her on the stairs of our house, trying to reassure her that her life was not over and that she shouldn't 'just kill herself' as the trolls were telling her to. To this day she can't talk about it without becoming extremely distressed.

Like so many others who suffered from Brexit Derangement Syndrome, my family were fair game for Geordie, something I was never able to come to terms with. It was also my first experience of someone who appeared to have Jekyll and

Hyde Syndrome. Most of the media sharks I had come up against thus far weren't afraid of showing their teeth from the start, but I couldn't reconcile this cultured, intelligent and in many ways extremely thoughtful gentleman, for whom I wrote a weekly column, with the person he showed himself to be on those occasions when he smelled blood in the water.

I would like to say that I bear him no ill will, and of course the journalist in me understands his motives all too well. But as a mother, the Beatrice thing was just unforgivable: the story itself was not of any consequence, but the trauma it caused on a personal level was lasting and there's no possible justification for putting a child through that.

As for the story about Michael being gay – with Dom or anyone else – that didn't bother me in the slightest. At frequent points in my marriage various people solemnly informed me that Michael was definitely gay. And after we split up, it was widely assumed that homosexuality (his, not mine) was the cause. All I can say, without going into too much detail, was that, as far as my own experience goes, Michael was enthusiastically heterosexual – and evidence since would tend to support that view.

What was, however, true, and remains true to this day, was that Michael enjoyed the intellectual company of men probably more than that of women. And he did have a lot of gay friends (still does), plus as a minister he had a habit of surrounding himself with incredibly handsome gay men such as Henry Newman and Henry Cook (a.k.a. 'the Henries') and Josh Grimstone. But that was all circumstantial. A few swallows do not a summer make. Some might still say, however, that an obviously winning touch in how not to be a political wife is to pick a partner who prompts such prurience.

So gay, no; metrosexual, oh yes. Compared to most of the men in the average newsroom (or for that matter the Commons tearoom), Michael was always suspiciously impeccably turned out. He was invariably more fragrant than even the famous Lady Archer (his favourite aftershave was Penhaligon's English Fern, alternating occasionally with Blenheim Bouquet), was always freshly scrubbed, wore nice shirts and smart cufflinks, was fastidious about his hair – and, of course, was (is) famously polite.

For some reason a lot of people mistook these attributes for proof of homosexuality, which I think probably says more about them than him.

His supposed lover, Dom, by contrast, was not notably nice-smelling (on the contrary: when he first started work in Michael's rather cramped and airless parliamentary office in Portcullis House, the ladies deemed it necessary to acquire some scented candles to dampen the scent of his masculine musk) nor, as a misguided proponent of the grown-up hoodie, was he well turned out. As for the seductive charm that might have caught a roving eye, I don't think anyone has ever accused Dom of possessing an excess of politesse.

Dom's wife, Mary, wrote a very funny piece in *The Spectator* in November 2016, in response to the allegations connecting Michael and Dom. It's still on the website: worth a detour. She correctly identified the source of the story as one-time chief whip Gavin Williamson, a man with the intellect of a prawn and the integrity of a rotten banana but blessed with a fox's cunning.

'Williamson had, said the MoS [*Mail on Sunday*], dashed into No. 10 "in the heat of the bitter EU campaign" to deliver news of the fling to the PM,' she wrote. 'Even before I knew

Dom was one of the Brokeback Brexiteers this seemed a very curious tale. What could have made Williamson so sure? Why did he rush to tell the PM "in the heat of the campaign"? The story was written as if somehow Williamson thought a gay romance shed light on the otherwise inexplicable success of Vote Leave.'

She then went on to make the very salient point: 'Not then, nor now, does David Cameron accept that his pal Gove – a lifelong Eurosceptic – chose to campaign for Leave for the sake of his country. Cameron's position on the matter, I've heard it said, is simply that 'Gove chose the wrong DC', Dominic C over David C, and that for this crime he will be forever dead to Dave. But what if Williamson, in the manner of all successful courtiers, was simply telling his leader what he thought he wanted to hear (an explanation as to how the 'wrong' DC could ever be preferred) in order to gain standing?'

That may indeed have explained Williamson's otherwise baffling promotion, but the point about Dave being completely unable to understand Michael's motives is correct: he reacted, to what he saw as Michael's betrayal, like a jealous lover. Not only, as we saw when Dave tried to deny Dom his place at Michael's side at Education, was he just plain anti Dom's influence, but he was clearly rattled by Dom personally. The Williamson anecdote showed that Dave was somehow collating Michael's personal life with his Brexit stance – pure emotion and quite in line with Dave's innate cronyism – whereas Michael saw the whole choice to Leave as a logical one, simply aligned with his wider political thesis and his personal beliefs.

I always liked Dom – well, the old Dom, at any rate. I first met him on a random night out in Soho with friends sometime in the early Noughties. For some reason I can't quite remember, the late Derek Draper was there, who at the time worked for Tony Blair; it was a fairly wonky (by which I mean policy wonky), non-partisan bunch. I got talking to Dom and found him fascinating, similar in many ways to Steve Hilton, fizzing with slightly manic energy and bursting with big ideas.

On the way home, I asked Michael about him, and he explained that he had been involved in Business for Sterling, which campaigned against Britain joining the euro, and was setting up a free-market think-tank called The New Frontiers Foundation. He also had an interesting connection to Russia, having lived there for a while in the late Nineties. Perhaps that is where he picked up his habit of calling everyone 'comrade'.

Dom was on the fringes of our marital friendship group, that is to say – along with many others, including Dougie Smith – someone Michael saw a lot of, but not with me. I think he thought I would be bored by the ceaseless political intrigue, and to begin with that was certainly true. Bored was perhaps not quite the right word: intimidated. Michael, Dave, George, Dom, Chris, Steve: they were all so self-assured and clever. I deferred to them on the subject of politics, not just because back then I was unsure of myself in that respect, but also because they had a way of making it clear that they were the experts.

The exception to this was Steve: he was always happy to debate with me, and always gave the impression he was genuinely interested in what I had to say. He was the opposite of a political snob – more of a political entrepreneur, always keen to explore new ideas – whereas George and

Dave were fundamentally traditionalists. It was a great shame when Steve was turfed out of No 10 not long after Dave became prime minister. Prime ministers need people like Steve in their lives, otherwise the Whitehall machine oozes over them like a giant amoeba, and it becomes less about doing the job – and all about keeping it.

The intoxicating effects of power are well documented; but for all the Boy's Own thrill of being able to scramble fighter jets at a moment's notice, or having dashing security officers following you around all day long, it's the luxurious extras that really go to the head. The chauffeur-driven car, the motorcycle outriders, grace and favours, the pick of the nation's arts collection, No 10 and No 11, embassies, grace-and-favours and, of course, a host of exciting new friends, all of whom have simply always been their greatest admirer.

CHAPTER SIX

THE INSIDER LOOKING OUT

'True love is being married for ten years and successfully resisting the urge to throttle him when he asks you where you keep the plasters ... or puts his dirty cups just next to the dishwasher but never actually inside it.'

Sarah Vine, *Daily Mail*,
October 2014.

It's hard not to be revisionist when looking back at the years when I was supposedly one of the top political wives in the country. From the outside looking in it must have seemed a life of unimaginable privilege and excitement, and, in many ways, it was: weekending at Chequers and Dorneywood, hanging out at Downing Street – but did I ever believe that I had a right to be there, in the way that I think Sam, Kate, Venetia and the like did? Not really.

Sam embraced the move to Downing Street with her customary élan. She didn't have long before the arrival of Florence, so she had to move quickly to get the place in shape and the older kids settled. It was no mean feat.

Downing Street is a funny old place. Without wishing to sound too woo-woo about the whole thing, it has a rather strange and slightly uneasy energy, the legacy, I suppose, of three centuries of high-octane political drama. People imagine it to be impossibly grand and luxurious, and some bits of it very definitely are. But a lot of it is like a run-down, old-fashioned guesthouse, rather more Fawlty Towers than Grace & Favour. The bits that the public don't tend to see – namely the back entrance off Horse Guards that most of the staff and residents use to avoid the press pack permanently stationed outside that famous front door (not to mention the resident lunatics with their placards and loud hailers) – is all Artex ceilings, grim carpet squares, lino and strip lighting; a rabbit warren of cramped offices with no natural light and primitive staff toilets. As for catering facilities, the only one I ever saw was an ancient, much-kicked and distinctly irksome vending machine stocked with items which looked as though their sell-by dates might have expired during Margaret Thatcher's time.

'Upstairs' was not much better. A lot of rather frowsty beige carpets and peeling paint, not helped by the fact that the windows all had to be hermetically sealed for security reasons. The outgoing incumbent, Gordon Brown, appeared to have lived a semi-monastic lifestyle, leaving virtually no trace of his existence save a giant TV placed, rather oddly, in the middle of one of the sitting rooms, with a single chair in front of it. All very Cold War. Elsewhere, the only concrete evidence of New Labour was in the No 11 flat – the bigger of the two – which the Blairs had occupied while in residence; it being far more suited to family life than the much smaller, more higgledy-piggledy and distinctly tattier No 10, which still had sniffable traces of Denis Thatcher's prodigious fag habit engrained in tar stains in the wallpaper.

There was a bespoke wooden kitchen, which must have cost a fortune and seemed frightfully chic back in 1997, or whenever it was installed – but it was in an odd place in relation to the flat, and very definitely not designed for the kind of open-plan family living and expansive kitchen suppers that Sam and Dave loved, more the sort of place that staff would cook before delivering food to a dining table.

But the oddest room, the one that had Sam and me truly baffled, was right at the top of the flat. It consisted of a full-length floor-to-ceiling mirror, with a ballet barre fitted the length of it. Sam and I immediately christened it the 'Carole Caplin Suite', after the controversial figure who had been a style adviser and fitness coach to the Blairs and a leading player in the so-called 'Cheriegate' scandal, in which a friend of Carole, an Australian called Peter Foster with a string of criminal convictions, was discovered to have assisted Cherie with the purchase of two flats in Bristol. Initially, Mrs Blair denied the connection, but was later caught out when Foster himself provided evidence of the deal. We imagined Cherie and Carole practising pliés in the mirror, while Tony worked on his guns in the corner. Happy days.

Anyway, it was quickly decided that the Camerons would live at No 11, the Osbornes at No 10, both renting out their respective London houses. There was a small yearly budget available for maintenance and redecoration costs – but Sam reasoned that since they were likely to be there for at least one term, it was worth investing some of her own money in making it a proper home. The entire place was given a refresh, including a new open-plan kitchen/dining room with stainless-steel work tops and fragrant seagrass to replace the old carpets (her signature style). It was not an easy task: everything had to go via the 'approved' contractors, who naturally charged like rhinos for everything.

Nevertheless, Sam got there in the end, and the result was a bright, modern family home, as normal a space for the children to grow up in as possible, given the circumstances. Meanwhile, upstairs, George and Frances set about defumigating No 10 – albeit in Osborne & Little's rather more flamboyant style.

Frances, though similar to me in her ability to side-eye the stupider sycophants, came from political royalty herself so was innately accustomed to the razzmatazz. I wasn't. Her father was the Rt Hon David Howell, now Baron Howell of Guildford, who was a senior minister in Tory governments from 1979 to 2012 and came from the same Eton–Oxbridge background as so many Tory grandees did – and do: he was patrician, a bit lofty, to the manor born, though, in fact, a kind man.

But here we were, in 2010, rocking up for drinks at Downing Street, Twixtmas at Chequers, and dipping our fingers in the font water at the christening of the prime minister's daughter, my goddaughter, as if this was the most normal thing in the world. I don't remember ever discussing the lunacy of this with Michael but, looking back, it really was as if we had taken a pact never to mention the sheer head-fuckery of our lives.

Me, Sarah the awkward 'Inglesina', friends with the prime minister, being waited on hand and foot by staff at Chequers, sitting at the chancellor's dining table at Dorneywood, hanging out with bona fide A-list celebrities like Helena Bonham Carter and her husband Tim Burton. I was Alice in Wonderland, still slightly over-large on the Drink Me potion, out on the black and white Chequers board with the sliding Knights, expecting any minute that the Queen of Hearts would topple through the scene, shouting, 'Off with her head!'

LESSON FIVE IN HOW NOT TO BE A POLITICAL WIFE:
being the grown-up, cynical one who persists in Not being that impressed by the empty trappings of power.

Chequers is impossibly historic and Dave loved that. He was the most enthusiastic of tour guides, pointing out the exquisite panelling, the Rubens supposedly 'redecorated' with a moustache by Churchill, the famed Long Gallery on the first floor with its stained-glass crests of former prime ministers, Cromwell's death mask and Queen Elizabeth I's ring. Above the fireplace hung the Lord Protector's sword: there was many an evening when, after one of Graham the chef's fine suppers and one or two wines from the peerless cellar, the temptation to take it down and brandish it seemed hard to resist.

It is, at heart, a Tudor manor house and even the origin of its name is a little lost in the mists of time: either it's to do with an earlier manor of the twelfth century being owned by a man whose name meant chessboard in Italian or, as historian David Starkey suggests, it's more likely to do with the 'chequer' trees that grow throughout the garden.

Like all good stately homes, it has a ghost; the legacy of one of the more colourful periods in the house's history. Lady Jane Grey, the ill-fated 'Queen for Nine Days' who lost her head at the behest of her cousin and rival, Mary I, had a sister, also called Mary, who later fell foul of the next powerful Queen, Elizabeth I, to whom she, along with her surviving sister, Katherine, was a lady in waiting. Elizabeth was unmarried and childless, and since the sisters were in line for the succession via their mother, Lady Frances Brandon (who was the daughter of Henry VIII's sister, another Mary), neither could take a husband without the express permission of the Queen. So naturally, the naughty little minxes both did.

Elizabeth was not amused. She banished Mary's husband and sent Mary to live under house arrest at Chequers, under the watchful eye of William Hawtrey, who built the house as it is today. Mary was imprisoned in a room over the entrance, at the top of the house (thereafter known imaginatively as 'The Prison Room'), over what is currently the main entrance.

There is a secret stairway up to this room from a side reception room, installed by Hawtrey so that Lady Mary could occasionally be allowed down, presumably for a little light luncheon and a turn around the quad. That first Christmas there, in the company of Tim and Helena, the three of us decided to slip up and explore.

From inside the house, the room is reached via the main bedrooms, up a creaking staircase and through various connecting rooms. There is a small ante-chamber, presumably for a maid, or maybe even a guard. In the crepuscular gloom of a late December afternoon, there was a spooky chill in the air and an unnerving number of dead or dying flies buzzing against the lead windowpanes. Behind the door there was an eerie handprint on the wall, supposedly Lady Mary's, now preserved behind Perspex, some illegible scribblings, also etched into the wall – and a small, beady-eyed portrait of Mary herself, glaring furiously at us interlopers (later, on the occasions when the children were allocated that room to sleep in, they always insisted that I cover this painting over).

A small, rather rickety bathroom led off it, again something of a fly cemetery. I couldn't help thinking about Sam's stories – less historical than Dave's – about Mary's ghost that supposedly prowled tragically around Chequers at night. I loved a Gothic ghost story as much as anyone and here I was, living one out with none other than the director of *Corpse Bride*, *Sleepy Hollow* and *Beetlejuice*. I looked at Tim; Tim looked at me. 'I can feel …' he said slowly. '… I can feel … a presence …' That was it for me. Not for the first time and not for the last in inappropriate circumstances, I got the giggles. To my amazement, so did he. Dave, coming up the stairs to find out where we were, thought we were all entirely insane.

Haunted rooms and dead flies aside, Chequers was efficiently run by a long-forgotten stratum of the Armed Services, the Women's Royal Naval Service, known as 'Wrens', and the general feel of the place was a curious mix of officers' mess and budget gentlemen's club. The decor had the 1983 hand of Maggie still clutching it: chipped skirting boards, faded chintz, the occasional rag-roll paint effect, suspicious amounts of magnolia paint; all shabby chic before shabby chic was a thing.

The bathrooms were decent, unlike the usual aristo country house, with good water pressure and deep baths, and as well as a tennis court (upon which Dave used to delight in crushing his opponents), there was a fantastic Olympic-sized swimming pool, heated and covered, built in 1973 under Edward Heath's tenure and paid for by the then American ambassador, Walter Annenburgh, as a thank you for hospitality enjoyed by Richard Nixon during two visits.

The insulation in the pool house was terrible and Sam, who took the environment rather seriously (again, before it was even really a thing), shuddered at the thought of the profligacy. But for a family with small children, whose guests often had their own nippers to entertain, that pool was a godsend. Many happy hours were spent splashing around in its bath-like depths. It was certainly a far warmer – if no less wet – alternative to the inevitable Sunday morning constitutional over the Chilterns to the Plough Inn in Cadsden, which was, come rain, shine or anything else the English weather could muster, always a three-line whip affair.

Dave's rabid enthusiasm for the long Country Walk was one of his more tiresome character traits. It made sense – the breakfasts at Chequers were monumental (my son *still* talks about them in awed tones), and something had to be done to walk them off and make space for lunch. Being a natural outdoorsy type with bags of energy, it never occurred to him, I don't think, that we weren't all jumping out of bed at 5 a.m. raring to pull on our wellies and yomp up hill and down dale. He even subjected Angela Merkel to one during a weekend with the German chancellor: he had to help her over the stile at the end of the field, an image that remains fixed in my mind.

It certainly irked his security staff, whose natural habitat was the mess room on the way to the swimming pool, where they would sit together watching telly, their shoes lined up outside the door, drinking tea and eating biscuits. Whenever Dave, as he often did, would leap off the sofa and declare he was off for a run they had about 10 seconds to ditch their mugs of tea and head out after him. He certainly kept them on their toes.

The walk to Cadsden would be undertaken at a more leisurely pace thanks to the merciful presence of children (never dogs: Dave was never a dog person; in fact, I would go so far as to say that he disliked them intensely, unusually). The path took us over fields and down a steep hill, which was popular with other walkers. A member of the public could always be depended on to whip out their camera phone and snap us in our wellies and I soon learned to avoid photo-bombing by walking a judicious 10 steps behind, or sometimes ahead. Unlike the Obamas or the Burton-Bonham-Carters, or some of the other VIPs I met at Chequers, I did not suit the hearty, outdoorsy candid camera approach. Where Helena Bonham Carter got some fetching colour in her perfectly alabaster cheeks, I went bright red and looked like I was about to have a coronary – and unlike her gorgeous eclecticism of colour, ruffle and texture, I wear sleek black and white only, neither of which play to anyone's best advantage when surrounded by bilious waves and folds of putrid-coloured anoraks.

Suffice to say that I soon learned to hang back with the security guys walking behind the PM: for one thing, they had fabulous tales of derring-do to which I merely needed to listen and ooh and aah – so, no puffing – and they scowled so mightily at any ramblers snapping them that it rarely happened, and certainly never appeared in next day's papers.

There is a famous photo of them all, baby Florence in a papoose, Helena and Tim smiling, Michael to one side, snapped by a walker that first Christmas. I am mercifully out of shot. Of course, the net effect of this is, unlike the ubiquitous Bullingdon photo which still gets hauled out of mothballs at least once a year as a constant reminder of how posh Dave and his mates were, I appear not to have ever been part of the Chequers crew because there is no public pictorial evidence of my presence. That was always my preference. Not for me the successful political wife's ability to be omnipresent, like Nancy Reagan or Norma Major.

In June 2012, the Camerons' love of walking to the pub for lunch came back to bite them on the bum, when they inadvertently left their daughter behind there – a story which the grubbier papers leapt on with alacrity a couple of months later, rubbing their figurative hands together at the realisation that this terrible abandonment had happened on the very same day the Government relaunched a £450 million 'troubled families programme'.

'David Cameron left daughter behind after pub visit' chided the *Guardian*, talking disapprovingly about him and Sam leaving in separate cars, and only realising that Nancy wasn't with the other parent when they got back to Chequers. 'Thankfully, she was safe and well.'

The *Sun* went even further, quoting a Plough bartender as telling the paper, 'Pub staff found his daughter in the toilet and didn't know what to do ... it's frightening that the Prime Minister of Britain can forget something so important as his own daughter.'

This story has always enraged me, probably because it reminds me of a similar one when Michael and I left William, who had just started secondary school, in a hotel room at the Cheltenham Festival in the autumn of 2016. We were there at the behest of *The Times*, and had gone to another venue – about three doors away – for a *Times* event. Will had elected to stay in the room and watch *Match of the Day* with the dogs, but at some point during our absence he got worried and went to ask the staff at the front desk whether they knew where we were. They knew exactly where we were (the party was in the sister hotel), since I had given them clear instructions and asked them to call me if there were any issues at all. I had also asked them if they were okay to keep an eye on him, since he was a bit too grown up by that stage for a babysitter (he was already going to school on his own, like many Year 7s), and they had assured me not to worry.

So I was mortified when one of the hotel staff – who I later found out was an avid Remainer – sold a story to the *Daily Mirror*, which spun it as 'Michael Gove's young son was left alone in a room at a posh B&B for six hours while his parents enjoyed a glitzy celebrity party'. It was especially embarrassing for poor Will, who was in his first term at Holland Park Academy, not the easiest of environments for the child of a Tory politician at the best of times, and even trickier when the story reported that he had been wandering the corridors of the hotel distraught. It was a politically motivated attack, designed to hurt Michael – but in truth the only person it really upset was poor Will.

The Cameron one was a similar below-the-belt story. Nancy was 8 years old at the time, not the toddler that the wording from each paper suggests – and, as we've established, the Camerons walked to this pub most weekends so all the children were well-known there and familiar with the environment. In fact, when Dave went back to get her, he found Nancy helping out with the staff. Afterwards, the other children in the other two families who had come to that Sunday's pub lunch were reportedly rather jealous that Nancy got to go behind the bar. In total, she was away from her parents for about 15 minutes and yet she will always be known as the child who was abandoned in the pub. Welcome to the toxic interface between politics and the media.

Lunch itself was never at the actual pub; after shandy and crisps, we would get a lift back to the house with security and then it was a traditional Sunday lunch, prepared by chef Graham: a roast, mountains of veg, ice cream for afters. Graham's homemade ice cream was the stuff of legends. Again, like the epic breakfasts, the children talk about it still.

Evening drinks were by the fire in the great hall under the watchful eye of various eminent Cromwellians and Dutch masters (not to mention a few mistresses), sprawled in the deep sofas facing each other, mags on the ottoman; swimming through White Ladies, the cocktail that Dave had really perfected: slugs of tart lemon juice, sweet Cointreau and an extra cosh of vodka. Unbelievably drunk-making and entirely delicious: I couldn't resist them, hence my habit of making rather unguarded remarks on those sofas, of which more later.

After dinner, there was none of that sexist rubbish with gents staying with port. We all hung out together in a strangely informal, feet-up sort of way, sometimes upstairs in the Long Gallery, occasionally watching reality TV and shouting at the telly. During that first Christmas and New Year in 2010, Dave had an idea, inspired by the X Factor finale, which had shockingly been won by Matt Cardle, soon to be forgotten, while third-placed One Direction went on to make boy-band history. I remember being told a scurrilous story by one of my *Times* showbiz colleagues that at the party afterwards, Harry Styles was seen whispering in Matt Cardle's ear, 'Think of how much p***y you're going to get.' A crystal ball would obviously have shown that this would, in fact, be Harry's own embarras du choix ...

Anyway, Dave decided that we should have our own *X Factor* competition, ostensibly to keep the kids entertained but also secretly for his own enjoyment (actually, not even that secretly). And so, the prime minister and I zipped off to a retail park on the outskirts of Slough to prowl the aisles of Curry's for a suitable piece of equipment.

When Dave was on a mission, he tended to move very fast, striding ahead in that determined and instantly recognisable Old Etonian way of his. Dawdling along behind, I had my first real taste of being caught up in the slipstream of fame. It was fascinating. People would walk past him going in the opposite direction; their brain would clock something, and they'd do a double take. Then they would turn to their partner, or whoever they were with, in amazement and silently mouth something along the lines of, 'Ohmigod, was that ...? Is that ...?' One or two of them would give him a quick 'Cheers, Dave' and a thumbs-up; others would giggle and scuttle off in the other direction; some would be all nonchalant; others would try for a selfie. Always Dave just took it all in his stride. As the years went by, the same thing started to happen with Michael, who always bustled through shops and stations faster than his retail-obsessed wife. 'Bloody hell, it's that Michael Gove. Bloody hell!' I would hear as I tried to catch up with him. I would smile at them. 'Yes, it is. And, bloody hell, I'm married to him!'

Anyway, Dave ended up buying an actual *X Factor* 'official merchandise' karaoke machine that plugged into the television and it was the hit of that Twixtmas and New Year. All the children obviously hogged the machine, obsessed as they were with Jessie J and Will Young, but most evenings after supper you'd find a few tipsy grown-ups warbling through 'Jolene' and air-guitaring madly through 'Stairway to Heaven'. I choose to draw a veil over who thought themselves Beyoncé and who would have sounded better as the klaxon in the factory at the end of the day ...

Sam really came into her own when she threw a party – and the party she threw at Chequers for her delayed 40th, in 2014, was probably my last truly happy memory of those gilded days, and almost certainly one of the best parties I have ever been to. Sam had transformed the Great Hall into a rave, with glitter balls, lasers and disco lights playing over about 150 people dancing wildly to the music of DJ Sarah HB, short for Hard Bitch. Dave and Sam ruled over the dance floor, always the best dancers, doing their Ceroc double act with enviable grace.

Everyone was beautiful and clever and powerful; but for once I didn't feel like Cinders at the Ball. Sam had already complimented me on my Diane von Furstenberg black wrap dress, even though it was a touch too tight around the middle – 'Those bosoms, Sarah!' – and I was having the time of my life, sipping mojitos and chatting to Sarah Montague in the Rose Garden. If I'd known the reference back then, I would have said it was just like the party scene in the film of *Saltburn*: effortless decadence, posh people knowing just what to do and say – except that for once I wasn't the one drinking the bath water: I was part of this enchantment.

It was, sadly, just a brief glimpse into a world of magic: Michael, for reasons I have never established, wasn't having a good time at all, and insisted on leaving early and returning to London. In the governmental car on the way home, never the best of passengers, I threw up, to the horror of both the driver and Michael. Clearly, it had got just too much for me.

It was all a little like being at an incredibly luxurious and fun boarding school; an attractive prospect from the get-go for the more institutionalised of the 'Camelot' lads. But I never forgot where we were and that we were being 'run' by a team of hard-working staff. The more we went, the more we were looked after: one of the 'Wrens' started to bring me cups of tea in bed in the mornings. This was because, for all Graham's friendliness, it was nigh on impossible to access the industrial kitchen, staffed by minions at all times, so there was no nipping in there for a cuppa or a snack.

This baffled the children: 'It felt like the opposite of privilege,' remembers Will, my son, who is always reassuringly candid about those days. 'We couldn't even get a pack of crisps!' I remember Bea being melodramatic and saying to one of the nannies, 'But I'm dying here! Can't I just have a cookie?' and the nanny wagging her finger at her and saying, 'You know perfectly well that we are not allowed in the kitchen; you'll just have to wait until lunchtime,' and Bea wailing, 'But that's awful, grown-up food and I don't want that!' at which we all fell about laughing.

Bea insists that she and Will were strange compared to the other kids – that they always stuck out and got into trouble. She hated the upstairs–downstairs life, was unnerved by having her bed made and felt watched all the time. 'I was freaked out by the staff,' she tells me now. 'I made things up about them all – even the bodyguards – how they were all living this strange parallel existence to us, spying on us and plotting to eat me in my sleep.'

It's the children's memories of Chequers and Dorneywood that give me perspective on those years. They weren't remotely impressed by the grandeur of staying at a sixteenth-century manor house with connections to historical superstars and every prime minister since 1921. They remember the house mainly for the endless games of Capture the Flag that they played in the warren of 'service' rooms and sculleries at the back of the house. The concealed 'library doors' in the bookshelves that led to the bedrooms staircase was absolutely my favourite feature; for them it was just a shortcut to sneaking about.

But they were blown away by the facilities: the indoor swimming pool, the football pitch that the Camerons created, the number of rooms with tellies. 'I do remember meeting Malia and Sasha Obama and frolicking with them in the incredible indoor pool at Chequers,' Bea tells me, 'but I only realised that there was anything extraordinary about this when you asked me what I thought of them when I got home. And I was never remotely impressed by the other kids: everyone wanted me to be friends with Nancy but she was the year below me, which seemed important at that age, and she was so unlike me; always meek and mild, keeping her head below the radar, never getting into trouble. I was the polar opposite; I was trouble, so there was no chance of us being soulmates.'

Ask Bea now about the grown-ups and she's hazier on the more high-profile names that came through the door; as unimpressed now as she was then, even Barack Obama only gets the most dismissive of namechecks. But she can skewer the usual suspects we went with, with observations that only a child could make.

'Dave? Dave never really spoke to me, I never liked him much. Sam was fine – she was like a totally normal mum to all of us; Frances Osborne was nice but nervy, like a bird trapped in a cage, fluttering against the bars. George had that menacing, Mr Burnsesque gleam in his eye. Venetia Lockwood was a gorgeous angel, always kind and protective of us, but I never saw what she saw in Chris: he was super-shouty and always telling me off, to the point where I could tell you would get really annoyed. But I have to admit I had a massive crush on his son Isaac, who turned out to be gay: just my luck!

As for Will, as soon as he was able to connect his foot to a ball, that was his only interest in life. So both Chequers and Dorneywood, with their football pitches, TV rooms, X-boxes and PlayStation and the similarly footie-obsessed peers Elwen Cameron, Isaac, Xandy and Seth Lockwood, Luke Osborne and all the James boys – enough to form two five-a-side teams against each other, or an actual team against the dads-and-coppers – were each nothing short of heaven on earth.

Asking him for his memories on those years is like asking for someone's Top Trumps: 'Elwen was a bit more rugby and cricket – posho – but he was the one who got his dad to put football nets into the field at Chequers so, yeah, he was okay – and he wasn't bad on the pitch. Luke was the best – not too much older than me and a Chelsea fan. The Jameses were slightly mummy's boys and sometimes a bit too obviously on best behaviour; Xandy Lockwood was a cool guy with a good goal kick – and Seth wasn't bad either. Will Finn was an ace striker. Really funny on and off the pitch.'

And what about the grown-ups, I ask him now, any memories there? Will is suddenly gripped by a very animated memory. 'There was an epic match at Chequers quite a few years in, when I was about 8 – "Tory dads versus Tory kids" – when the dads suddenly obviously decided that they didn't have to let us win anymore. It was my dad, Dave, George, Boris, Chris Lockwood and Alex Finn against me, Elwen, Will Finn, Isaac, Xandy and Seth – and we battered them.

'Will and I both got hat-tricks and we were flying, then suddenly Boris took me out and fell really heavily on me. It was just the worst tackle ever. I was lying there, struggling for breath, and you, Mum, you weren't even near the pitch, but suddenly you were yelling from an upstairs window of the house, shouting at him to get off me. It was funny but I was actually really grateful.'

I remember watching that post Sunday lunch game from the Long Gallery with the other mums – and it was striking just how nakedly competitive Boris was, especially in the general vicinity of Dave. As for Will, there's not many lads his age who can say they've had Boris Johnson knock the wind out of them.

The differences between Will and Bea's childhood and mine and Michael's couldn't have been starker than in these years – not just because of the golden circumstances we were all finding ourselves in but because, at the end of the day, when we climbed into our Skoda and drove back down the Chequers or Dorneywood drive to West London, we were back into our usual unit as a family and often we chuckled together about the weekend's stranger moments.

For my parents, the high life was everything; for us, being together was our true life. Rosemary and Roger were very definitely a couple, with two hanger-on kids making a nuisance of themselves; we Goves worked well as a foursome. As Bea said, when talking to me about this book, 'My childhood was fun. No matter what you were going through, there were no dark periods for us; we were just tight as a family – tight and crunchy.'

That hasn't stopped both of them making some fairly perspicacious observations down the years about how they saw us behaving with 'the grown-ups' …

'Dad always cared about status and getting it right,' says Bea now. 'He was so confident in his own cleverness and intellectual stature but I realise now how on edge he often was when we were out and about in polite society because he wanted to get it right – and, more importantly, he wanted us to get it right. It was like he'd made these rich, clever friends at Oxford so he'd got himself into all the right circles, bought a house in just about the right area, bought himself the right telephone number – so now it was up to us not to let him down.

'It was funny because he couldn't have been nicer to any friends from school who came for playdates, no matter who they were or where they were from, so he totally wasn't a snob – but it was just so important to him that the political lot didn't ever think us poor and silly. It made me laugh because he knew little things that would otherwise have given us away – like cut flowers being the thing and houseplants being common, or how to say ASS-cutt not Ass-COT – but would have been horrified if we had teased him about actually caring about it.'

Bea is equally unsparing when it comes to me during those years. 'You were better but I could tell when you'd put your big-girl socialising pants on,' she says, with a touch of icy wither about her. 'You would go all glittery and sparkly, with a tinkling laugh that you didn't really use at other times. And I really noticed how much more relaxed you would be when there were fewer people around – and even better if they were arty, like Tim and Helena, not political or old-school.

'In all those holidays in Ibiza, you and Sam were so tight together. I mean, I know now that you did all the heavy lifting beforehand in organising everything' – I nod, thinking wryly of the dozens of online procedures for air tickets/catering/car hire/villa hire that every trip to Ibiza had entailed – 'but when we got there, you were in your element with Sam. You and she loved cooking together, you would gossip non-stop around the pool, put the world to rights and still have time to lark around with us. It was so much fun – for everyone – and I don't think you should ever forget that.'

Painful as it is to think back to those prelapsarian days, and biased as she so obviously is in my defence, my daughter is right about one thing: Sam and I did have fun together.

I think it's that first State Opening in May 2010 that sums up everything about me being both insider looking out and outsider looking in – and the surreality of both positions. There's a famous photo of Sam and me in the balcony in the House of Lords at this event, flushed with excitement and quite clearly delighting at the occasion. I remember it well – our mutual recognition of how moving and solemn it was watching the Queen's Speech, that feeling that we were witnessing the building bricks of ceremony that made up our constitution, the richness of the tableau before us, the sparkle of the king's ransom of tiaras – but also our shared tendency to lapse into mortifying hysteria at the daftness of some of the rituals.

We both had a sharp eye for the pantomime touches, the striding about, the banging on doors, the campness of some of the declamations, how good Black Rod's legs were in his stockings (oh God, do you think they're hold-ups or tights, don't you wish men wore Spanx sometimes, just to save us from the eye-bleeding sight of their spare tyres rolling over the top of their knickerbockers?), the rising smell of moth-balls from all the ermine capes and the occasional whiff of old wee, which reminded me of Debo Devonshire's revelation after the 1953 Coronation that a number of peers had actu-ally peed in their capes, so long had they had to wait in their seats. It was all so gloriously unquotidian, larger than life and daft in that peculiarly British way.

My journey to get there that day had been similarly eccen-tric. We had arranged to meet inside the Palace of Westminster rather than take me through the circus of getting into and then out of Downing Street, where they'd just moved in. So I'd taken the Tube to Westminster and emerged into a Parliament Square that was absurdly crowded with the crowds that gather there for every State Opening. I could barely move.

I looked rather helplessly at the clogged 200 metres that lay between me and the entrance to the House of Lords and thought that I couldn't possibly fight my way through there, so I flagged down a policeman. 'Excuse me,' I said, with my most charming smile. 'Could you possibly help me get through to the St Stephen's Tower entrance? My name's

Sarah Gove and I'm the guest of the prime minister's wife at the Queen's Speech.'

There was a short pause, and then he burst into laughter. 'Prime minister's wife, you say? Go on, love, pull the other one, it's got bells on it.'

I hadn't expected this and stumbled slightly. 'But, um, no, really …' – but it was too late: the policeman had gone and I was no closer than before. I inched my way through the packed ranks of people – excuse me, excuse me – while simultaneously trying to call someone who could help me. Finally, I got through to the switchboard at No 10 and wailed at one of the SpAds, who were all watching the whole thing on television in the offices there. He said he would come and rescue me and get a policeman to escort me over.

While I waited for him on the corner of Whitehall, I reflected on the irony of having suffered from classic imposter syndrome all my life and here I was, on the one hand the choice of the prime minister's wife as her plus-one so, yes I'd made it, and yet here I was being jostled powerlessly by crowds of people like me – imposters, all of us – and I couldn't even persuade a policeman to take me seriously enough to let me in.

When I finally made it into the House of Lords, somewhat red-faced and rather sweaty (that is why, in those pictures, I am fanning myself with a programme), Sam thought it was entirely hilarious and made me tell the story to every friend we met before – and afterwards – at the overheated and over squashed reception in the Speaker's Room with the gruesome John and Sally Bercow. She was right – it was funny, but it also summed me up as still the outsider, even when I was so demonstrably an insider.

She always got it right, I seemed always to get it wrong – like her agonising over whether to wear a hat that day and eventually deciding not to – so obviously I didn't either, out of deference to her decision. Which was fine – but meant that my increasing hair loss was then on display for every photographer to capture; which is why I love and loathe that photograph in equal measure. This was a repeated theme in these years that, just as I seemed to be getting the hang of being a political wife, something would happen to remind me how foolish I was for thinking that.

Take the Black and White Ball of 2012. This was the Tories' annual fundraiser, held in a cavernous steel and plastic pavilion inside Battersea Park: wall-to-wall thrusting young Tory types all courting aristos and arrivistes alike. Honestly, you've never seen so much plastic surgery or second wives all in the same place at once. Michael was hosting a table, so there was no escaping it.

I don't remember an awful lot about who we shared a table with or the speeches (no doubt excellent) that were made; but I do remember one person very clearly: Joan Collins. It was Sam who pointed her out to me, and we admired her from afar, a true star in a firmament of tinsel. I'd had a few glasses, so, imbued with Dutch courage, I decided to introduce myself. Drawing on my *Times* beauty editor experience (still my favourite ever journalistic gig), I waffled animatedly about makeup and wigs, which La Collins loved, being a devotee of both. It turned out she was working on her own beauty brand – appropriately named 'Timeless Beauty'. Somewhat to my surprise, I found myself asking if she and her husband Percy would like to come for supper at Barlby Road. To which she responded, even more to my surprise, that she'd like that and she would get Percy to organise it.

That said, the evening was not an unmitigated success. For a start, I don't think either Joan or Percy had ever been to North Kensington, the expansive playgrounds of Cadogan Square and Saint-Tropez being more their usual speed. I couldn't help but see a slight look of horror flit across their faces as they walked up our rickety garden path and took their seats in our modest sitting room. Not that I hadn't done my homework: Percy had been in touch beforehand so I knew to offer Joan only white wine, not to feed her red meat and to be generous with the cheese board; nevertheless, I was as nervous as hell.

I covered up any discomfort by revving around with the homemade canapés (eat your heart out, Meghan Markle), including some quails' eggs that I had foolishly hard-boiled and peeled myself (another life lesson learned – never boil your own quails' eggs: if you're going to go down this route, just throw caution to the wind and get the boiled and peeled version). I presented them to Joan with a little pot of celery salt on the side, and she took one, exclaiming 'How delicious!' as she held it between her crimson-tipped fingers. She bit into it. Oh the horror, the horror, as Joan's selected egg turned out to be rather more soft-boiled than expected. It exploded all down her spotless white silk blouse, covering her in yolk. We all sprang to her rescue, but it was too late. She was charming about it, of course, but clearly put out. Faux pas number one.

It got worse. Faux pas number two: as luck would have it – and as I type this, I still can't believe I was this stupid – my parents were in town that week, so I decided it would be fun to invite them. Quite why, given my father's track record for misbehaving, I do not know; I think perhaps I just thought they would love to meet her, being of Joan's generation. I thought my mother especially might enjoy it: my grandmother Ruth had been a huge fan of *Dynasty*, which my grandfather rather disparagingly called 'Die Nasty'. Perhaps I imagined it would be some sort of bonding exercise. I could not have been more mistaken.

My father started off by acting like a lovestruck schoolboy. This was most peculiar: a) I had never seen him like that, he was always Mr Braggadocio; b) his flirtation technique was a cross between Alan Partridge and Mr Bean. I saw Percy blench slightly as Dad lunged forward to help Joan clean her shirt.

I'd assumed Mum and Joan would get on famously, cast as they were from the same mould: both beautiful, ferociously disciplined, quick and funny, no stranger to a shoulder-pad or four. But something about my father's mooning eyes clearly got her back up, because it was like watching cats prepare to fight; all waving tails and rictus grins. Neither of them was prepared to share the limelight; my mother was, after all, the Joan Collins of her social set back in Italy, a status which the real Joan was obviously not going to acknowledge.

Usually socially accomplished, Rosemary also failed to read the room because she was so busy glaring at my father for making a tit of himself. Which he duly did, as we sat down to eat, falling back from the failure of his seduction technique into the safe embrace of his usual bad-boy blustery bullshit. At one point he must have truly offended her because I saw Joan's face set into glacial lines of fury. My mother shot him a very hard stare. I started to feel a little sick and I hadn't even eaten anything yet.

What to do when a diva looks ready to detonate in your kitchen? Why, call in reinforcements: I decided to let the children come down, all soft and pink in their pyjamas in the hope of defusing things. Faux pas number three.

'Oh, I know who you are!' says 7-year-old Will, well-scrubbed and clutching his Moomin. 'You're the lady from the Snickers advert.' Joan's eyes widened in mild horror; the ad to which he referred was doing the rounds at the time, with Joan playing a football coach being a bitchy diva, before being sweetened back into his male body by his favourite chocolate bar.

But worse was yet to come. Will carried on in his piping treble, perhaps sensing that he hadn't quite struck the right note. What was needed, his child mind reasoned, was a compliment. 'I must say,' he said, 'you don't look like you're 80 at all!'

LESSON SIX IN HOW NOT TO BE A POLITICAL WIFE:
have children who are both seen and heard, more's the pity.

Miraculously, Percy and Joan had us back – without the kids, funnily enough – to their palatial lateral flat in one of Chelsea's grandest mansion blocks. That first time we were invited with Christopher Biggins (whom I have adored ever since) for an evening of pure old Hollywood – but if you'd told me on either night that I would actually become friends with Joan, I would have laughed in your face. She is an absolute inspiration, not just for her sharp mind and dress sense

– but also for her razor wit. We were once having a conversation about Ozempic, the weight-loss jab drug. 'Oh, I love Ozempic,' I said gaily. 'I've been on it for years!' Joan looked me up and down. 'Really?' she drawled, raising one of those incomparably well-drawn eyebrows, and pausing for lethal effect. 'I'm not sure it's working terribly well, darling …'

Notting Hill Set we could do, Old and New Hollywood we could do, but there was one element of Camelot that we could never quite crack.

The prime minister didn't just hang out at Chequers and Downing Street, he was also still a constituency MP, so he spent a fair proportion of his time down in Oxfordshire in his seat of Witney. As the years of power rolled on, the more what became known as 'the Chipping Norton Set' coalesced like gobbets of grease around them. At first, as described brilliantly by Peter Oborne in the *Telegraph*, these were 'an incestuous collection of louche, affluent, power-hungry and amoral Londoners, located in and around the prime minister's Oxfordshire constituency' – characters like Jeremy Clarkson and the power couple Soho House founder Nick Jones and broadcaster Kirsty Young.

But these then attracted the newer masters of the universe, who started to acquire some proper Cotswold gems as their weekend homes. Chipping Norton was the limestone British Camelot. Who would have dreamt it? The gentrification of these honey-coloured treasures went into overdrive, complete with saunas, wet rooms, firepits and helipads, of course. Rebekah Brooks and her husband Charlie lived a few miles from Cameron's constituency home. Matthew Freud, the PR guru then married to Elisabeth Murdoch, also had a weekend home in the area, as did Dom and Tiffany Loehnis, on the doorstep of Soho Farmhouse, itself a magnet for Cameroons and cool kids. We couldn't possibly keep up: we were already living wildly beyond our means.

Yes, this was, for me, the recurring motif of these years: the muffled sound of silicate in my ears as I buried my head deeper and deeper in the sand. The fancier our weekends got, the grander our weeks, with me cooking vast banquets of roast lamb haunches and Tuscan beans for the cognoscenti crowded into our warm kitchen, or dinners out in the favoured bistros of Notting Hill, Michael often grandly footing the bill because he loved the idea of either repaying the hospitality of our political friends, or impressing our media friends.

Nick Boles was a friend who fell into both camps. He has known and loved Michael since their Oxford days, although Nick himself opted for industry over the media, and was struck down by the political bug at about the same time as Michael, starting down the traditional (non-Cameroon) route of being a local Conservative councillor in Soho, founding the well-respected think tank Policy Exchange, fighting off Hodgkin's Lymphoma along the way and finally becoming MP for Grantham and Stamford five years later than Michael, in 2010. His own passage through politics has been nearly as bumpy as Michael's, both of them hampered, in my not very humble opinion, by their principles, which is why I still adore them both, along with their third Naughty Nineties flatmate, Ivan Massow. And unlike He-Who-Shall-Not-Be-Named (Cameron, for those who had to go and make the tea), despite their equally radically different views on Europe, Nick and Michael themselves have remained the fondest of friends.

'Michael has always been excessive and extravagant in rather odd, old-fashioned ways,' says Nick now, when we talk about those days of largesse and bravura. 'It wasn't just about buying endless vast tomes of biography and political history – I mean, does anyone need to read every single analysis of American politics since the 1930s? – it was the fact that he bought them from Heywood Hill, bookshop to the Quality, at full price, always in hardback! And it wasn't just that he always bought the most expensive cut of meat from the poshest butchers or bulk-bought marvellously expensive claret from Berry Bros., it was the fact that he then drank the wine like Ribena and ate as if he couldn't wait to finish so that he could re-join the conversation.'

If this makes Michael sound like someone out of his time, like a Georgian Hellfire Club rake tossing bones over his shoulder to waiting lurchers, then I think that's about right. I can picture him togged up in full Beau Brummell pantaloons, cutaway coat and Waterfall-knotted necktie, keeping the Prince Regent entertained with his prodigious brain and easy ability to be the court raconteur. The trouble was that, like the Prince Regent, Michael had a greedy grasp of extravagance but no head for budgeting.

Keeping up with the Cameroons became so much part of our lives that I have to admit I stopped even wondering at the discrepancy between our incomes. Had I not had my hands firmly clapped over my ears, I couldn't have avoided the simple blaring fact that neither of us were taking home anything like the pay we'd had when we met: Michael because even a minister's pay packet was less than his final *Times* P60 and me because, as mentioned before, the cost of childcare meant that I nearly paid to work at *The*

Times. So what made me think we could afford the same lifestyle?

On one dark and deeply tucked-away level I knew. But growing up with my father, Roger the Dodger, Mr Boom 'n' Bust himself, meant that this was a reality that I was well-versed in avoiding. I'm quite sure, though, that my unvoiced fear of the inevitable reckoning with the financial fates contributed materially to the allure of the *Daily Mail*, when they came fishing for me in 2012.

Since the expenses scandal in 2009, I had often felt like I was falling between two stools: stranded between my career at *The Times* and Michael's in politics. Depressingly, it seemed, my colleagues on the paper had believed what they read. In their eyes, I had crossed over, from independent journalist to wife of evil politician – and nobody understood how dehumanising that was for me. The shortening shelf life of *Times* editors did me no favours either: from the lovely Peter Stothard, who had promoted me, and Robert Thompson, who was an amazing editor and a great champion of mine, I was then faced with James Harding from 2007 – and I felt like he didn't really see the point of me. Harding once asked me what I wanted to do on the paper and I said, flexing my muscles, that what I really wanted was to write a 'shouty woman's column'. He laughed at me and instead gave me a jolly bla-bla column in *The Times* features and lifestyle section. I enjoyed it thoroughly, was hugely grateful and even (I hope) wrote amusingly about universal issues like husbands who couldn't drive, but that shouty woman hadn't gone away, hadn't even quietened inside me.

The shouty-ness nearly burst out of me the day late in 2010 when Will Lewis joined *The Times* as general manager.

This was the man who, when he was editor at the *Telegraph*, had wilfully stitched together a thin skein of (in the end) spurious expenses headlines to net 'just another corrupt Tory' without thinking of the cost to that unjustly accused man, my husband, causing Michael to doubt everything about himself as a public servant and to withdraw into a hard-cased shell from which, ultimately, I was unable to extricate him. To say he ruined my life is, as the lingua franca has it these days, *my truth*. To see him walking the corridors of what had been my safe space made me want to spit nails.

I soldiered on, telling myself I didn't have a choice, I needed to work, but deep within me the worm was beginning to turn. So when, in 2012, Ted Verity, then one of the senior editors at the *Daily Mail*, reached out to me and offered me almost double what I was earning at *The Times* to have my own opinion column at the *Mail*, from an office a hop and a skip from the children's school at the bottom of Kensington Church Street, it seemed like the stars were finally aligning in my favour.

Not everybody saw it that way. At a party at Downing Street shortly before I made the move from *The Times*, Emily Sheffield, Samantha's sister, gave me the third degree about it. How could I possibly even contemplate working for such a man as infamous as Paul Dacre? The *Daily Mail* was evil and I should have nothing to do with it. You know, the usual virtue-signalling claptrap that people tend to believe about a newspaper that they hardly ever read beyond the online headlines.

But as she figuratively wagged her finger at me, I realised something more; that – to these people – I was just Mrs Gove, not actually a person in my own right, at best just 'a *Times* journalist'. Steady, Sarah, you can't blame her, I thought, keeping hold of my temper. But still: it's that thing of people like them not realising that people like me have their own life, their own needs and, more importantly, their own bills to pay. Not everyone has a baronet for a daddy; we commoners have to take the opportunities as they come. Our conversation had the precise opposite of the intended effect: it strengthened my determination, and lit a fire in me that has never quite gone out.

So when I was later asked to go and meet Dacre, then in his 20th year as editor of the *Daily Mail*, for him to give me the once-over, I was mulishly predisposed to like him. Dacre's reputation may have preceded him but I'm often resistant to prejudgement, having been prejudged myself so often. I knew that he was a shouty man, with a reputation for verbal abuse and, according to Christina Odone, 'a drill sergeant's delight in public humiliation'. I'd listened when he appeared on *Desert Island Discs* in 2004, when Sue Lawley teased him about his methods, to which Dacre responded, 'Shouting creates energy; energy creates great headlines.' A writer called Nick Davies, in his book *Flat Earth News*, was ruder, citing that Dacre's staff called the morning conference the 'Vagina Monologues' because of the master's habit of calling everyone a 'c**t'.

Yet the man that greeted me at the door of his elegant mews house in Belgravia couldn't have been more charming. Granted, there was a certain gruff professionalism to his manner: when I thanked him for his generosity, he assured me that I would be expected to earn 'every penny' of my salary. And although I could tell he was far from convinced of my suitability for the role (the slot that I was earmarked for, the so-called Wednesday witch column, had been previously held by Lynda Lee-Potter, Allison Pearson and Sandra Parsons, among others: these were sharp stilettos to fill), I instinctively liked him. He had that same irrepressible energy I had first come across all those years ago at the *Daily Mirror*, that absolute passion for his craft. He was a hard taskmaster alright; but he also read every single word of his newspaper before it went to press. In every aspect of his role as editor, he was just extra. And I'm a person who likes extra.

After the veiled contempt that had crept into my relationships at *The Times*, Dacre's plain speaking was refreshing and his interest in my brain, not my husband, was seductive. Of course, he was being clever. Of course, he was hoping that by getting me on board, he would gain a modern Mata Hari with some insights into the machinations of government to which only the *Mail* would now be privy. I'm not, nor have I ever been, *that* naive. But our interests were aligned, the potential benefits were mutual. I wanted a voice, he wanted to give me that voice.

Dacre had also done his homework. He had read an article I had written in *The Times* the week before about women my age becoming invisible, about folding the towels, feeding the dog, remembering the children's gym kits – all the unseen, unthanked parts of a mother's life – and he held it up to me, tapping it firmly.

'We'll make you work hard for this,' he said, fixing me with a gimlet glare. 'But you're not going to be invisible anymore.'

I don't think either of us had any clue just how prophetic these words would prove to be.

CHAPTER SEVEN

BOILING THE FROG

'The notion that if a frog is plunged suddenly into
boiling water, it will jump out; but if the frog is put in
tepid water which is then brought to a boil slowly,
it will not perceive the danger and will be
cooked to death.'

OR

An unfortunate series of events ...

There was a moment during Michael's turbulent stint as Secretary of State for Education, in 2012 or thereabouts, when I realised that the ripple effect of politics was boundless, mindless, endless. I was sitting in A&E at the Chelsea and Westminster hospital in the early hours of the morning, having been there since the middle of the night, with a husband greyfaced with pain and in the foetal position on a trolley.

185

We had waited several hours in the emergency room, as various drunks came and went (after hours the place doubles as an unofficial shelter for the incapacitated and inebriated) until eventually – after some remonstrating by me – Michael was admitted. I must admit I was a reluctant Florence Nightingale: Michael's recurrent bouts of hypochondria had become a feature of our marriage, and while I was not unsympathetic to his plight, I half thought it would probably turn out to be trapped wind.

I was wrong. In actual fact he had kidney stones, which probably explained why the two paracetamol which the Cerberus of a reception nurse had reluctantly handed him during the interminable wait had failed to lessen his agony.

As the sky lightened to morning outside, the registrar – a wiry, Rory Stewart type wreathed in a strong aroma of ciga-rette smoke – strode into our cubicle and picked up Michael's notes. He did a double take. The name had meant nothing to any of the junior staff who had so far examined Michael (and neither I nor Michael would have ever dared say anything, lest we be accused of seeking special treatment), but this guy obviously read the papers. 'Are you *the* Michael Gove?' he asked. Michael nodded yes.

Having thus realised that not only had a government minister been kept waiting almost five hours in the dead of night, but had also been left in excruciating pain, he immedi-ately ordered a scan and prescribed morphine, to be administered via a suppository. Satisfied that Michael was at last in good hands, I nipped to the loo. I came back just in time to overhear 'Rory' announcing to the nurses' desk, 'Right, which one of you wants to stick their finger up Michael Gove's arse?'

LESSON SEVEN IN HOW NOT TO BE A POLITICAL WIFE:
realise too early for anyone's mental health that when you step
over the salt circle into the five-pointed star coven of politics,
you have ceased to become a person. You are now a c**t.

Doctors can shed what's left of their bedside manner with you. Ordinary people no longer need have any consideration for you. Friends no longer trust you. Children are taught to despise you, not respect you. Journalists and policemen no longer need to be impartial – or accurate. You have lost those human rights and protections because you are no longer human, you are a politician and you are now the legitimate prey of the only big game hunting still allowed in this country. I can see the ads now: 'Public Servant Safaris: Stick Your Finger Up the Big Five!'

Politicians simply can't win. If they're nice and cuddly, and become best known for wearing leopard-print kitten heels, like Theresa May when she was at the Home Office, then nothing gets done and they are castigated for being dull. If they're keen as mustard and charge in to effect change, so that people's lives and outcomes actually stand a chance of improving within the short five-year term of one government, the public reacts with shock and heels-dug-in hysteria. For the vast majority of un-politicised Brits, therefore, Michael Gove will forever be associated with his time at the Department for Education (DfE) and it wasn't difficult to see why he became so unpopular so quickly, unfair though I still think that was.

Not for the first or last time, he polarised public opinion into stark camps of fan and foe. It was his first cabinet post and he came in hard. The National Curriculum was over-thrown entirely; GCSEs and A-levels were hurled back to more rigorous exams; and grade inflation was smashed by a new numeric system. The underperforming swill of compre-hensives were shaken up by the expansion of academies and the introduction of Swedish-style free schools and held up to the light themselves by a rebooted Ofsted framework, putting the 'ooof' into the proof of inspection. Most daring and derring-do of all, Michael went head to head with the flabby and complacent teaching establishment, planning to rip away the protections of the unions and putting a harsh spotlight on teacher performance management, believing that improving teacher quality was key to raising standards.

'Gove's Mad Exam Shake-up Slammed by Teachers' (*Sunday Times*, 21 June 2012). 'Gove's Crazy Curriculum Reforms Under Fire' (*Star*, 12 February 2013). 'Gove's Free Schools Failing Our Kids' (*Mirror*). 'Ludicrous', 'Barmy', 'Fury'. The headlines that reacted to the new educational reforms saw Michael pilloried and blocked at all turns. 'Kicking the wasps' nest,' was how one friend described it to me, speaking in tones of mingled awe and disapproval.

I had the same mixed reaction myself, not that I showed it at the time. (I was *trying* to be a good political wife, remem-ber.) I'd been educated at so many schools, here and in Italy, that I knew from bitter experience the difference between some of the waffly rubbish that some state school teachers thought would turn their charges into nice little lefty liberal citizens – not caring that they couldn't get a job at the end of it – and the brilliance that truly rigorous, exacting teachers in any sector could extract from their classes if they built educa-tion from the basic bricks up.

So I applauded the Government's determination to raise academic standards and get tough on teachers across the nation – and could see the attraction – from a small 'c' conservatism point of view – of increasing school autonomy from politically biased council control by expanding academies and free schools. I was all for how radical my husband was being – I had always loved the man of principle within him – and couldn't help but be awed by the reading and research (and the number of zeroes at the end of our Heywood Hill bookshop bills) that he plunged into for months and years. What I couldn't help but roll my eyes at inwardly from time to time was the headstrong manner in which he did it, the way he merged a desire for change with a lack of understanding of how best to achieve it.

Of course, with hindsight, I can see that there was more than a little of the dread hand of Dom at play here. Cummings was well known for being a blunt instrument and not suffering fools even remotely gladly. He operated mad-professor style out of a frowsty little cell in the Department, surrounded by scattered files, discarded musty clothing and the unlit scented candles placed in there by tactful underlings, and has been accused of everything from bullying to describing colleagues as being 'thick as mince' to being accused by a *Guardian* journalist of using 'dark arts' to get his way.

Much of this is true: in 2012, the DfE had to settle with a senior female civil servant accusing Cummings of bullying, to the tune of £25,000, and Michael had whiplash from turning the other cheek to the methods Dom used to ram things through the inertia of the Blob.

I blame myself a little for Dom being so important to Michael because it was I who had suggested that Michael hire him back in 2007, when Michael was shadow education secretary. When Dom moved home to Co. Durham in 2006, I had heard it was to lick his wounds after his break-up with Kirstie Allsopp and, remembering Dom from parties, always with a notebook in hand, rather sweet and a little lost but always fizzing with ideas, ideas, ideas, I felt rather maternal and protective towards him. So, when Michael said one day, 'I need some policy wonk work and can't find anyone good,' I said, 'What about Dominic?' My mistake. My big mistake, to misquote *Pretty Woman*.

Mind you, the Blob would have tried the patience of Job: Michael himself regularly tore his hair out, when going through his red boxes in the evening, at the sheer incompetence, the staggering inability of some of the Blobbier career DfErs ('Shall we call them Duffers?' I suggested sweetly one evening) to answer the questions that Michael was asking and provide the data he needed.

Or was the incompetence more sinister? Education was known to be stuffed tight with the sort of wishy-washy wonks who, having enjoyed their own superb private or grammar school then university education, believed (patronisingly) that education for those who came after them should be 'better' ... That learning should be about the 'discovery' of knowledge by children not yet tainted by the capitalist need to earn a living, not the 'force-feeding' of the underclasses and the unnecessary provision of university places that they felt were the aims of Gove and Cummings, childsnatchers. So perhaps their inability to deliver decent data to the ministerial team was deliberate crumb-dropping to clog up the broom of reform?

I can therefore sympathise. Every day of work for Michael

and Dom must have felt like Butch Cassidy and the Sundance Kid busting out against the Mexican army – and that's before the public started coiling their lynching ropes. But as the fate of Butch and Sundance demonstrated, coming out all guns blazing never ends well. Besides, it's such a very *male* approach.

Any woman will tell you that the route to getting your own way is not to crash in high-handedly and tell anyone entrenched in their own brilliance (in this case, civil servants) how to clean their house; you have to convince them that it was all their brilliant idea in the first place. Any mother can tell you that the way to handle spoilt, entitled, though adored, children (which is my default view of teachers and most civil servants) is not to go head to head with them but to sidle around them, sweetening your bossiness and determination to get them to see sense – with flattery, championing, negotiation and an iron hand in a velvet glove.

I am obviously both woman and mother and knew all of this, but it would never have occurred to me to tell Michael and Dom that they were going about this all wrong. They were the experts, used to dealing with the mandarins, the boffins and the wonks – what did I know?

For one thing, unlike the vast majority of his cabinet colleagues, Michael had been state-educated himself in Scotland, before he got his scholarship to a private school, Robert Gordon's College in Aberdeen. He felt very strongly that all children, regardless of their start in life, deserved a chance at a good education right from the start, and that meant only one thing: improving standards in the state sector.

Unlike some of his colleagues – and unlike the Labour politicians of today – he wasn't as interested in scoring political points and blaming everything on the previous government as he was in getting these reforms right – which is why he took lessons (as it were) from overseas governments across the political spectrum, and why he was guided more by rigour than by expediency. His championing of state education had nothing to do with class warfare. He didn't regard the private sector as the enemy, a privileged elite to be crushed on principle; he saw independent schools as the gold standard to which *all* schools should aspire, and from which useful lessons could be learned.

No one, then, could accuse him of taking the easy way out. Which was lucky, because they accused him of everything else: of high-handedness, for being dogmatic *and* for doing U-turns (you can't win), of marginalising creative subjects, of putting people off teaching – and, more depressingly, of his idiocy in taking on the educational establishment in the first place. Michael himself was able to shrug off most of this criticism – unlike the slings and arrows of the expenses scandal, this sort of sledging never troubled him much because he knew that he'd done his homework and that, intellectually, he was on the right track. But his unpopularity soared and teachers swore they would never forgive him: which meant that, closer to home, politics started to rear its head in all our lives more regularly.

She'd had the odd run-in at primary school but in September 2013, after a year of headlines attacking the planned reforms, Bea started at secondary school, at Grey Coat Hospital in Victoria. The news of her enrolment had been made public in the press, and she felt the pressure of being 'daughter of' immediately, although not in a good way.

'I didn't notice it so much on my orientation day, though I did notice how bemused some of the kids in the year-above class were by me, but it turned out that there had been some gossip about me because someone had read in the newspapers about where Michael Gove's daughter was going for secondary. So for the rest of that term and over the summer, all the pupils had the chance to ask their teachers and parents who Dad was – so by the time I started in September, everyone knew to hate me. The only saving grace was that my own year had no clue what had gone on, so they were oblivious – unless they had older siblings at the school. But it was quite a way to start – with all the teachers and most of the pupils just automatically hating me for who I was.

'Even then, I only realised that people knowing who I was could have an impact beyond the school gate the first time a school friend came to my birthday party and screamed so loudly in my ear that I shouted at her to shut up – and her mum then threatened to go to the *Sun* and tell them that I tried to stab her daughter. That was interesting.'

I remember this. The girl in question was not a very nice piece of work, one of those who get invited to everything not because they are especially fun or popular, but because if you leave them out they make your life hell (i.e. a bully). And she behaved like one throughout the entire party, monopolising the whole thing by almost immediately bursting into tears, accusing Bea of not really liking her and creating a massive drama centred around herself. Then, while everyone else was downstairs and in the garden, she snuck upstairs with a couple of her acolytes, and went into Will's room, where they proceeded to have their own little party. By the time I discovered them, they had pulled the entire room apart, and ripped the curtain off the rail. Needless to say, not a word of apology.

Her thuggish behaviour continued to dominate the party, and I could see that it was making Bea miserable. When the time came to do the cake, she muscled in next to Bea, practically knocking her off her chair, and blew out all the candles before Bea had even drawn breath. Then she screamed like a banshee right in Bea's ear. Bea, like me, does not cope well with loud, sudden noises. She was holding a (very blunt) knife with which to cut the cake and she brandished it – jokingly – in the girl's direction.

That evening, as I was reading in bed, my phone rang. It was the child's mother, screaming blue murder down the phone at me. 'Your daughter threatened to stab my girl!' she yelled. 'You need to get that bitch under control!' She then informed me that she had filed a police report, told the school and was going to inform the papers that 'Michael Gove's daughter is a psycho'.

There followed a Kafkaesque inquiry in which Bea was interrogated and I was called in by the headteacher to explain myself. The fact that this absolute brat of a child (and her horrible mother, which was obviously where she got it from) had the agency to put my daughter through such an ordeal, when it was *she* who had behaved like a delinquent, taught me a valuable lesson: it doesn't matter how kind or tolerant you are, some people will always screw you over if they think they can get something out of you.

Bea can talk tough now about such memories, but she wasn't anything like as tough then and it makes my blood boil that she was being put through such treatment aged just 11, a sensitive age. Will was always more sanguine, partly because he was younger and partly because, like Michael, it's much more water off a duck's back for him.

'The only thing I remember about him being Education Secretary,' he tells me now, 'is that at primary school, nearly every day, some kid or teacher would say to me, "If your dad's so clever, why can't you get him to change the school dinners?"'

'Funnily enough, it was one of the school's dinner ladies who really picked on me for who I was – I learned to keep my head down because if she spotted me, she'd shout, "Oi, Gove! Back of the line!" … What she didn't know is I actually thought that was hilarious because to avoid her seeing me I'd just practise my spymanship, my covert skills, trying to pass by her undetected.' Ah, my little James Bond …

By 2014, it was clear that Michael was one of those figures that the man in the street was now being taught by the media to hate. Not only was he booed on *Question Time* just for appearing, but commentary in the papers was branching out beyond his education remit into a general criticism of him. A female comedian on Radio 4's *News Quiz* in 2013 began her remarks about that week's fight over the English Baccalaureate by referring to 'that foetus in a jar, Michael Gove'. Sandi Toksvig (for it was she) then followed it up by saying he obviously had no friends and 'a face that makes even the most pacifist of people reach for the shovel'.

Now hear me out here but I have a little theory about this that I've tried out on those close to me. My thesis is that the media decided to make the public hate him, above any other Tory contenders, because Michael didn't fit the cookie-cutter mould of what the public thought a public figure should look and sound like. They did it with Fergie, they did it with

Meghan, they did it with Ed Miliband, they tried to do it with Boris and the endlessly repeated photo of him zip-wiring, but he's a special case. I was cheered by Janice Turner writing in my alma mater, *The Times*, that 'we need politicians with big brains, not square jaws' but hers was a lone voice above the jeering of the crowd.

This is not a pity party, nor is it special pleading. Michael isn't the first person this has happened to and he certainly won't be the last. Handsome Justin Trudeau was far more popular overseas than he ever was for his actual policies back home in Canada, whereas poor old Ed Miliband will always be mocked for his resemblance to Wallace (or Gromit?) just to pick two examples. But it was an easy Achilles heel to pick – to slam Michael, not only for the unpopularity of his reforms, but to include his cherubic looks, his lack of 'pedigree', his non-Savile Row suits, in a kind of holistic condemnation.

I also happen to think the media was misguided in singling him out from the unpromising ugly pageant that is the Tory Party but that's obviously the personal bias of someone who was married to him and who can see his features every day in the undeniably beautiful face of our daughter Beatrice. The fact remains that, from 2012, just like they've always done for the poor Duchess of York, any picture editor would always choose the least flattering picture of Michael (and me, by extension), the moment when he pulled a face or was caught jogging, to go with an article – even if it was about the serious business of politics.

This obviously reached its nadir when *Spitting Image* returned to our TV screens years later in 2020 – once seen, never forgotten, Michael's scrotum face – but it was during the DfE years that it suddenly became not just okay, but expected, to hate Gove. Will remembers, albeit with merely a shrug, the years of going to Chelsea football games with his dad, when even the winos on the way in had a go at Michael. 'Oi, are you that Gove?' they'd all say and when Dad nodded and smiled, they'd draw themselves away and snarl, 'Well, you can fuck off then!' Dad would be quite funny and would say to me as we walked on, 'I think maybe he'll feel better about me after another one …'

Only when I steeled myself to read Cameron's memoir, did I realise that Michael's perceived unpopularity also gave Michael's critics inside the Government some kindling with which to eventually smoke him out. I read with some amusement that I am only mentioned by Dave as 'Sarah Vine, a *Times* journalist', as if I were simply a stringer in the press corps but, revisionist as *For the Record* is, further in is when Dave doesn't do Michael justice and I think the less of him for it. In Chapter 36, 'The Long Road to 2015', Dave soon begins to change his tune from describing Michael as his 'best friend' and 'the reforming minister of his generation' to subtly undermining him, describing him in the next couple of pages as 'this zealous and charming eccentric' who was starting to be 'a threat to all our reforms … so unpopular that that wasn't just a danger to the politics but to the policy.

'"Just get on with running Education Department and stop commenting on everything else under the sun," I told MG on the phone,' reads Cameron's account. 'But he couldn't help himself.' Shades of Ms Sheffield when she told me off for writing an opinion column for the *Mail*.

Meanwhile, as we plunged on into 2014, the more shifting the sands became, the warmer the water beginning to boil the frog, the more controlling Michael became about my *Daily Mail* column, now into its second year. 'You have to learn to say no,' he said to me once as if it was something being imposed on me by my evil *Mail* masters, rather than an opinion that I – and quite a slice of the rest of the country – could have independently from the *Mail*. It was the first presentiment I had that he now believed his work mattered more than mine; that politics was, in effect, gaining the upper hand in our marriage.

And to be fair, a part of me agreed, the part of me that still felt like an imposter, who still thought everything I said and did was wrong, that everyone else *was* better than me. But there was also another part, increasingly confident and growing bolder with every piece I wrote, that resented these attempts at censorship, as well as the notion that, as a wife, I should be a wholly owned subsidiary of my husband's career.

What I should have cited back at Michael was not only the growing success of my column inches but the number of occasions on which I *did* stand up to the *Mail* about what I wrote. At first, I think I was even a disappointment to Dacre because I wasn't the pushover he and the other editors might have thought I would be. I would never write about the Camerons; I treasured my friendship with them, especially with Sam, about whom I have never written – and will never write – a bad word; mainly because there isn't a bad word to be written about her but also because I considered her a true friend, and I don't bitch about my friends.

But the very fact that I had accepted the offer of a job on the *Daily Mail* in 2012 seemed to have been taken almost as an act of aggression by the Camerons and their immediate circle, who were ever warier of Dacre. Emily hadn't just been spouting hot air when she tried to put me off back in 2013; Samantha herself had reason to dislike the newspaper. As she had repeatedly explained to me, they were always trying to run stories about her business and work connections, always trying to paint her as some sort of latter-day Cherie Blair, opportunistically seeking to profit from her husband's jobs. This drove her mad, and over the years it turned from irritation to real anger and thence to actual paranoia.

Even so, I could see no reason why that should mean I couldn't write for it. After all, you would never expect your best friend to stop being a theatre critic just because you were married to an actor, would you?

And besides, the truth was that at the paper I was her and her family's staunchest advocate. I was forever putting my neck on the line to defend the Camerons, both politically and personally, and on more than one occasion I successfully argued stories down. I felt – as I still do – that if you don't like something you should engage with it and do your best to change it from the inside. To lean in, as Sheryl Sandberg so famously said. That was what I was trying to do at the *Mail*: introduce a different point of view into this very reactionary, male culture. And, almost to my surprise, the editorial voices asking me to spill the beans on politics soon quietened when they saw that I could more than hold my own on the wider issues of the day.

That my friends couldn't understand – or appreciate – this infuriated me. Most things I wrote in the *Mail*, no matter how positive or unrelated they were, seemed to be taken negatively. What annoyed me even more was the notion – unspoken but very much implied – that I should somehow act as an unpaid spokesperson for the Cameron government, that I should be a sycophant and a courtesan rather than, as I had always been, a true friend, an equal, able to speak plainly and honestly. I began to wonder whether they saw me differently to the way I saw them. If I helped out with stuff – organising our Ibiza holidays, or taking up the slack on the school run, or performing other administrative duties, it was because I cared about them and we were mates. But now the worm of doubt began to creep in: was I a friend or just a fixer?

Even worse, was I … staff? After all, there was that time when I'd been helping out in my usual way at a very 'Chipping Norton Set' party at Dave and Sam's house in Witney, buzzing around keeping an eye on the food, making sure glasses were topped up, keeping a weather eye on the kids and I saw Jeremy Clarkson talking to, I think, Rebekah Brooks. I drifted up to say hello to them, but Clarkson took one look at the bottle of white in my hand and, without looking at me directly, waved his hand and said, 'Actually, can you get me a glass of red?' Being a very good waitress, of course, I did. At the time I'd thought it was hilarious but maybe a server was essentially how they all thought of me …

Above all there was a sense that my career – and my husband's – didn't matter as much as theirs. That we had to compromise our beliefs and views in order to facilitate their life at No 10. For me, this was perhaps the most insulting notion of all, not least because before any of the politics and grandeur had ever really happened I had always bent over backwards to help my friends when they needed it. But also because it just smacked of entitlement, which was not something I had ever associated with Samantha. I was deeply upset about the growing distance between us, a distance that I just couldn't seem to cross anymore.

This first came to a head in the reshuffle of 2014. Dave writes about it quite honestly in his memoir, his highhandedness coming through loud and clear.

'I needed Michael in a top job but I was beginning to think that a different, less high-profile role might be better for all of us,' writes Cameron. 'Two weeks before the reshuffle I got him into the Downing Street flat and put it to him. He agreed but the next day my plan hit the barriers. Michael emailed to say he had changed his mind. What had happened? I smelt Dominic Cummings and totally flipped.'

About one thing he is right. Michael did row back from a conversation he and Dave had had – a year before. They had chatted idly that if Michael were to step away from Education, then the chief whip role would be as good a place to go as any, suiting Michael's bonhomie, popularity with backbenchers, non-cronyism and keen observation skills. As reshuffle time approached, rumour reached us (via two civil service drivers chatting to each other) that the PM was actually serious.

Michael went to Downing Street for dinner and Dave went further and presented it to Michael as a 'Chief Whip Plus' role, even drawing a *Game of Thrones* analogy, saying Michael would be the 'Hand of the King', knowing that my husband shared his *Thrones* obsession. There was talk of Michael being given access to the 'Box Returns' – the read-out of the PM's decisions from each box of paperwork he went through – which was presented as 'proof' of Dave's insistence that this was a key insider role. I had agreed with the theory of this – and Michael did initially agree with the chief whip move – but, under close re-examination, it was a terrible idea.

For one thing, it was a clear demotion – forget some paltry Box reading, Michael would no longer be part of the cabinet – and, much more catastrophic, it meant an annual pay cut of over £36,000. Had I known either of those things, I would not have been so positive about the prospect. Our nostrils were barely above water as it was and our finances couldn't handle any drop at all, let alone such a huge one. Dom agreed with me, told Michael that it was a dick-move by Dave and, with 12 days to go – nearly a lifetime in politics, after all – Michael went back on his earlier assent to the move.

Dave did flip. Later, Michael said he had never heard Dave lose it like that. He rang and shouted at Michael down the phone, then followed it up with a text. 'You must realise that I divide the world into team players and wankers. You've always been a team player. Please don't become a wanker.'

Have you ever noticed that when people start talking about team players, it's more often than not because they want the rest of the team to agree with them? Take out the 't' and the 'a' and you get a 'me' player. And that's what Dave always wanted, which is fair enough, but as my son Will would say, 'Mate – don't dress it up as teamwork.'

Cameron forced through the move. Michael was demoted. Instead of moving him alone, as promised, it was done as part of a general reshuffle, in order to publicly humiliate and punish him for his rebellion. Worse, in my eyes, the PM was insultingly casual, in an entitled way that I didn't often see in him, about the devastating effect that this would have not only on Michael's income, but also his morale. When you've never once had to worry about how to pay the mortgage, it must have seemed ok for him to, as he says in his own words, 'offer Michael a flat in Admiralty House to help make up the difference', the idea being that we would then rent out Barlby.

I played nice and went along to have a look at the flat; it was lovely, actually, and much more spacious than our house in Barlby Road – plus it would have been incredibly convenient for Bea at Grey Coat. Part of me also felt that the proximity to Parliament would work to our advantage as a family, as it would mean that Michael would be able to drop by in the evenings before voting and see a lot more of the children. But Michael felt – entirely reasonably – that accepting such a bauble would not only put us in an invidious position, the 'grace and favour' optics of it would not be great. We walked away along the tourist trap that is Whitehall and thought resentfully that Cummings was right. Another dick-move, Dave.

So far, so politics. But enter Sarah Vine, stage right. Not Sarah Gove, wannabe Political Wife (I was still a wannabe because I still wasn't getting it right), but Sarah Vine, *Daily Mail* columnist and (getting to be) voice of Middle England.

Max Hastings, grand old man of Fleet Street, political and cultural arbiter, had written a piece in the *Mail* condemning the demotion of Michael as 'worse than a crime', going even further than the rest of the over-ridingly negative press, which saw the move as simply a betrayal by the PM, giving up on Michael's education reforms and punishing Michael for no good reason. After all, for a man who supposedly prized his friends' loyalty so much, Dave had shown precious little to Michael on this front.

I read the Hastings piece and applauded every word, taking to Twitter/X as I so often did – and do – under my @WestminsterWag handle, to record my reaction to the news events of the day and requoting Hastings saying, 'A shabby day's work which Cameron will live to regret.'

The retweet aspect of this was soon lost and the quote was soon attributed to me alone – sorry, Max – to the delight of the talking heads and the fury of Downing Street. I had no idea until I chatted to Kate Fall, Dave's gatekeeper, soon after, just how stubborn Dave had been and how livid he was with me for the retweet. She and George Osborne had discussed Michael's U-turn two weeks before the reshuffle and had concluded that ramming through the chief whip appointment against both our wishes was not worth the pain – but Dave had dug his toes in and insisted. The 'shabby day' remark had then lit the kindling: Dave apparently yelled with fury when he was told.

Suddenly our friendship seemed at breaking point and maybe it was all my fault. We still got invited to stay at Chequers but there was a new wariness between me and Dave. For the first time, I think now, he had seen that I was a force to be reckoned with in my own right, a force that couldn't necessarily be cut down to size by him or his flunkeys – and that realisation didn't suit him. Dave had felt threatened by the Michael–Dom C axis, now broken because Michael couldn't have a SpAd as chief whip, but he now resented what he saw as my interference – and Michael felt let down by Dave.

What had been a tight team where everyone, as I now think Dave saw it, knew their *place*, was now stretched to breaking point, making the future less certain; the suggestion of trouble at t'mill not helped by a story that reached us about Will, who had spent a weekend at Chequers on his own at the invitation of Elwen, running into breakfast and asking the grown-ups, 'Isn't it true this house will be ours when my dad's prime minister?' Will, of course, denies that this ever happened. Not that Kate Fall bothered to check with him (or me) when she repeated the story in her book *The Gatekeeper*. I must confess I was a little disappointed in her on that front. In my book, it's below the belt to tell tales about other people's children in an attempt to get at the parents.

Dominic, meanwhile, had not helped matters by briefing all and sundry after his exit from Education about the lags and lickspittles that had plagued his time in politics – the implication being that he and Michael had been a force of two against these lesser mortals. He even applied Bismarck's famous put-down of Napoleon III – 'a sphinx without a riddle' – to the prime minister, which we did think ranked up there with Ann Widdicombe's 'something of the night' remark about Michael Howard.

Michael missed Dominic's wit and ideas but, as more than one of Michael's close advisers observed, he profited from his absence in terms of calming down the aggressive feel of his governance. He kept his head down as chief whip, even – I think – enjoying some of the more baroque aspects of effectively being the party's priest confessor (unlike subsequent chief whips, he has always respected the sanctity of that privilege). He obeyed the 'steady as she goes' dictum being put out by Downing Street as they navigated the rocky shoals of the Scottish Referendum – where Michael's roots and Scottish bonhomie were vital and entered into the final approach for landing the 2015 election.

What had started out as a nail-biter – the Tories needed to shed the Lib Dems coalition and win in their own right but all the signs pointed to another hung parliament – turned into an unexpected majority victory of 10 seats, helped by the loss of ground by Labour to the SNP in Scotland and the worst Lib Dem result since their formation in 1988. We were back into two-party politics and, better news still, the Labour Party disastrously elected Jeremy Corbyn as their new leader. Best of all, with lots of jobs on offer, Michael could come back in from the cold to a new cabinet position, this time as Lord Chancellor, the Secretary of State for Justice.

These were halcyon days for us. Michael's salary leapt up again; I was stretching myself and being stretched at the *Mail*. Ted Verity was a fantastic – if exacting – editor and mentor, and I began to broaden my writing range.

As self-made 'parvenus' both of us adored the rich ceremonial nature and look of Michael's new job. I had the *Private Eye* cover of the 2015 State Opening (he, robed up to the nines and nodding respectfully to the Queen, attended by small posh pageboys, including the tiny Marquess of Lorne), blown up to poster size, despite the mocking message about him being a champion leaker (which everyone knows now was always Dominic Cummings). Even better, I let the blood rush to my head and spent a small fortune I didn't have on commissioning a full-length portrait of Michael, in his velvet and ermine full regalia, from the very talented artist daughter of a friend. I loved that portrait, loved everything it represented, and am almost sad I didn't get to keep it in the divorce.

Meanwhile, Michael was like a pig in shit, snuffling happily through acres of research, theories, histories, ideas, all to do with the big issues of Justice: prisons, the sovereignty of the law and human rights. His first job as court reporter back in

Scotland, on the *Aberdeen Press & Journal*, gave him a small leg up in terms of legal nous, but at Justice he had a Gordian knot to untangle. He had inherited a Department in turmoil, almost on the brink of revolt after Chris Grayling's disastrous tenure, where among other disasters a planned initiative to crack down on drugs being smuggled into prisons in personal possessions was suddenly misframed as an attempt to ban books in prisons. Throw in a prison system that was clearly failing, an influential caucus of magistrates who'd had their noses put entirely out of joint by Grayling and the encroachment of the European Court of Human Rights into centuries-held British legal precepts prompting calls for a British Bill of Rights, and there were almost more naysayers ready to trip Michael up than there had been over at his old job.

One thing was certain: he had learned his lesson from Education, so to speak. Without Dominic egging him on (he admits now that he wouldn't have had him back, even if he could have done), he was less antagonistic, more predisposed to listen to even the feistiest campaign groups, and clearly relished the intellectual challenge of working *with* not against the vested interests. And I think he even surprised himself with how much this new brief inspired him; the notion that Justice could in some ways be seen as an extension of Education, and that run correctly, for some, the prison system could prove an opportunity as well as a punishment.

Michael duly got himself back into Dave's good books, obeying the PM's diktat to 'take the noise down' at Justice, soothing the magistrates bitching into Dave's ear, changing the mood on prisons with his idealistic (and rather wonderful, in my humble opinion) proposals to turn prisons into second-chance universities, working more collaboratively than he ever had with Dom at his side, with good politicians like Dominic Raab was back then and *Birdsong* author Sebastian Faulks's brother Lord Edward Faulks in the Lords.

He played to Dave's love of decentralisation by giving prison governors more control; setting up league tables to see which prisons performed better at both prisoner life and recidivism afterwards, and visited dozens and dozens of penal institutions, both here and overseas, from Germany to Texas. I remember joining him for the first time on one of those trips – he probably did nearly one prison a week – to the Clink Restaurant at HMP Brixton, which is run by inmates as part of a scheme to help build skills back in the real world. It was then that I realised how few resources prison governors have to work with, how leaky and run-down the infrastructure, how insurmountable the scale of the challenges they face.

This was also when the Henries joined our family. Henry Newman, known to be super-bright at CCHQ, had worked as a SpAd for Francis Maude and had come into our lives socially through Simone; Michael snapped him up as a departmental adviser when Maude lost the right to have SpAds after the election. Henry is thought by both of us to be probably the smartest policy brain there is – and one of the most modest. He's also disarmingly good-looking and has outlasted the slings and arrows of Life with the Goves to become a lasting friend to both of us, divorce notwithstanding.

Michael had worked with Henry Cook both at Education and during his time as chief whip, and equally quickly got him on board. The two Henries were instantly thick as thieves and, along with Beth Armstrong, his parliamentary and party adviser, Michael's team was a happy one. I adored all of them and loved the flirtatiousness of the handsome Henries, the fact that they were already friends with friends of mine, like Simone and Carrie Symonds (now Johnson), and felt entirely comfortable having them lounge around our kitchen table, shooting their mouths off and taking political ideas for a ride in this safe space.

But there was a dark cloud looming. Contrary to the advice of Michael and so many others in his close political circle, flushed with the (close shave) success of the Scottish Referendum, the prime minister had included the promise to have a referendum on whether Britain should leave the European Union in the manifesto for the 2015 General Election. Now that they were safely in government, Michael and many others counselled against a hasty fulfilment on this promise but Dave, once again, was determined.

At this point, the frog was merely enjoying the warmth of the water. No one had even coined the word that was to haunt my dreams for the next five years:

BREXIT.

CHAPTER EIGHT

BLOWING THE BLOODY DOORS OFF

'The people of this country have had
enough of experts.'

Michael Gove, during an interview with Faisal Islam
on Sky News, 3 June 2016

And now we come to it: the countdown to the Brexit vote, one of the most over-analysed periods in recent political history, minutely documented by countless observers and participants, all of them confident that they remember every twist and turn. In truth, few paint an even half-accurate picture of events – mostly because, in politics, more than perhaps any other walk of life, people have a habit of making things up to suit their agenda. As a general rule, the more self-assured the account, the more self-serving and the larger the pinch of salt required to digest it.

I can see the holes, the vanity, the justifications and the spin in those other accounts because I was there for so much of the headlong descent into Brexit – into the vote and then into the long drawn-out agony that was the delivery. That said, at the time I was painfully naive. Close to the incandescent heart of the action, yes, but also clearly blinded to some shenanigans, that to those on the outside might have seemed nefarious but to me, on the inside, just felt like business as usual.

The difference now is that I am neither caught up in mainstream politics anymore – which gives me perspective – nor am I married to a politician, so there is no line for me to toe. I can tell the truth and shame the devil, and no one can really stop me because I'm done with the lessons of being a political wife.

In other words, I really have no fucks left to give.

Of course, that isn't the whole picture either. I still owe my children a duty of care – an accident of birth put them into these events and they don't deserve any ricochet egg-splats. But I've been completely transparent with them all through the process that this book has involved, not least because it's their story too, with their voices heard. They may have had the amusing times at Chequers or at Dorneywood when they were small children, but they were older when Brexit hit – Bea had just become a vulnerable teenager when the Vote Leave campaign scooped the EU Referendum and Will had just started at Holland Park Comprehensive, so both paid a harsh price for the whole of the country suddenly really hating their dad. And, in many cases, their mum too.

'I am annoyed that you're publishing this though,' said my son Will, back when we were first discussing the book. 'I was kind of hoping that I would one day get to write my own memoirs of life as a political brat. It would be called,' he said with a threatening gleam in his eye, '*The Boy in the Corner* – all those things I heard, with no one ever suspecting that I was listening.'

I wasn't exactly in the corner but not even the most deluded of politicians would be stupid enough to think I wasn't listening – not least because from time to time I would offer the readers of the *Daily Mail* my unique take on events. I never kept a meticulous, detailed diary – partly because I'm not a self-obsessed navel gazer – but also because the whole thing was honestly such a nightmare that at the end of each day the last thing I wanted to do was plod over it all again: I just wanted the blessed amnesia of sleep to descend as quickly as possible. Besides, I didn't have time: I was busy looking after children, dogs, a house and my own job, all while battling ill health and periodic bouts of depression. I was only just able to hold onto the mane of the galloping horse of events piling in on top of my responsibilities, let alone free up a hand to write a diary.

I'm really not one to make excuses for my failures, but my health was a big problem. It's funny, but now that I'm in my late fifties, I genuinely feel brighter and better, more energised and saner, than I did in my supposed prime. My underactive thyroid, which had plagued me since I was a sluggardly teen, had by the mid-2010s changed up a gear into a full-on auto-immune condition, leading to severe joint pain, weight gain and other debilitating and unsightly issues; all exacerbated by stress. My hair, which had been falling out also since my late teens, had decided to give up the ghost almost entirely. I looked and felt terrible. Just getting out of bed in the morning was a physical grinding of gears. On top of that, I was peri-menopausal which, as any woman who has ever gone through it knows, is a shit show (that's a technical term). It was all I could do to get through my day, let alone take stock of the momentous events unfolding around me. My body felt like a cauldron of pain and anxiety, turned up to critical heat by the mounting pressure of life in the spotlight.

Also, back then, trying to be a good political wife, I felt an obligation to hold some of my fire, mainly so as not to cause trouble for Michael. There was, after all, precedent that punishment would be doled out, as when Cameron fired him from Education and took it out on him when I had had the temerity to have an opinion about it.

Once we divorced, my opinions became less encumbered, although out of residual respect for the man who is, after all, the father of my children and also to spare them any (further) embarrassment, I have refrained from dragging him too much into my writing. But now that he too has finally seen the light and left the toxic swamp of politics, there really is very little in the way of reasons to stay schtum.

So now it's my turn.

Buckle up for my take – truthful but chaotic – because this is how it was for me. I also understand what people mean when they say it can feel eerily calm in the eye of a storm – that is exactly how I felt. I had very little sense of the importance of individual events – things which now, when I look back, appear pivotal, at the time just seemed perfectly mundane.

For me, there is something of a soft furnishing theme in the run-up to the vote to Brexit. The trickier the conversation, it seemed afterwards, the softer the sofa in which it happened, almost as if the downy embrace of baggy upholstery could relax the players into a loose-lipped revelation or conceal the daggers of the smiling assassins tucked into its corners.

The first stirrings of unease had come during a gloriously sunny weekend in August 2015, on a break with friends in Norfolk. Having announced in January 2013, as part of their re-election manifesto, that the UK would have a referendum on staying in Europe if the Conservatives won the next election, Cameron had pinned his colours to the mast early.

Too early, said Michael, who never wanted (nor thought it necessary to have) a European referendum, especially so soon after the 2014 Scottish Referendum, which was appallingly close and risky, right up to the wire, when suddenly all the gloomy predictions evaporated into a 55.3 per cent vs 44.7 per cent win for the Tories' NO vote. The margin was convincing for all that it was unexpected, but in the warm afterglow of victory the PM seemed to forget almost instantaneously how close a shave it had been.

Michael had always been very clear with Dave about referenda in general – that they were dangerously polarising and created more problems than they resolved – but now he advised very particularly against this one. Nevertheless – flushed with his success in defending the Union and of defeating Scottish independence for a generation – Dave insisted that the Eurosceptics would never quieten down unless they were thrown the bone of a referendum, after which they could all similarly shut up for a generation (cue hollow laughter).

Timing wise, it was obvious to me and my friends that the May 2016 date – so early in the parliament, so hot on the heels of the Scottish vote – was also being pushed hard by

George Osborne, who was impatient to get the poll out of the way and his own leadership ambitions launched.

This, by the way, was by no means a betrayal on George's part; Dave was ready to hand it over. I think that had it been just him on his own, he might have been perfectly happy to carry on. But the one thing Dave always prioritised over everything else in his life – including power and politics – was Sam. After six years as First Lady, and with all the general fuckwittery and stress, and people poking at you that comes with that utterly thankless role, she had just about had enough. She had supported Dave in his ambition to become prime minister, and there was a distinct feeling in her mind that enough was enough. She – like me – was acutely aware of the pressures of her husband's job on their children and their growing need for privacy away from the glare of Westminster. She also had her own ambitions, to start a clothing label.

Indeed, while trapped in the role of dutiful political spouse, she had taken advantage of the imposed inertia to do a full-on pattern-cutting course. I would go around to No 11 for coffee or a drink and find her beavering away in her sewing room, listening to her favourite radio station – Radio 6 Music – and conjuring up ideas. Being a yoga aficionado – it was, she said, the only thing that really kept her sane in the fishbowl of Downing Street – and therefore slim as a pin, toned and (to my mind) enviably flat-chested, I served as her model for the boobacious versions of her dresses.

Ironically, Sasha Swire, who could surely have found something more inflammatory to write about me, given my general level of disgrace as a political wife, chose precisely this period of interactions with Sam to write about in her grubfest (but generally rather entertaining) diary – and got it completely arse about tit.

'Poor old Sarah Gove,' she wrote condescendingly, which is her first mistake as I was ever Vine, 'who bends over backwards to please the Camerons, was lumbered with cooking all the food while Samantha was upstairs learning to cut patterns (she wants to set up a fashion business). She then had her hair done! Turning up at her own party feeling perfectly relaxed while Sarah is laden with dishes of fish pie she has herself cooked.'

It just goes to show how someone who calls themselves an observer can get entirely the wrong end of the stick. I only met Swire a few times, but I always found her notably self-obsessed, one of those women who tends to assume every man in the room is hopelessly in love with them and as such prone, especially after a few drinks, to tiresome innuendo. So perhaps that explains her lack of perception.

Anyone who really knows me knows that I am never happier than when I'm in a kitchen, especially at parties. It means I have an excuse not to have to speak to people like her (or her bumptious husband), and I get to do my favourite thing (i.e. cook). As to bending over backwards, why wouldn't I want to help out a friend under pressure? If that makes me a poor old sap, then so be it. The Camerons were by no means singled out by me for that treatment: I'm an inveterate people pleaser. That said, I have no memory of this incident, or the supposed fish pie. Fish pie is not generally in my repertoire, so perhaps it was another one of those anecdotes she simply misremembered.

But of course, despite misfiring this particular arrow, Sasha does know how to hit where it hurts. When our friendship was placed under strain – by me working at the *Mail*, or by the 2014 reshuffle, or when our Ibiza holidays together were shelved in favour of the Camerons being hosted for free in Ibiza by uber-hairdresser John Frieda – a shadow of suspicion did flit across my mind that perhaps, for the Camerons, the job had become more important than their old muckers, that Michael and I could outlive our usefulness under the wheels of the prime minister's fanatical need to get his way.

Anyway, for the referendum to work as emphatically as he wanted, Cameron needed to be seen wielding influence on the EU from within, so that a Britain staying in Europe could be seen as operating from a position of strength not subjugation. Earlier in that summer of 2015, at the June European Council meeting, David had been ebullient, buoyed up not only by the success in Scotland in 2014 but by the unexpectedly generous margin of the Tories' win in the election a month beforehand, and so had laid out precisely what he wanted, with the arrogance of one who expected to get nearly all of it.

And so it was that under the bright glare of a Norfolk big sky on that August 2015 afternoon, lounging on garden couches, Michael and I and our friends discussed the hubris of that approach to the European Council. Michael, as always, took the position that Cameron was on a hiding to nothing: that instead of negotiating ourselves in closer, we should have been putting distance between us and European interference and entanglement.

I must confess, I actually agreed with Dave's approach, not Michael's. As someone who had grown up in Europe and understood the continental drift, as it were, I had always been of the opinion that we Brits needed to lean in with

Brussels. Get in there, gain influence, double down – and change things from the inside instead of flouncing off in a huff. The continentals don't do things like the Brits, all bravado and bluster and grand declarations; they prefer a softer, more flexible, buy-me-a-coffee approach. It's probably something to do with the weather – and the coffee.

On a weekend break in Antwerp – one of the last happy memories I have of our marriage – it had occurred to me that Michael could be the perfect person to turn around Britain's relationship with the EU from the inside. Blissfully tripping around the cobbled streets of this Belgian jewel, I fantasised happily about moving the family to Europe, about the kids learning to speak French, of returning to life as an ex-pat. Little did I know that this was now becoming the furthest thing from my husband's mind.

Back when Michael and I got engaged, friends expressed surprise that my fiancé, arch-Eurosceptic that he was known to be at *The Times*, should have fallen for a girl like me, who grew up in Italy. The answer then, as now, was that Michael wasn't a sceptic in a Little Englander sense, believing that British was best; he loved Europe – especially its vineyards – but just didn't want Britain to be run by an unelected cabal in Brussels. As a result, in our chats that weekend in Norfolk, Michael was already musing, in that abstract, historian way of his, about whether the UK should actually stay at all in a trade organisation that didn't seem to want to listen to it.

Our host had been close to Michael for years, especially since they had worked together on education in 2013, but even he glanced worriedly at Michael when he said this out loud. This was a dangerous trajectory. Both of us tried hard to persuade Michael that he should not get carried away by thoughts of resistance to the Cameron/Osborne juggernaut, partly because it seemed so futile, the Remain verdict such a shoo-in for the Cameron master plan, to the point where resistance would just be a petard upon which all Eurosceptics would be hoisted.

'Mhu-mmph. Mhu-mmph,' said Michael. Always his vocal accompaniment when challenged, this sound – what I call his 'listening but not hearing sound', almost a verbal tic – is a beautifully conciliatory but characteristically opaque mixture of an affirmative yes-mm, a thoughtful hmmm and, finally, an ambiguous hmmph ending. It is a sound that is Michael to a tee. Non-confrontational, not actually disagreeing, even (to the uninitiated) appearing to agree, but ultimately unenforceable as agreement because it is so utterly non-committal. He mostly uses it when he's trying to read and people keep bothering him. He also tends to deploy it when he thinks the interlocutor is talking utter bollocks, but doesn't want to have to point this out.

Our host and I, however, were satisfied that we had headed this particular Gove moment of intellectual free-ranging off at the pass. In the sunshine that day, there was nothing concrete about his stance, no outright opposition, merely a weighing up. There were other conversations through the autumn and into winter but always, it seemed, with more of his old leader-writer's hat on than with his newer ministerial cap.

There were no nefarious plots, no gathering of dark forces, and certainly no Movement, despite Nadine Dorries's most torrid imaginings. Or at least if they were, I never had sight of them. For one thing, there was no time: Michael was still working all hours of day and night, with his usual laser focus on his brief as Lord Chancellor, developing ideas for prison reform that were breathtaking in their scope. He now saw that prison for young offenders could be an extension of education – a second chance for youths already let down once by the system, and a second chance for governments to take advantage of a literally captive audience to hook prisoners' curiosity and intellect into education and qualifications, and thus reverse the polarity of a life heading south. It was the sort of long-lead, far-reaching policy that Michael lived for, and had he had the opportunity to pursue it I can't help but feel – as I later told him – that Brexit would merely have been a footnote in his lifetime's index.

Which is why, when Dave cornered me at teatime on the last day of that year, on New Year's Eve 2015, I felt entirely relaxed. For one thing, I was, once again, lounging. This time, we were cosied up – just the two of us – on the sofas in front of the large fire in the great hall at Chequers, resting our digestions momentarily before the next meal, our children happily parked in front of the telly or a gaming screen, the PM and I idly chatting about the different personalities that were there already or were about to descend on us. All the usual enjoyable flimflam of a weekend at Chequers.

'Everything's going to be okay, isn't it, Sarah?' Dave said suddenly. 'With Michael, I mean. And the referendum?'

'Oh, I think so,' I reassured him. 'You know what Michael's like. He likes to noodle things through and he's always believed that we needn't be intimidated by life outside Europe, but ultimately he's onside.'

Much has been made of that moment. I meant what I said. Michael hadn't shared any other view with me – just the fading memory of those ambivalent 'mhummphs' in Norfolk. Most of all, being frightfully middle class about it all, and in that cosy setting, I didn't want to start a row, or even rock the boat. But I had forgotten two crucial factors, both of which were interwoven with one another: Michael's family background and his need to make a difference, to have a legacy.

Michael has always felt very strongly that being adopted was his second chance in life: 'I owe everything I've achieved to my father. I was very lucky to have him,' he has said in many an interview. He adored his adoptive parents, Ernest and Christine, and always felt so fortunate to have been one of the lucky ones, that he owed both his parents and society to make it big in life, to show that theirs wasn't a poor choice, that he wasn't going to waste this chance.

So Michael's thirst to leave his mark wasn't (just) the usual politician's vanity but a yearning to stand tall to his parents – his saviours – and leave a legacy to be proud of. The fact that his father had to sell his fish merchant's business because of the EU and the common fisheries policy in the 1980s had made a deep mark on the teenage Michael and left him with a visceral loathing for the impersonal sweep of federalist policy making. He was very clear that, for him and his family, the CFP from the EU was directly responsible for the destruction of the Scottish fishing industry and for the loss of thousands of Scottish jobs, not to mention the proud seafaring traditions that stretched back for generations in his adoptive family. The idea that good, solid working men like Ernest, who had never done anything but the right thing, could have their lives and livelihoods upended by flabby fat cats on the Continent rightly riled him. For Michael, the EU was personal, all tied up with his love for his father and his need to do him proud, with his roots into Conservatism and his intellectual respect for British history and sovereignty.

As his wife, I should have understood this, and understood his depth of feeling. But, very possibly because of my own European slant, I failed to see how deep these particular waters ran. And in truth, it was not as though he talked about it an awful lot. He preferred to come at the problem, as he so often did in other aspects of our life together, from an intellectual standpoint.

I think if he had just been honest with Dave and said, 'Look mate, I know what you're trying to do with this referendum, and I totally get it; but what you have to understand about me is that the EU totally screwed over my dad, and he never quite recovered, and for that I can never forgive them and so if you do go ahead, you need to know I won't *ever* vote for those fuckers in Brussels' (or words to that effect), Dave would have understood. If he had made it personal, which it was, and which Dave certainly felt later, it might have been okay. But instead he made it political. Which was not okay.

In my stupidity, I had not yet worked all of this out. Or maybe I had and just didn't want to admit it to myself. Either way, it was with all sincerity that I reassured Dave at Chequers, feeling not a qualm when the PM then announced a week later, in January 2016, that his government ministers could vote freely in the referendum, that there would be no party whip, because I still didn't imagine that this made the slightest bit of difference to my husband, he being one of Cameron's right-hand men. Silly me.

Part of the trouble, of course, was that all of Michael's own right-hand men – Dominic Cummings, everyone around him – were committed Leavers from the moment that word became the label. So nearly all the opinions he was getting at work were very one-sided.

I have occasionally tortured myself that Michael didn't share with me his mental machinations in the following months leading up to the referendum. I even distinctly remember a conversation with him that Christmas, talking about the work he was doing at the Ministry for Justice, and saying rather fan-girlishly, 'I think the work you're doing at Justice is far more important than your educational reforms – far more important than anything else you could do about Europe. This is legacy stuff – actual outcomes that could become positive.' But again, I should have known better than to think that he would divulge his thoughts to me. Michael has always been a person who lives inside his own head: convivial, friendly, outgoing, yes, but also intensely private, never feeling the need to externalise his thinking and fearsomely good at compartmentalising.

His ability to park everything in neat stackable (and occasionally lockable) boxes was how he was able to saunter through the brickbats of politics with a smile on his face, how he could live so easily beyond his means, apparently untroubled by a low bank balance or the privations of a politician's salary. It was both part of his charm – he wears life lightly – and part of his ability to madden me with his apparent insouciance. Part of the frog-boiling for me was how gradually, in retreating behind his armour after the 2009 expenses scandal, he was increasingly failing to come out for anyone, even for me.

I also think that he liked to put me in a box, one marked 'home' rather than 'work', which meant that, again, contrary to certain feverish imaginings, we didn't talk all that much about politics. Most of our conversations revolved around the domestic – stuff to do with the kids, friends, the day-to-day practicalities of family life. I think he thought the political stuff bored me, or perhaps he assumed I wouldn't really understand it, or be interested. This wasn't a sexist thing – Michael is the least sexist man I know – and he had plenty of close female advisers, such as Pamela Dow, who worked for him at Education and later became his director of strategy at the Ministry for Justice, who were crucial to his political conversations. I just don't think I occupied that space in his head.

Michael was also deeply non-confrontational, all part of that same need to compartmentalise – in this case, in head, in sand – so none of us should have been surprised that his apparent compliance with Project Referendum wasn't quite what it should have been. He has always had the tendency to avoid conflict until the last possible moment, presenting contrary plans as fait accompli, saying 'Surprise!' with a big smile.

When I asked him afterwards why he hadn't at least discussed with me the way his thoughts were going, he flannelled me with talk of wanting to spare me the drama of it all. Which is somewhat ironic. In his podcast revelations, *Inside the Room*, Michael himself admitted to 'moral cowardice', both for not disabusing Cameron, when Dave told him about our New Year's Eve conversation, and for not coming clean with me.

George Osborne was more suspicious. At this point, in the early spring of 2016, Leave was still a motley crew, a ragtag gang of old-style patrician Eurosceptics, mixing uneasily with immigration bores and disenfranchised right-wingers. George was clearly worried that if Michael jumped ship and joined them he would legitimise the 'brand' and give intellectual heft to what was now being called Brexit.

As well as sharing a love for Wagner, George and Michael have always been very closely aligned politically. George knew what even the London-bubble media hadn't quite worked out: that Michael had standing among his peers in Parliament and a thick layer of grass-root support among Conservative Party members, as being someone who Got Stuff Done. Worse still, ever the arch strategist, Osborne knew that if Michael lit the way and left the Cameron camp, he might well be followed by that famously unreliable loose cannon who had the maddening ability to appeal to millions of voters: Boris Johnson.

So even though the mud-slinging was in full swing, we were nonetheless invited to lunch at George's weekend residence, Dorneywood. Perhaps George thought he might have one last ditch attempt at getting Michael back on-side, perhaps he just genuinely wanted to spend some time with his old friend, who knows. A bit of both, I suspect.

Dorneywood is very different from the prime minister's weekend residence, Chequers. The latter is laid out on a grand scale, every inch steeped in history and officialdom. By contrast, Dorneywood is much more like a very large family home, rather higgledy-piggledy in parts and with a warm, friendly atmosphere.

Originally a Georgian farmhouse, it was variously expanded over the years by various eminent Victorians. The house itself is cosy and comfortable with an odd hallway/dining room entered via a small porch stuffed with coats and wellies, leading on one side to the kitchens – catering-grade to cope with grand dinners – and a small family sitting room. On the other side is a somewhat draughty morning room and beyond that, in what must be the older part of the house, a large, wood-panelled drawing room with trompe l'oeil panelling and a beautiful set of windows looking out onto the gardens.

From here, there is a door leading onto a small patio furnished with curious three-legged white metal chairs which, I recall, are fiendishly hard to stay upright on, especially after a few lemonades. Beyond that is the croquet lawn on which John Prescott famously played and on which, somewhat less famously, our late Jack Russell whippet cross, Mars, had rather ignominiously dispatched Gordon Brown a few years previously. Not *the* Gordon Brown, you'll be relieved to know, but his namesake, one of the Dorneywood flock of rare breed chickens named after former chancellors of the Exchequer. Not clan Gove's finest hour, I must confess.

Upstairs there is a warren of bedrooms, each with a different, quirky name. Ours was always Hard to Find, as I remember, which it was, especially if George had decided to crack open the Government wine collection.

Anyway, it was outside on the little terrace adjoining the drawing room over drinks that I argued with George about what they should do in the event of the Government losing the vote. I was adamant that it needn't spell the end of Cameron's premiership. This referendum was not a vote about *him*, a judgement on his abilities as prime minister, I argued; it was a simple binary vote about whether to stay in or out of the European Union. Everyone was being far too hysterical, I said; they just needed to calm down, wait for the vote – and then implement the result.

I remember George looking at me as though I were completely insane. I wonder now whether it was yet again a male/female thing. Women – and in particular mothers – are so used to making the best of bad situations, we do it all the time. Men, especially powerful men, are so much more uncompromising. If they cannot have it their way, they won't have it at all.

So in February, George and Dave planned a pincer movement on my unsuspecting husband to make sure that he stayed on board. Once again, soft furnishings were the deceptively welcoming setting: in this case, the Osborne & Little sofas in George's flat in Downing Street. According to Dave's own account, George went in strong on Michael, speaking starkly about how he thought the Leave camp would start off with all the best intentions, be open about their liberal, sovereignty-seeking aims, but that they would soon descend into a sub-Farage rabble. 'If you go for Leave,' Osborne later revealed he told Michael, 'you will confer respectability on that mob. Boris will have to join, you'll splinter all the Cameroon friendships and alliances, Dave will have to resign and my career will be over.'

'Michael seemed torn and really pained by our conversation,' writes Cameron in his memoir. 'He told us despairingly, "My head is in a strange place. For once, I find it hard to articulate. But if I do decide to opt for Brexit, I'll make one speech, not much more, and play no further part in the campaign."'

Michael says now that he meant every word of what he said on the yellow sofas that day. He says that from the moment Dave brought up the subject of a referendum, he repeatedly told him that it would be a mistake – partly because, he says now, 'I feared I would be on the other side.' For him, the parting of political ways was inevitable; every fibre of his being then wanted to make his leave as pain free and uncomplicated as possible. But, as I wrote at the time, the PM was not only his boss, he was also an old friend. It doesn't get more awkward than that.

I've often wondered if things wouldn't have taken a different turn had Dave not deliberately humiliated Michael so publicly over Education. After all, Michael had been doing what Dave wanted him to do, and doing it at considerable cost to his own political (and personal) capital. By treating him the way he did when the going got tough, Dave demonstrated in no uncertain terms that he had no particular loyalty towards Michael, either as a friend or a political ally. That was the point, I think, when the shard of ice entered Michael's heart. Michael would never have gone out of his way to damage the PM; but when it came to something that truly mattered to him – in this case, the referendum – he was not going to abandon his principles for someone who had not only abandoned him, but also and very deliberately fed him to the wolves to save his own skin.

Others were clear-eyed about the duplicity of the leadership, sometimes from the perspective of having gained a little distance. My son, the 'Boy in the Corner', remembers a weekend at this time, when Steve Hilton flew in from LA for just two days, arriving at 9.30 a.m. to talk to Michael about his next steps. 'I was playing *FIFA* in the sitting room,' Will says now, 'and I remember having to turn it down because they had to talk – so obviously I listened, especially when Steve started leaning quite close in towards Dad and his voice got deep and really serious. "Just don't listen to George and Dave," he said. "They are not your friends, they are *politics* friends. Do what you believe in – because they surely will." I think it was the first time I'd heard the phrase *politics* friends.'

Michael's beliefs were taking shape to an ever more detailed degree. Throughout the winter, I had watched his usual mutterings – about the profligacy, the back-scratching, the bureaucracy and the tentacles of Brussels working their way towards a stranglehold over British government – get louder the more he worked on his red boxes and tried to line up his ducks on his big prison reforms and human rights adjustments.

At the same time, obscure books such as a scholarly analysis of the 1975 Referendum by David Butler and Uwe Kitzinger and Roger Bootle's *The Trouble with Europe* began turning up on his bedside table. Before my eyes, I could see him making the transformation from common or garden Eurosceptic to someone who might be getting ready to jump ship from the Cameron galleon.

Nick Boles remembers a Barlby Road dinner during this tense period, when Octavius Black and his wife Joanne Cash, both passionate Europhiles, had a bit of a go at Michael for what they saw as his spurious arguments about Europe. Michael, very rarely for him, became very heated, shouting about fisheries. Octavius especially, who had known Michael since they were 18 years old and debating at the Union, was very taken aback by the hammer and tongs suddenly being waved in the air.

For my part, I tried time and again to introduce the subject of Dave and how, if Michael decided to openly support

Leave, the consequences for our relationship with not just the Camerons but others like the Lockwoods would be disastrous. I repeatedly urged him to have an honest conversation about it all with Dave, to really have it out with him, man to man, to make it crystal clear how he felt about it all. I was certain that if that could happen, they would be able to reach an accommodation. But the more I pushed, the more he retreated back into himself. It was as if he just didn't want to hear it. I became wary of even bringing the subject up.

By the time we got to Aberdeen for a half-term long weekend with his family, Michael was like a cat on a hot tin roof, locked in an internal struggle of agonising proportions. He talked to his father, spent hours on the phone with Dominic and MPs like Douglas Carswell and Owen Paterson. Meanwhile, I was doing my usual juggling act of working remotely, being an attentive daughter-in-law and a half-term mum. There's nothing like seeing your husband wrestling with potentially career-breaking decisions of vital national importance while also entertaining an 11-year-old and a 12-year-old with games of Monopoly and trips to rain-lashed activity centres.

We returned south for a dinner, arranged a few weeks earlier, with Boris and his then wife Marina at their house in Islington. Much has been made of this dinner as evidence that Michael and Boris were always in cahoots and had their Vote Leave campaign planned from the outset. Pundits have pored over the events of that evening time and again – they've even been dramatised, with mixed success.

It is perhaps worth remembering that at no point have any of the people who have written about what happened ever bothered to ask me about it, which gives you a sense of how reliable and well researched these accounts are. Mind you, the dinner is also a prime example of me having no sense at all on the night itself that momentous decisions were actually being made. I presumed – foolishly – that it was just more brain-farting by both my husband and Boris over yet another rambunctious kitchen supper. My main memory is of feeling mystified as to why on earth Evgeny Lebedev, the proprietor of the *Evening Standard*, was there (I still have no idea, to this day) and I do remember he said about three words, and that I couldn't stop staring at his beard, which was most impressively pruned.

I certainly didn't know that Boris was having the grand existential crisis that he later claimed – although I obviously knew that Brexit was on the menu. We had drinks upstairs in the drawing room, a classic jumble of books, papers and dog-eared furniture typical of all upper-middle-class houses, then repaired to the basement kitchen (again, textbook), for dinner. A succulent slow-roast lamb, as I recall, plus lashings of good red wine. It was there, in the slight gloom of the dinner table lighting, that Boris and Michael noodled away, weighing up the pros and cons of the former joining the Leave campaign.

All those who have conversely framed Boris's decision as a kind of ill-thought-out whim will be disappointed to know that he was forensic in questioning not only the political practicalities of Leave, but also whether it was, in fact, legally possible (an important consideration which later turned out to be crucial) and, if so, what the processes by which the UK would detach itself might be. Timescales, economic consequences, trade options, regulations, Northern Ireland: these were all in the mix. I saw no flibberty-gibbetry that night, none whatsoever. Boris sought the counsel of various third parties – a cabinet minister, a lawyer – barking loudly into his mobile (on speakerphone) in between mouthfuls, Michael listening in and occasionally contributing.

I listened closely for a few minutes, but it really was a very lawyerly and quite technical conversation and the aroma rising from the slow-cooked shoulder of lamb was beginning to torture me more than any future of the EU, so I tucked in. Marina and Evgeny followed suit, and Marina and I spent the next 20 minutes attempting to make dinner party conversation with Evgeny in stage whispers, Boris shushing us whenever we got too loud.

It was all a little surreal and intense but, while it was definitely an interesting evening, it was not unusual. Just another table-top tap dance around all the issues, I thought. What astounds me once again, as I look back at this point, is my naivety. Or maybe it was stupidity. It's ironic that I chose this moment to be a good political wife: to hear no evil and see no evil – at precisely the moment when I clearly should have been paying close attention.

Either way, whatever it was blinded me to the truth of what was really going on. I knew Michael was struggling between his loyalty to Dave and his beliefs. I could also see that Boris's dilemma was more self-centred, concerned with what would be best for him, but I thought it was all, at worst, a political conundrum. I just had no idea how personally they were all taking it.

Meanwhile, Downing Street drafted in some soft-skills agents to work a parallel persuasion campaign. The Lockwoods messaged both of us repeatedly – Chris with an increasing shrillness, Venetia more mournfully, with a sense of 'please don't let the boys throwing their toys out of the pram wreck it for us'. I was invited by Kate Fall, Dave's gate-keeper, for a drink at her house for what she actually said was 'a quiet word'. And all the time, the sands were shifting underfoot; I could no longer tell who were friends and who were foes-in-disguise. It's also ironic, therefore, that when Kate wrote about me in her book, she cast us in roles rather reversed to the ones I had assigned us. From being quite a mate – I always liked her and she describes me earlier in the book as 'a clever, funny, powerful and forceful woman who is used to proactively managing her brilliant but not very down-to-earth husband' – she changes her tune when talking about the early months of 2016.

'Sarah is always so compelling,' she writes. 'Even if you profoundly disagree with her, she has a way of wrapping her narrative around you like the coils of a python, until the way of least resistance (her way) seems the only sensible option.' All this from the Dave acolyte who did precisely this to me with her 'quiet word' coiled around me like a noose; the only difference being that I did resist. The message was becoming clear: don't get above yourselves, you are foot soldiers not ranking officers like us, so just get out over the top and do what we say, there's a nice Gove.

That February half-term week, Simone Finn, Michael's ex-girlfriend-turned-political-confidante and a good friend of mine, happened to be at Frances Osborne's birthday party, shortly before the PM's ultimately unsuccessful trip to Brussels to secure the negotiations for which he had laid out his wares the previous summer. Tensions were high – battle lines were clearly and openly being drawn up between

Remainers and Leavers, from the backbenches right up to cabinet level – and it had become increasingly obvious to everyone that No 10 were very keen indeed to swing Michael back to them.

Frances was still married to George at that point, though we all knew it wasn't always a happy experience for her, and he lost no time, when Simone arrived at the party, in rather imperiously demanding that she had a word with Michael to get him back onside. After a short exchange, Simone being emollient but noncommittal, Osborne's tone turned petulant.

'But ... but ...' he spluttered. 'We *made* Michael Gove. Who was he before? He owes us his whole bloody career! How can he *not* support us?'

Not only was this patently, foully, untrue, but never have I heard so pithily proved our eternal suspicion that neither Michael nor I were ever quite good enough for the public-school nabobs who made up the true inner circle of David Cameron's ruling elite. Suddenly those cosy chats at Dorneywood, all those years of friendship, of school runs, of shared holidays, of helping out on every level, looked a little empty, two-dimensional. Perhaps Sasha Swire had been right after all.

When I was a timid teenager, I used to have a recurring anxiety dream in which all my friends and family would gather around, tell me they never liked me and always thought I was an idiot, then point and laugh while my world crumbled. Suddenly, it felt like that nightmare had become reality. I felt stupid, used and humiliated. But above all, it finally confirmed a very important and deeply depressing truth, one which I had previously felt did not apply to us.

LESSON EIGHT IN HOW NOT TO BE A POLITICAL WIFE, THE MOST IMPORTANT LESSON OF ALL:
there's no such thing as a friend in politics.

Meanwhile, Michael's political chums and advisers at work also got to see him deliberating. Michael's scorn for the creaking judicial bodies of Europe was well known by them; he had spent the months since taking the job at Justice being like Canute, trying to hold back the waves of EU overreach on human affairs at the Council of the European Union and the European Court of Justice, saying disgustedly afterwards that they were simply 'unreformable institutions' and that the meetings were pointless, ever-decreasing circles of what Michael derided afterwards as 'just smiles and nice coffee'.

Back inside the Department, the rules of engagement for the referendum were being written on the back of an envelope. What became clear early on was that despite the supposed 'free vote', any ministers backing the Vote Leave campaign would immediately be excluded from governmental procedures, protocols, even from materials and resources within the Department. This was overstepping on an outrageous scale, not to mention the fact that it would have left the Ministry for Justice without a secretary of state.

Dom Cummings was outraged by this and ramped it up to Michael that this was symptomatic of the PM's contradictory attitude to the 'free vote'. Dom clearly wanted to bounce Michael into joining the Leave campaign and the Henries were always convinced that it was he who leaked to the press about how Michael had already made that his decision (he hadn't, not officially), which happened while the

PM was still in Brussels. A move straight out of the Cummings playbook.

What was becoming ever clearer was that the ramifications of the referendum had not yet been fully considered. There was a moment when Laura Kuenssberg was in Michael's office, interviewing him about his role as Justice Secretary, when she asked him whether the British legal systems would fare better if we were outside the European Union. When Michael thought and said, emphatically, that 'Yes, they would be better', there was a feeling in the room among his team that a lid had just been lifted. 'It suddenly struck home,' one of them told me later, 'that this referendum was going to snowball out of control – that all public policy would be gathered up and smashed by it'.

Boris, meanwhile, was still wavering. Famously, as revealed in Tim Shipman's book, on the Friday before the referendum date announcement, ever the writer, he sat down and wrote two articles – one in favour of remaining in Europe and one in favour of exiting, in a classically Boris the Academician's attempt to tease out the issues in his own head. His detractors have long and tiresomely argued that this was confirmation of his self-serving venality on the subject; but as a writer myself, I know that sometimes the only way to come to a decision is to argue it over with yourself on paper. No one has ever, to my knowledge, seen either article but we all know the outcome of his last-minute deliberations.

On Saturday, 20 February 2016, the prime minister announced that the EU Referendum was going to be held on 23 June. Later, the cross-party Vote Leave team was revealed. Michael and Gisela Stuart, the Labour MP for Birmingham Edgbaston, were the Co-convenors of the Campaign

Committee, with Gisela doubling up as chair. The rest of the Committee was comprised of 23 MPs and Peers from all parties and crossbenches, plus some wheeler-dealers like Dominic Cummings, part of the team since the moment the 2015 election had wrapped, now firmly in the limelight as campaign director, and John Longworth, former director general of the British Chambers of Commerce.

Tucked in halfway down the roster was the name of the man who had left it to the very last minute to reveal his direction of travel: Boris Johnson. Simone tells me that apparently Dave became very emotional when he saw the list and – astonishingly – was reduced to tears when it was confirmed that both Michael and Boris were on it. While George was dependably cold and emotionally detached, this was the first time I'd had an inkling of how this might go for our friendship with the Camerons.

It was extraordinary how quickly the blame game started. It got very nasty, very fast. Andy Feldman, then still chairman of the Conservatives and a great friend of both Michael and Dave's, had a party for his 50th, at the end of February 2016. Despite the fact that already people in our wider friendship circle were beginning to take sides, Gabby Feldman, Andrew's wife, had invited us along to a swanky East End sushi restaurant.

I had real reservations about going. Various friends had already made it clear in no uncertain terms that they considered Michael's decision to join Vote Leave not only politically irresponsible but also personally treacherous, and it looked like the Cameroons were closing ranks. It had been a relentless few weeks, and I was in no mood for a party. I just thought it would be better off all round if we kept our heads down and stayed away, not least because I didn't want to ruin Andrew's birthday celebrations.

I texted Gabby and suggested it might be better if we didn't come. She was adamant that we should, and that it would be fine. Kate Fall also got in touch to say that Samantha and Dave were very much looking forward to seeing us there. It felt like a three-line whip, so I resolved to go. But something told me it wasn't going to be much fun.

One of the problems, I knew, would be the 20 February column I had written for the *Daily Mail*, in which I did my best to explain the rationale behind Michael's decision to back Leave. Against a backdrop of sustained threats and pressure – and when I say threats, I do mean threats: at one point I was told that if Michael didn't back down, I would find myself 'in a very cold place indeed' – I had written in what I thought were calm and conciliatory terms about the difficulty of the decision he had made. I hoped it would shed some light on the complexity of emotions around it – and act as a bit of an olive branch to Dave and Samantha.

Reading it back, I still don't think there was anything in it that was either indiscreet or unfair. But perhaps I touched a nerve when I wrote the following passage:

'Opening up a box, I came across a stack of photographs from our wedding, back in 2001. Sixty or so of our good friends gamely schlepped to the South of France for a knees-up. There was George Osborne chatting to, of all people, feminist author Caitlin Moran, and Ed Vaizey, now the longest-serving-ever culture minister, delivering his brilliant best man speech.

'And Samantha Cameron, radiant and pregnant with her first child; she and David laughing on the coach back from the church. Not the Chancellor or the famous writer or the Prime Minister. Just a group of people from all walks in life who had in common one thing: us.

'It was as though fate had intervened to remind us what we were risking.

'The Camerons are some of our dearest friends. We had been through so much together, both personal and political. I am godmother to Florence, their youngest.

'Now David would inevitably feel let down. Michael was between a rock and a hard place. Be true to himself and disappoint his friend; support the Prime Minister and betray his principles.'

I was trying to explain the impossibility of the choice Michael had faced. That none of this was personal, that we could, if the will was there, overcome this and remain friends. But I was wrong. If anything, it seemed to have the opposite effect. Because, for the Camerons, it was held to be deeply personal that Michael had gone with his principles. As Kate Fall, to whom I spoke that same night, wrote later in her book, 'Perhaps it [was] naive of David to think that Michael, who was always anti-EU, would be prepared to sacrifice his political beliefs for personal loyalty.' In other words, Dave couldn't believe Michael had defied him. This, to a man like Dave, was not principle but betrayal.

And I was soon to find out, that February night, that political and personal had just become inextricably enmeshed.

The evening started off badly enough, when Michael and I travelled separately to the party, leaving me to face the lions' den alone. As misfortune would have it, I arrived just as the Camerons did and, faced with two small lifts up to the restaurant, the protection team took one and the three of us took the other. As the lift doors closed, and before it even started up, Dave looked at me with daggers in his eyes and said, through clenched teeth, words that turned out to be the last I ever heard from him, face to face.

'You have to get your husband off the airwaves, you have to get him under control. For fuck's sake, Sarah, I'm fighting for my political life here.'

For the first time since I'd known him, that charm and levity of touch that I associated with Dave was nowhere to be seen. He was angry, deadly serious, outraged even. He spoke to me as if he was neither a friend nor an equal, but as someone who clearly felt he had an absolute right to his superior position.

Also, for the first time ever, I felt the abyss of class between us. There was no attempt to speak to me as an equal on this matter, no indication that he wanted a proper conversation. This was an order, not a request, master to servant. And the quivering fury behind his voice, the anger in his eyes, was down to one thing and one thing alone: Michael was defying him. It wasn't just that he didn't like it. It was also that it did not compute.

That is the thing about the British class system. There is a group of people, Dave among them, for whom failure is simply not a reality. Their class and their money insulate them from all the day-to-day disappointments that affect ordinary people, and so when things don't go their way, they just can't understand it. It's not malicious, it's just their reality. Dave's response to Michael's decision echoed that: it was as much incredulous as it was anything else. He simply could not understand why Michael, who on many issues was generally very much a team player, had on this occasion decided to defy him.

The answer, though he never understood it, was simple: Dave was indeed fighting for his political life. Michael, by contrast, was fighting for his political belief. The two things are very different.

But back to that night. Michael arrived, all bonhomie and calm, and we sat down to supper. I remember it was a long, thin room, with the door at one end. I was seated quite a long way in, several places away from Samantha. There were warm speeches and delicious food, but the conversation was aggressively Remain, and there was quite a lot of what my dear friend Imogen likes to call finger-jabbing in my direction (she always says that the problem with me is I'm only ever three glasses of wine away from a finger-jab, and I'm afraid she's not wrong).

I was tired and uncomfortable and, as soon as I could, I signalled to Michael that we should probably go. As I walked past the backs of my fellow guests to get to the exit, I paused to say thank you to Andy, who was sitting next to Samantha, and that's when it happened. In the lift with Dave, Sam had not said anything; now she must have been a few drinks down, and so she let rip.

The incident was later reported, leaked presumably by a fellow guest, in the newspapers. According to the *Sun*, Samantha launched into a tirade, accusing me of 'betrayal'.

I don't think I said very much as she laid into me, although the *Sun* wrote that the pair of us 'ended up raising their voices and effing and blinding'. I don't recall much swearing, but then the memory is vague, clouded by emotion. I do recall she felt very strongly that I should not have put her name in the paper, that the *Mail* and Dacre were the enemy, and I was therefore complicit in their general evil and what she saw as their mission to bring down Dave. They had always had it in for her, she said, right from the start, and she couldn't believe I had betrayed her by working for Dacre.

There were so many things I could have said. That the *Mail* was a great paper and that I was proud to work there; that she had no right to tell me what I could or could not write; that if Dave hadn't treated Michael so cavalierly at Education then perhaps he might have acted differently; that she had no idea how much I stood up for her, how many times I had advocated for her and Dave at the paper, defended her corner; but also that all this was just bloody ridiculous. We were friends, grown-ups. Our children had grown up together. Surely, I could have concluded, that was worth more than a stupid political disagreement?

But I didn't. I was too shocked to really argue, suffering from the curse of the writer whereby you think of a stunning riposte a day later, acutely aware that everyone was watching us, and conscious that in this room I had no allies. She was Queen, this was her moment. I just had to stand there and take my punishment. Besides, I had written the piece, so in that respect she had a point. But what I had thought might serve as a carefully worded kind of apology, an explanation if not a justification, albeit a public one, had clearly been interpreted as an attack. I knew I shouldn't have come – but maybe that was why Kate and Gabby had been so insistent: maybe it was a deliberate ambush, to give Sam the opportunity to dress me down. I was embarrassed and upset and fled the room, mumbling an apology, not quite in tears, but on the verge.

Even then, I didn't realise the finality of our rift: that politics – and the potassium-on-water conflagration that

happened when politics and media collided – would ultimately be the grim reaper of all the friendship that had come
before. To me, it still felt like a chapter, not the end of the
book.

After that, the floodgates opened. The Remain teams were
quick to cry foul on Michael's increasingly obvious leadership of the Leave campaign, citing his 'promise' to Dave and
George on the yellow sofas that day that he wouldn't actively
lobby or campaign for Leave. Amber Rudd, in turn, famously
laid into Boris, trying – not unreasonably but over-personally
– to attack him for being flaky. 'He's the life and soul of the
party,' she told an ITV debate, 'but he's not the man you
want driving you home afterwards.'

At the same time, Michael was discovering what a sack of
ferrets the Vote Leave camp was and, having made this most
momentous decision on a personal level, found himself calming down the infighting and pulled inexorably into being the
face of the Leave campaign as he did so, as the original cast
of characters fell away or onto their swords. When asked by
George years afterwards if he didn't think he had deceived
them about the level of his involvement with the Leave team,
Michael admitted that he hadn't intended to make any
speeches, sit on any TV sofas or take part in any of the tele-
vised debates that he ended up doing, as he had told them
that day on the sofa.

'But during the course of the campaign,' he told Ed Balls
and George Osborne in their podcast in April 2024, 'Dom
[Cummings] would say, "If you don't do this debate or
appearance, they'll just get bloody Farage on", and then
Dom would sweep his arm wide, encompassing everyone
working in the team room behind us, a tight-knit group of

people I had worked with and trusted for years. "You just can't let these people down," he would press. What choice did I have?'

Once again, the Hand of Dom was being felt. With the perspective of 10 years, I see now that, while Michael's judgement can rightly be impugned as often impulsive and sometimes misguided, the disastrous Dom-ination during these months was really the hand at the tiller steering us onto the rocks.

Gallingly, Dave's earlier misgivings about Cummings and his baleful influence were on the money. For one thing, I remain convinced that it was he who drafted the open letter that was sent to the papers in May 2016, with Michael and Boris as the undersigned, which criticised the prime minister's immigration policy but was taken by Dave as a personal broadside.

What is undeniably true is that Dom had upped the ante throughout the campaign, being the one to come up with the infamous claim that Brexit would free up £350 million per week for the NHS; dismissing Remain's economic warnings as Project Fear (an evilly brilliant touch); and framing the referendum as a battle between ordinary people and the establishment, writing off the reservations of the Bank of England and the Treasury as the reactive jitters of the elite, tapping into the public distrust of politicians and experts.

So when Michael said his now infamous quote about how he thought the country had had enough of experts, I wasn't the only one who heard Dom's influence there, with Michael adopting a Cummings turn of phrase to describe his own disgust with what he saw as the disconnect between the real world of British people and the metropolitan abstractism and bureaucracy, that he'd seen as a secretary of state in three departments. Most damagingly of all in the long run, throughout the Leave campaign, it was Dom urging Michael to row in behind Boris, insisting that he was the magical populist ingredient, that nothing else mattered.

Key to understanding Vote Leave was this belief in Boris. The other erroneous – and equally startlingly trusting – belief was the team's miscalculation, as it turned out, about Life After Victory. It's not true that there was no plan, as has been said. They had a plan. It was the personnel that was the issue. The reason roles were not worked out beforehand was partly because Michael really never believed that Leave would win, but also because to his mind that would have seemed presumptuous. Dom, Boris and Michael all assumed that Dave would stay on as prime minister, no matter what the result and that if, by some miracle, Brexit was the chosen outcome, they would simply serve under him, and under his direction. It would be up to Dave to appoint whomever to whatever role in the process. As they saw it, to have made plans would have been disrespectful to their leader. Never would they have predicted that they would be left in charge.

Added to that was Michael's refusal to directly engage in any conversations at all about Life After, with the team sharing with me their frustrations about seeing him clam up if they ever tried to pin him down or make him take a view. This was something I could recognise – increasingly – in my day-to-day life with him, the feeling almost from the start of the Leave campaign that whenever I tried to get him to hear my views and fears about Brexit and its consequences, he would simply retreat into his shell and blank me out. It was something that even the children cite now – his remoteness then, his inability to be open about issues that were tricky and nuanced. It would eventually prove to be the death knell of our marriage for me.

As the weeks of the Vote Leave/Better In campaigns unfolded – through Farage's Armada of little boats on the Thames, through the £350 million claim being emblazoned on the well-travelled battle bus, through the inaccurate polling that found in favour of the Remainers – I could only hope that my friendship with Samantha would recover. She and I were the true friends out of the four of us. Michael and Dave may have known each other longer but political ambition had always been the third wheel in their relationship, even back at Oxford. Samantha and I were joined by the strongest ties of shared motherhood, of grief, of wiping children's noses, bolstering each other up against the storm of public opinion.

When, on 16 June, with just a week to go before the Brexit vote on the 23rd, the Labour MP Jo Cox was murdered by a right-wing nutter, those bonds seemed more important than ever. Campaigning stopped in its tracks as the country stepped back in shock. A mother of two, a wife, a daughter, had been murdered in cold blood and in cold daylight, for what reason? Because she was a Member of Parliament.

Not widely known on a national level – even Kate Fall said she had never heard of her – Jo was universally popular among her Commons colleagues. MPs on all sides of the house mourned and clustered together to gain mutual comfort. Over supper in Barlby Road one night with the Henries, we took a sober look at what life could look like beyond the referendum, beyond this cataclysm. Idle speculation about Life After no longer seemed appropriate. Henry Newman was, moreover, of the view that Jo Cox's murder would kill Vote Leave: that no one would want to vote for something that had seemed to have attracted such horrific controversy.

The subdued gathering around our kitchen table, Michael included, could not have imagined what would happen a week later. Even on the day of the vote, when Nick Boles and Michael had lunch together at that tapas restaurant, the two of them talked less about Brexit and more about the need, as Michael saw it, to pull back together as a party, regroup and heal. Nick himself went to a Remain party that night and remembers it being a grim event, full of high nerves and deep depression. For all the oxygenated bluster and beef of both campaigns over the previous few weeks, it was as if this murder in the name of politics had deflated the hot air, momentarily leaving both camps with a bad taste in their collective mouths, and highlighting that there were things more important than Europe. As Jo Cox had said in her maiden speech as an MP, 'We are far more united and have far more in common with each other than things that divide us.'

For me, almost as strong as the feeling of shock and grief that this lovely woman had been killed, was the realisation that this was the final nail in the coffin of my respect for politics. How could being an MP ever make up for the danger and horror of being attacked, not just every day in the press and on social media, but in real life, chopped down simply for doing one's duty?

CHAPTER NINE

LADY MACBETH

'Ultimately, Michael's view is that true friends can have differences of opinion without letting it affect their relationships. I hope and pray that will turn out to be true.'

Sarah Vine, *Daily Mail*, 25 February 2016

To the victor, the spoils. Sadly, this time, the Bible was wrong. In just 24 hours, winning the Brexit vote turned us from victors into Britain's Most Wanted.

'There was this block of about 50 men with cameras outside our front door, all yelling, and me wondering what we were going to do about that,' says Bea now. 'Then I thought back to how, a year or two before, there had also been paps there one night when the Rothermeres came around for supper. Claudia and Jonathan didn't want to be photographed so my friend Evie and I ran out ahead of them and capered about in front of the paps, knowing that the photographers couldn't take pictures of kids, so we ruined all their shots. So this time I offered that Will and I should do the same – and I remember you looking a bit frazzled and saying something like, "I don't think that will work this time, darling" and I thought how unlike you it was to sound so defeated – especially since we'd won!'

On Thursday, we had beamed dutifully at the amassed paps outside our front door as we went to cast our vote on the referendum, albeit with me dying inside at how I looked and felt. But this was the next morning, and everything had changed. There had been a victory but it didn't yet feel real, and it certainly didn't feel it was ours. Michael escaped like a spy on the run, out the back through the garages that lined the back of Barlby Road and being bundled into a waiting taxi back there by a frantic Henry Newman, speeding off to the Vote Leave HQ to take stock.

I set off with the children on the school run not long after-wards, my stomach churning with anxiety not so much about how I looked – once again that seemed of piffling importance – but about whether I would bump into Sam. The thought filled me with panic. It was bad enough that many of the other parents at the school gates were Remainers. We sneaked into the car behind the paps' backs and made the journey in a sort of dazed silence, even the children, for once, paying forensic attention to the news on the radio.

'Pound crashes at shock Leave result,' intoned a gloomy John Humphrys in his special official BBC Voice of Doom, 'but Gove and Boris remain silent.' I remember thinking how irritating it was that we had Humphrys on the *Today* programme that day: only he could make it sound so reprehensible that neither Michael or Boris had released a statement. (Little did we know that there had actually been a fight at *Today* HQ that morning: Nick Robinson and Sarah Montague had been meant to host, but John Humphrys muscled in, pulling rank as lead interviewer, to Nick's fury.)

I could see the way the narrative was turning. 'Oh, fuck off, Grumpfries,' I raged at the car radio. 'Give them a break, they only found out themselves less than four hours ago.' There was a giggle from Bea. 'Mum,' said Will sternly. 'There's no need to swear.' I'm always loath to directly contradict my children but this time I was tempted: there was every need to swear.

How had this happened? Even with the obvious collapse of any Labour leadership on the question of Europe, leaving millions of voters spinning in the wind, the polls had still been (narrowly) in favour of Remain. Michael himself had been convinced that Leave would lose as we went into the final week, though I did notice that he went very quiet the last couple of days, always a sign that his cogs were in full whirl. At midnight, based on exit polls and early Remain returns, Nigel Farage had actually conceded that Leave was likely defeated, out-twatting himself once again, when he then had to eat his words after the 4.40 a.m. announcement that Leave had actually won by a margin of 52:48. This he did with typical Faragist air-punching, hailing Friday, 24 June as 'Independence Day' and the result as 'a victory for real people, a victory for ordinary people, a victory for decent people'. I heard that – and had a slightly hysterical reaction: which were we? Which, dear God, was he?

My father's worst fears had come true. Britain was leaving the European Union and the markets were in free fall, with the FTSE 100 down by more than 8 per cent and the pound plunging to its lowest level in 30 years. Boris was essentially hors de combat; having attended his daughter's graduation from St Andrew's the day before, he had hightailed it back to London late the night before. Nigel Adams was detailed to go and pick him up and drive him to Westminster for a hastily thrown together press conference at the Vote Leave HQ.

Michael was, meanwhile, entering a whole new world of surreal. 'From the moment the referendum result was called for Vote Leave,' he says now, 'it felt like politics sped up. The carousel got very, very fast.'

By 8 a.m., he was in Westminster, being clapped and applauded into the Vote Leave offices by equally dazed and overwhelmed activists. No time to take stock (or face a grilling from John Humphrys, thank you very much) it was just before 9 a.m. when the switchboard of Downing Street called. 'The Prime Minister is on the line for the Secretary of State,' said a disembodied voice. 'Putting you through now.'

Observers still remember now how pale Michael went, how formal the call was, as the PM coldly conceded that the EU Referendum had been won by Vote Leave. There was no acknowledgement that they were friends, no mention of future planning, no suggestion that they meet to discuss next steps. There was certainly no mention of Dave resigning, quite the opposite: when Michael said he hoped that, at the very least, the PM wouldn't trigger Article 50, the start of the legal process to prompt Britain's actual exit, Dave merely assented curtly and left it at that.

And yet, resign he did, less than 40 minutes after that, marching out into Downing Street with noble words about fighting head, heart and soul (and tongue lash, I thought, wincing) to keep the UK in the EU. He did say that he would not be the one to trigger Article 50, but with no mention of that being at Michael's specific request, just that he would leave that to 'fresh leadership'. I might have had a sympathetic frog in my throat listening to him end his speech, visibly emotional, with the words, 'I love this country, and I feel honoured to have served it', had I not passed Go and gone straight to Fury Street on that morning's Monopoly board.

What a massive man-baby. What an impossible, irresponsible child, throwing all his toys out of the pram because he hadn't got his own way. Of all the shabby days I might have tweeted about in Dave's premiership, he'd saved the worst for last. Et tu, Pontius Pilate, don't forget to clean under the nails there as you wash those hands. In the months and years afterwards, it almost amused me to see all the guff printed in all the Cameroon politico memoirs – about how this was the honourable, only option – but on the day, I was not remotely amused. Er, no. Abandoning the ship after you had deliberately steered it into the iceberg was by no means the only option. The grown-up, statesmanlike thing to do would have been to go out there, say something along the lines of, 'I'm sad that this didn't work out the way I wanted, but the British people have spoken, and as your prime minister I have a duty to make sure your wishes are respected. I will therefore work with the leaders of the Leave campaign to begin the negotiations and remain in my post until such time as things have sufficiently stabilised for me to hand over to a successor.'

He certainly knew he had Michael and Boris's support, because a few days prior to the vote, they had both signed their names to a letter saying as much. The truly honourable option was always open to him. He just wasn't big enough.

Instead, he did the precise opposite – and plunged the country into chaos. It was because of him, because of his inability to swallow this admittedly very bitter pill, that we ended up with the disastrous Theresa May, and that Brexit itself was so badly handled that it could only ever be seen as a disaster. That, I'm afraid, was Dave's legacy: offering the British people a choice and then, when they made that choice, punishing them for it.

But maybe it wasn't entirely his fault. Every politician goes on a journey, you see, with the journey of a prime minister admittedly a particularly difficult one. In a nutshell, you start out being a relatively normal human being, full of plans and ideas – and you end up quite bonkers, obsessed with very little else save your own survival and, failing that, your legacy.

It's got nothing to do with character – even the best succumb. It's just the nature of the beast. Power is the ultimate drug. Those who are hooked on it will, like any addict, go to almost any length to get their fix, prioritising it above all else – friends, family, colleagues.

Dave, while in many ways very grounded, was no exception. It was crystal clear to me as we had exchanged words that February night at Andy Feldman's that nothing mattered more to him in that moment than winning the referendum; not so much because he passionately believed in staying in the EU but because he knew that if he lost it would be the end of him politically.

LESSON NINE IN HOW NOT TO BE A POLITICAL WIFE:
start thinking (dangerously) that you know better than the
politicians how to run things.

In their April 2024 podcast *Inside the Room*, George
Osborne and Ed Balls had Michael in with them and they
discussed this precise moment in recent political history,
Dave's decision to resign. George said that the Cameron team
were surprised by the flak Dave copped for stepping down. I
remember back during our conversation at Dorneywood that
George had looked at me as if I was entirely mad when I had
said that, in the then unlikely event of a Leave victory, the
serving prime minister owed a duty of care to the country to
avert instability and the potential hell of a general election
and stay in post. It was clear that in George's mind – as in the
minds of many others around Dave – that the idea of not
resigning in the event of a defeat was out of the question. It
was simply a given, a political imperative – something that I
just really couldn't understand, and quite honestly still don't
to this day. I guess it's that old Men Are from Mars, Women
Are from Venus gender difference. Or in this case, Tory Men
Are from Mars, The Rest of Us Are from Venus …

Ed Balls, you see, agreed with me in that podcast chat, that
the PM should not have gone; that it was his job to pull
together all the players in the weeks after and provide some
leadership through the uncertainty that he had plunged us
into. Who cares that he felt embarrassed about dealing with
the likes of Merkel and Juncker after his defeat? Man up,
Dave, face the music, heal the party, embrace the challenge
of the result – and, if you can't face it yourself, appoint a
Brexiteer to be your negotiator in Europe.

Actually, forget that phrase 'man up'. Make that, 'Woman up, Dave.' How else could we possibly be mothers, wives, daughters? Yet again, I feel like the male ego here was a huge part of the problem, that being a woman – or at least listening to one – would have equipped Dave better at this moment. Because men, let's face it, have a great deal of difficulty admitting when they've screwed up. Women, by contrast, are much better at it. We're trained in it from an early age. We're also used to failure, and well versed in the art of compromise. We women have to admit we are wrong all the time and under the most testing of spotlights. Do not, under any circumstances, give me any pain relief during my labour, we say, mostly because I want to feel every connection with my baby. Sod that, we howl on the day; give me every jab, puff and drip going – just make it stop. Welcome to womanhood. We fail, we succeed, we push our sleeves up, we fail again, we succeed again and so it goes. That's life.

So, laboured analogies aside, Dave should have parked all his vanity, his pride, his dogma and his misplaced sense of the importance of his legacy. Greedily, he wanted to go down in the history books as the man who saved the Union for a generation in one term (tick), *and* saved the Tory Party's fracture on Europe for a generation in the next term. Well, it didn't quite work out. Get over it, mate.

In the podcast with Osborne and Balls, Michael says that he doesn't criticise Dave for going but that, 'like Ed, I do believe it would have been possible for him to stay … there are precedents of other prime ministers losing other referenda and staying on'. This is mild Michael-speak for the total shock he felt about being bounced into a situation where two people suddenly blinked in the glare and realised they might have to lead the country at a moment's notice.

Dave must have known this. He's not stupid. He must have known that resigning would cause utter chaos, and that in doing so he had the best chance of ensuring that Brexit would be a disaster. Was that why he did it?

I remember my father telling me a story once – again, sadly not one that necessarily casts him in the best light – about how he'd sat next to an American woman on a plane once. She was, he said, loud and annoying and wouldn't stop talking. When he ordered a large gin and tonic, she made a snarky comment, which didn't exactly endear her further to him. Anyway, when they brought around the in-flight meal, he refused his. 'Excuse me,' she said, 'can I have it if you don't want it?' He turned to her and said, with great relish, 'I'd sooner throw it away than give it to you.'

It felt a bit like that with Dave, like he'd sooner bring the entire country down than let Leave have its victory. And he did.

An hour and a half after Dave retreated behind the black door of No 10, Boris finally made it to London just 15 minutes before the press conference they had pulled together. Dom Cummings grabbed him and Michael and bundled them into the equivalent of a broom cupboard, just off the room where the press was already gathering. It was a short, one-sided conversation: Dom said that Boris was going to stand for the leadership, with Michael supporting him as his No 2. 'That's it in a nutshell,' Dom concluded. 'Right?' Boris and Michael simply nodded and that was that. Such are the great affairs of state agreed. In a broom cupboard.

Ten minutes later, Vote Leave held their press conference, fronted up by a shell-shocked looking Boris, Michael and Gisela Stuart. Boris downplayed the drama, saying there was no need for haste, calling for unity, averring that the UK would not 'pull up the drawbridge' and downplaying any questions about whether he would stand to be prime minister. Michael followed with some equally sober remarks, saying cautiously just that the UK now had a chance to 'take back control' and reshape its laws.

By then I was in the office, watching open mouthed with the rest of my colleagues. There is an assumption that it was a riotous day of celebration at *Daily Mail* Towers; in fact, feelings were very mixed. Dacre himself, of course, was pleased as punch, striding in via the back lifts as usual and stopping at the desk I shared with Andrew Pierce and Richard Kay to express his astonishment and delight, before chortling on towards his office, humming 'Land of Hope and Glory' loudly as he went.

But elsewhere there was not universal rejoicing; in the Femail department, several members of staff were actually in tears. Maggie O'Riordan, the departmental boss, was not at all convinced; Tobyn Andreae, now head of communication for King Charles III, wasn't either. Even among those who had voted Leave, there was a definite sense of 'be careful what you wish for'.

This apprehension was shared across town, at Vote Leave HQ. Even the biggest fans of the Gove–Johnson axis were hard-pushed to find the joy of victory in that room. 'It felt like a big moment,' said one of the Vote Leave team to me afterwards, 'but a big moment that was being held at a wake.' Afterwards Michael told a friend, in my hearing, that it was only after that call with Dave that he fully recognised that their friendship, which he (and I) thought might, in time, overcome these political differences had actually been irrevocably lost and was now over – forever. He was in mourning.

At the press conference, with the astounded eyes of the globe upon them, this feeling of shock, dearth of excitement and lack of tangible plan from two men who had always imagined they would be the off-set architects of the change, not the CEOs out front, spooked the markets even more. Ruth Davidson, the best thing about the Scottish Tories and on whom I always had a bit of a girl crush, came out with the line I wished I had thought of myself: 'Boris and Michael looked like two young arsonists who suddenly find out they've burned down the school and don't know what to do next.'

Michael now rebuts this quite firmly and insists that the note of caution was a deliberate move to avoid gleeful triumphalism, not only to distance themselves from Farage (who was notable by his absence) but also to reflect the closeness of the vote and the gravitas of the decision that had been voted upon by so many. 'Of course, in our desire not to punch the air Neil-Kinnock-Sheffield-rally style, not to look exultant in the wake of David's fall, people then inevitably thought we looked like naughty schoolboys.

'People were attributing to us all sorts of feelings and projecting onto us all sorts of intentions,' he told George Osborne and Ed Balls, 'and I'm long used to pundits trying to second guess us, so I ignored that, but we did have a plan, details of which were even in Vote Leave's outline of what should happen. The fact that that plan was not put into place until much later was as a result of … well … other events.'

Ah, events, dear boy, events, as Harold Macmillan once said: the greatest challenge for a statesman; the idea that even the best laid plans can be derailed in an instant by the unexpected – crises, global developments, scandals, personal enmities. How different the world might be today if Dave, instead of deserting his post, had called Michael and Boris into No 10 and said, 'Right: you won. Didn't see that coming. So what's the plan?'

Vote Leave were on their knees. Michael himself was in better shape because at least he had had a good night's sleep the night before, but the rest of the team were in tatters. It's easy to forget now, especially with the tortuous slog that came afterwards in the name of 'Get Brexit Done', but it had been an exhausting campaign, dogged by bad feeling and contrary claims, pitching brother literally against brother, best friend against best friend and, at the last, a murderous, gun-toting, knife-wielding ultra-right-wing lunatic against an elected representative of democracy and innocent mother of two.

Not since the English Civil War had the country been so discriminately divided within families, within county lines, outside the usual boxes of self-interest. Unlike general elections where the secret ballot is sacrosanct, Brexit was one of those ballots where everyone seemed to know how their nearest and dearest were voting, and that provoked terrible rifts. Wives moved out of husbands' beds. Students refused to talk to their parents. Grandparents were ostracised by the younger generations. My own family was simply one of many: Michael's parents staunch Leavers, his adoptive sister a Remainer, my own parents rabid Remainers, my brother hardly speaking to me he was so cross a Remainer; our children agnostic all the way, pleased to be in the team, not really au fait with all the nuances but obviously loyal to their dad.

And me?

To this day, I remain conflicted. I was perfectly prepared to accept that some of my friends felt very strongly that Michael was in the wrong, and that leaving the EU would be a big mistake. What I failed to appreciate was that they could not – or would not – separate that political opinion from their friendship with us. Pressure from the Camerons played no small part in this: I was told in no uncertain terms that the order had gone out to send us both to social Siberia.

The Lockwoods, the Jameses, many more: within the space of a few days almost my entire friendship group – the people who had been the weft and weave of my life – unravelled. Messages went unanswered, calls not returned, emails ignored. As promised, I did indeed find myself in a 'very cold place'. There were a few exceptions, to whom I shall always be grateful. Of all our 'BB' ('Before Brexit') friends and acquaintances, George and his now ex-wife Frances had remained the most neutral throughout the campaign, despite the sinister brand of pressure that George had occasionally brought to bear. Unlike Dave and Sam, who had made their feelings so painfully clear, George always tried to separate the personal from the political.

While his explosion to Simone had confirmed that he was furious about Michael's choice to join the Leave camp, George otherwise behaved like a consummate grown-up whenever we saw him socially. For her part, Frances was one of the first people to text me to see if I was alright on that Friday morning – which, given the circumstances, meant a great deal. We had been scheduled to spend a week together in South West France in the summer – in the event they ended up cancelling, but it was for perfectly understandable reasons. I think it might have been a bridge too far for us all at that point but later we resumed our easy relationship with them, donning silly hats for a New Year's Eve party in 2017, for example. Later they had their own domestic dramas, as their marriage collapsed and George behaved quite abominably towards Frances, but she and I are still close friends – and comrades together in the How Not to Be a Political Wife league, though I always manage to surge ahead in the general uselessness stakes.

Our other close friendship, however, was not so easily negotiated to a truce. As I've already said, the events during the first half of that post-referendum Friday had confirmed to Michael that this was more than a political disagreement between him and Dave, that this was the end.

When it had come down to it, the very thing Dave cared most about – his power, his reputation, his legacy – was the very thing Michael was willing to sacrifice in pursuit of his own long-held belief that the better course for Britain was to leave the EU. I knew this because I had tried very hard to persuade him otherwise, and failed. Dave saw it differently: that Michael was prepared to sacrifice their personal friendship and his loyalty to Cameron's Camelot for a political mirage.

When it came to Samantha and me, I hadn't believed that we could possibly be over: that our families, once so close, would now be forever far apart. No matter what the result of the Brexit vote, I had been planning to contact her after the referendum, to cajole our mutual friends into intervening on my behalf, to pursue peace in our time. But when I watched

Dave resigning outside Downing Street, I realised that a Rubicon had been crossed. And when I thought back to that night at Andy Feldman's party back in February, my heart quailed.

Quite simply, I had never seen Samantha like that. So angry, so embittered, so full of vitriol. And it was more than just anger at a piece I had written; it was the anguish of a woman who, like me, had seen her life twisted out of shape by politics, a person who had no choice but to choose between her husband and her friend, because politics and power had made it impossible to choose both.

Samantha wasn't just angry with me because of what Michael had done, or because I had let her down. She was angry then – and, I think, had been for a long time – because of the enormous pressure her position had placed on her. The price of being the superb political wife that she always was, in deprecating contrast to my own failures, was the price of our friendship. So that sharp exchange our fellow guests at Andrew's had overheard wasn't just a row. It was the final shattering of a deep and close amity that had been slowly buckling under the pressure of politics.

And actually, it broke my heart.

When the smoke cleared from the Brexit vote, this all became abundantly clear, so, within 24 hours of that 4.45 a.m. phone call on that fateful Friday morning, it was in a strangely elegiac, dressed-in-black mood that we headed into the weekend. It was to be a weekend – and the week that followed – that would decide both Michael's political fate and, in the end, twist the final knife into our marriage.

Michael was jittery, febrile and, quite frankly, a bit bonkers that weekend. It turned out that as they'd left the press conference that Friday lunchtime, he had turned to Boris and, still slightly dazed by the speed of the swings and round-abouts that morning, had muttered that, yes, he was indeed 'minded' to support him for the leadership. It was, once again, one of those little-thought-out throwaway remarks that would come back – very quickly, this time – to haunt my hapless husband.

'There was a fatal sense of drift about Michael's support for Boris after the referendum,' one of his team told me when we did a post-mortem in the months afterwards. 'I remember saying quite early on, "Listen, if you don't want to do it, you shouldn't do it, Michael!" And he just didn't … engage.'

I wasn't privy to the conversations between Michael and George that took place on that Saturday but I wasn't surprised that they took place. Michael called George to tell him that he had to get behind Boris, that Michael had seen how much he'd changed, how hard he'd worked on the Leave campaign, how he was bound to want George in his team and that, for Michael, George could be the hands-across-the-divide magic ingredient.

What was fascinating was that I had always thought of George as being like Michael: all about the abstract art of politics, but it turned out that even George had his red line. 'Anyone but Boris' was, Michael told me much later, George's basic line in these conversations. What I was surprised hadn't happened was that Michael and George hadn't, at any stage, considered that the two of *them* together might be the magic ticket. Not that Michael's team would have tolerated Big Dog Osborne bossing them around: Nick Boles (who, now that Brexit was done and dusted, was able to put his own Remain loyalties aside and come back into the inner circle of

Team Gove) had a visceral loathing of him; and the Henries and Beth were rightly wary of him.

Whatever, George made it clear that Saturday that he was going to support Theresa May, that all his 'people' were going to do the same and that the momentum would surely stay with her. So far, so Dave: if Remain wasn't going to be on the cards, then let's do our best to kibosh Leave.

But I think that George's distrust of Boris must have played on Michael's mind an awful lot, possibly because part of him shared it too. Michael had huge respect for George – in many ways he was something of a mentor to him, politically. But that was not strictly true of Boris. Michael had always seen the flaws in Boris, often up close. I remember once driving together to work at Wapping, Michael balancing a cappuccino in one hand and a Pret almond croissant (of which he was excessively fond) in the other. The previous evening, Boris had been the star guest at a fundraiser for his mayoral campaign, organised in part by Simone. A lot of work had gone into getting the right people in the right place to promote Boris. But he had shown up late, been less than charming and had delivered a lacklustre speech. As we rounded Buckingham Palace, Michael laid into him on the phone, chastising him for not taking the evening seriously, telling him it just wasn't good enough, and that if he didn't get his arse into gear his campaign was going nowhere. I was quite taken aback at the fierceness of Michael's rebuke, and at Boris's sheepish response – 'Sorry, Gover, sorry.'

So when it turned out that, post-vote, post-Dave's resignation, post-everything, while Michael and his team were tearing their hair out over what to do, Boris had spent half the weekend playing cricket against Earl Spencer's Althorp team in the grounds of the Spencer family's ancestral home in Northamptonshire. I had a real sense of foreboding.

It was partly for this reason that I stayed behind when Michael went over to Boris's house near Oxford on the Sunday for their Project of War; that, and the fact that our two children needed some parent time. Besides, I was slightly reeling from my own latest WTF? moment: somehow the *Mail on Sunday* – sister paper to the *Daily Mail* and at that time under the stewardship of arch-Remainer Geordie Greig who, you may remember, went on to take over the daily after Dacre left – had got hold of my brother, Ben, in Madrid.

In an article headed 'Thanks for ruining my idyllic life in Spain, says Gove's fearful brother-in-law as Tory Minister celebrates Brexit vote', Ben bemoaned the outcome of the referendum. 'I live in Madrid and my son was born here,' the article quoted him. 'I always took it for granted that I could just live and work here, but that may no longer be the case. I may be in a situation where I can't live and work in the country where my son is.

'I married a Spanish woman, but I don't have dual nationality. So there's a remote possibility that I would have to give up my nationality to continue living and working in Spain.' Ben went on to say that he 'was now an immigrant from outside Europe. They've suddenly changed my status.'

I was livid. Not so much with Ben – my brother is not a malicious person, and although I knew how pissed off he was about the whole thing, I don't think he said anything untoward or, for that matter, unfair. No, it was more the fact that my own bloody sister paper had weaponised my own bloody brother against me. Another dick-move by Geordie Greig – and not, as it turned out, the last.

Anyway, back to that Sunday. It was a gorgeous day and when the convoy of Henry Cook and Michael in Henry's Mini, Beth and Henry Newman in her car, both loaded to the gunnels with laptops, tablets, spreadsheets, policy White Papers, turned up to Boris's house, they found Boris's advisers sitting around barbecuing sausages, knocking back the rosé and generally having a jolly old Sunday with the boss. 'There was such a contrast of styles between the two teams,' said Michael later, 'with my guys all action stations and stats and schedules while the rest just partied on and I did wonder why Boris wasn't saying to his team, c'mon chaps, we've got work to do. It was all just too lackadaisical. A tiny worm of doubt entered my mind.'

What was worse, fattening up that worm of doubt, was that Boris pulled Michael aside that afternoon and meandered through an explanation about how, despite them both assuming that Michael would run his leadership campaign, that, er, actually, he may have offered that job to Ben Wallace as well. 'He's a great guy, though,' Boris apparently enthused, 'so you can do it together – that will be fine, yah?'

Michael was livid. Boris clearly wasn't taking this – or him – seriously. All the knuckling down he'd done during the Leave campaign had been as naught; BJ was right back to being his old Pinball Wizard self, just careering around and winging it. But it only got worse.

I don't know Andrea Leadsom and I have nothing against her so I'm not 100 per cent sure why she effectively became the touch paper by which Michael set fire to the Boris leadership campaign and thereby, eventually, to our lives together, but this does appear to have been the case. The entire team, including Michael and Dom, had apparently discussed with

Boris at some length how he was not, repeat not, to make any firm offers of ministerial roles in his putative cabinet: that this would be jumping the gun at best, and a crazy hostage to fortune at worst.

So, when Andrea Leadsom told Boris and Michael that she wouldn't stand and would support him if he gave her either the job of chancellor or chief Brexit negotiator, Michael gave Boris a warning shake of his head and mouthed at him not to say anything. To no avail. 'No, no, sorry, Andrea,' said Boris blithely, 'Gover's going to be chancellor *and* the negotiator.' Cue fury from Leadsom.

Michael said later that he could have throttled him but satisfied himself with suggesting to Boris, through gritted teeth, that the only way out of this and to keep her support was to handwrite a letter to Andrea, asking her to keep schtum and hinting that the negotiator job would be hers afterwards. How the tone deaf Leadsom had thought herself a contender for these top jobs, having held only two rather junior ministerial jobs herself, is beyond me, but it was clear that she needed to have this letter to clarify the realpolitik of the situation.

That Sunday night in Barlby Road, the chat around our kitchen table veered from the whirling world stage: the machinations of a grimly gleeful Juncker and the collapse of confidence in Labour's leader Jeremy Corbyn, to the spinning backstage: the grubby trading of favours and the sycophancy surrounding the incoming Court of Johnson, to the frankly theoretical: how could the energy and populism of Boris be harnessed for good? These were tumultuous times and I could see that things were moving very fast.

I nodded and chimed in at the time but I think better when I've written things down so, before I went to work on that

Monday morning, and before he was up, I wrote an email to Michael that clarified my thoughts. He was due to have a meeting with Boris that day, before Boris formally announced his claim to the leadership, so I focused on that – as much as anything, to focus *his* thoughts on that.

In the email, I tried to summarise what we had all discussed the night before; the need to pin Boris down about what he had offered Michael, to get guarantees to ensure that no one else was being fobbed off with the same offers, as well as reminding my still-idealistic husband of the lessons we had so painfully learned over the last few months: that loyalty was important but that we needed to be more politically pragmatic.

'Be your best stubborn self with Boris,' I urged him, knowing all too well that the flannelling, waffling charm of BJ could often divert even the most determined from their intended path, like forgetting why you're there when the GP asks you what's wrong. 'You must get specifics from Boris, otherwise you cannot guarantee your support,' I reminded him. In an effort to build up his confidence, I also wanted to remind him that it was his credibility, not Boris's, which would ensure the backing of a Johnson campaign by the ever-crucial media interests, so I cited both Paul Dacre and Rupert Murdoch as important players who I knew would only throw in their lot with Boris if Michael was to put his intellectual ballast behind him.

All the time I wrote, I wasn't even thinking of my own role here: I was simply encapsulating what we had all been discussing around the kitchen table the night before, like a secretary sending out the minutes of a meeting. I cc-ed those who had been there, pressed Send, snapped the laptop shut and rushed to work.

Except that I hadn't cc-ed the team. Not all of them. Instead of one of the Henries, I had accidentally cc-ed another Henry, some random PR I had in my contacts. We've all done it, typing out the beginning of a contact's name and assuming that the auto-prompt email address that then pops up is the correct one. In this case, PR Henry was still recovering from caning it at Glastonbury so it took him a day to open it and realise my mistake. At which point he momentarily stopped writing about lipsticks, shimmied out of his budgie-smugglers and put on his big boy pants; deciding to leak the email to the papers on Tuesday, 28 June. I do hope he was paid enough to upgrade from a tent to a Glasto campervan the following year.

To me there was nothing wild about this email. It was dealing with the Boris we all knew: all fire and flash, foibles and flaws, and it was simply the type of bolstering, hold-your-nerve billet-doux that any wife would send their jittery husband. But the press, needing some human frailty in a week of Big Stuff Going On, capered with glee.

The leak prompted a media frenzy, with numerous outlets portraying me as a malign, manipulative force, puppeteering behind the scenes and controlling my poor put-upon husband's political decisions. The *Telegraph* questioned whether I was 'a latter-day Lady Macbeth, secretly directing the fate of the Tory Party with her "poison pen"'. Similarly, Forbes called what I had done a 'treacherous act' in political history, further cementing the 'Lady Macbeth' comparison.

Rachel Johnson, Boris's sister, wrote a fully fledged attack on me – at the behest of … you guessed it: Geordie Greig. Yes, once again, the sister paper to my own paper was carving me up for public consumption. 'Michael Gove is now cast in the public mind,' she wrote, 'as a sort of Westminster suicide bomber, whose deadly belt of explosives has been detonated not by his own hand, but by his own wife.' What follows is a 2,000-word diatribe, the main thrust of which couldn't sustain the treachery theme for every word but took that peculiarly Westminster-bubble tack that we, the liberal elite who know everything, know that we shouldn't be doing Brexit – even if the country, the un-liberal knuckle-dragging idiots that they were, voted for it. To be fair to Rachel, she later apologised very sweetly. But at the time it felt very personal, and rather too close for comfort.

It also upset me because the whole Lady Macbeth thing was – is – such a lazy, sexist trope. It's the one thing I actually have rather a bit of sympathy for Meghan Markle over: this idea that, somehow, it's all her fault that Prince Harry turned out to be such a spoilt, vindictive little brat. Why, because he couldn't manage that all by himself?

Anyway, it was becoming clear that Michael and I were to be blamed for this general failure: that we hadn't fallen into line and nor had the country. Apparently, I had taken advantage of this febrile time in my witchy way to plant doubts about Boris's reliability, crack open the internal rifts in the Tory Party and highlight the influence of media endorsements for political candidates. It was almost as if no other commentator had ever thought to question Boris's commitment or competence, comment on the feral factionalism of the Tories or acknowledge the role played by the media.

Seriously? As I told *Tatler* in an interview in 2022, this attack on me was 'fundamentally misogynistic. It's only the wives that receive this treatment. When husbands get involved it just seems like they're being helpful.' A husband offering his wife advice is seen as kind and insightful, quite rightly; but me offering Michael the benefit of my journalistic acumen and my wifely support was Lady Macbeth? Oh, would you ever all just fuck off?!

There have been times, we can all agree, when I have been the walking, talking, writing apotheosis of How Not to Be a Political Wife but this was not one of them. This was me being A Wife, nothing more complicated. A partner, a sounding board, an other half. I was not poisoning anyone, pen or otherwise, I wasn't abjuring my Scottish man to murder anyone and there was no treachery in that email, all headlines to the contrary. Once again, truth was all too much the still, small voice in this particular wilderness – and instead we got shrill, tall tales. I would laugh about it now, as I try to laugh about most things; but the Lady Macbeth label has stuck, in all its sexist, bloody, woman-hating, denigrating glory – and I still don't quite see the funny side of that.

Michael did appear to think it was quite funny and was certainly as scornful of the media frenzy as I was, but it contributed to the general spiral of lunacy that week. Our son remembers it well. '"I am mad!" I remember Dad saying in the bathroom one morning,' says Will now. 'We were both brushing our teeth and he was gurning at himself in the mirror: "I'm going mad!" he'd say, with a wild look in his eye.'

As is often the case, the final straw was a light but fatal blow. I had forgotten about Andrea Leadsom until Michael arrived home on, I think, the Wednesday of that fateful week. He was spitting nails. 'One job,' he kept saying, pacing up and down the kitchen. 'One bloody job.' It turned out, of course, that Boris had not sent the letter. In fact, as it turned out, he hadn't even written the bloody letter. Or he had written the letter and somehow Nick Boles, who was deputised to hand deliver it to her, hadn't managed to. No one quite seemed to know, but the outcome was all too clear: Leadsom was still very much the thorn in their side.

I didn't quite understand why this was the final coup de grace but I was still smarting from the fuss over the email leak so I called in back-up in the form of the Henries. They arrived and tried to calm him down but Michael shrugged them off and rang Dom Cummings. Dom was at home in Co. Durham, having promised his wife Mary that he would give it a bit of a rest after the referendum and not get immediately involved with this farrago. Apparently, this promise might have been why Dom later denied he was specifically consulted and even had the nerve to present himself as a critic of Michael's decision, but he was on speakerphone and we all heard his response to Michael's gibbered reiterations about how he was done with Boris's hopelessness and incompetence, how he couldn't trust him to step up to the mark – 'this is just how I feel' he concluded rather forlornly.

'Well, in that case,' said Dom, 'you should do your own thing.'

Looking back, that was a key moment. Michael trusted Dom's judgement implicitly. His approval meant a lot, maybe even everything. If Dom had argued against, I'm pretty sure Michael would have shelved his misgivings. But he didn't.

That night I slept the sleep of someone who was exhaustedly deflated from the thousands of pinpricks of criticism, mockery and sniping from the press and public. Michael, meanwhile, the man who had slept the sleep of the righteous on the night of the Brexit vote just a week before, didn't sleep at all, having instead what he described to a friend who came to supper the night after as a 'long dark night of the soul'. She asked him what had prompted this.

'I gazed into the abyss,' he told her, 'and thought, "This man cannot be trusted to run the country. He has neither the focus nor the élan. Nor is he actually competent enough." And then I shook with fright, literally sweated with terror, at the thought that I was helping to put him into that position. And I knew I couldn't do that.'

Michael had repeatedly, eloquently and often amusingly told the nation that he did not want to be prime minister himself and that he would never run for leadership. 'If anyone wants me to sign a piece of parchment in my own blood saying I don't want to be PM, I'm happy to do that,' he said in 2012. 'I'm not equipped to be prime minister, I don't want to be prime minister,' he said another time.

But if he was to take Boris down – as he felt he needed to, having been the main culprit behind lifting him up there – then what else could he do? Simply withdrawing his support from Team BoJo and stepping aside from the campaign was not going to be enough. Boris was a speeding train and Michael felt that he had no choice but to hurl himself onto the tracks to derail the disaster that would inevitably follow if he didn't. To him, it felt like the only logical course of action.

What happened next, we all know. Michael called a press conference saying that he could no longer support Boris, saying that Boris could not provide the leadership needed to steer Britain through the changes ahead. In a shock move, he then announced his own bid for the leadership – a candidacy that was later that afternoon confirmed, against Andrea

Leadsom, Theresa May, Liam Fox and Stephen Crabbe, after a 'betrayed' Boris announced he would not be standing. 'I'll explain to anyone who asks,' said Michael with bravado, 'why I think I am the right person to be PM.'

The subsequent bunfight took place relatively swiftly. With the nation's outrage at 'throwing Boris under the bus' ringing in his ears, Michael pushed on, but the damage was done: the prevailing narrative was that Michael had plotted the whole fiasco for his own nefarious ends and always wanted the job – almost certainly egged on by his villainous, ambitious witch of a wife. Cue thunder and lightning, very very frightening.

Again: seriously? As if anyone would have plotted this farce. Michael didn't want the job; he just didn't want Boris in the job. I also wonder to this day if there hadn't been a thread of hope in Michael's mind that George might have crossed back over if Boris went – and brought the ex-Cameroon cavalry with him. Perhaps subconsciously that was part of why he did it. But this never happened, the mud clung to Michael and in the end the leadership contest was both swift and sure. Theresa May emerged as the front runner, Fox was eliminated in the first round of voting, then Crabbe withdrew from the race. By the second round of voting on Thursday, 7 July, it was all over for Michael and the leadership campaign was down to the final two: a rock and a hard place choice between the gimlet-eyed Theresa May and the dreaded Leadsom.

Still the Boy in the Corner, Will remembers us huddling round the television in a friend's house while he was doom-scrolling on his phone, half-listening to the numbers coming in: May 165, Leadsom 66, Gove 48. 'I remember thinking this might go wrong for Dad … so when the results actually came in, I made some joke about how it would all be okay if those numbers were the candidates' different ages,' he told the Rev. Richard Coles in the podcast 'The Apple & The Tree' in April 2025. 'It fell very flat.'

To be honest, a big part of me was relieved. The idea that I was salivating at the prospect of moving to Downing Street, 'measuring up the curtains' as some people put it, couldn't have been further from the truth. Firstly, I knew how restrictive and intrusive the role of prime ministerial spouse could be from Sam's experience, and I knew I would have been ill cut out for it, plus it would have been very hard for the children; second, I would surely have had to give up my own job in journalism, which I really did not want to do.

And Michael? Later, much later, even after our divorce, we finally talked: not about the events of that rollercoaster couple of weeks, but about his feelings. Every MP, at some stage, will have dreamt about becoming prime minister and they're lying if they say otherwise. Michael was no exception, but this was not that stage: he knew, he said, that everything about this timing was off, that this was not his moment. When Andrea Leadsom did a disastrous interview with *The Times* over the weekend between the first round and the second round, there was a twinge almost of fear that he might be into the final two, but he knew that even had that happened that would have been as far as he would go, that May had clinched the leadership because she was seen as the safe pair of hands in stormy seas. 'I felt curiously numb,' he said. 'Just numb.'

So May won, but she was utterly graceless in victory. She dispatched Michael with truly impressive brutality, almost wagging her finger at him and refusing to let him speak in their final meeting, in her tiny parliamentary office. 'I knew I was going to be fired when I got the call to go there,' said Michael wryly later, 'because if I was going to be retained or shuffled about, she would have called me to Downing Street.' It ended with her telling him to go away and have a think about loyalty. 'I felt like a delinquent schoolboy,' he told a friend afterwards. 'So I simply said, "As you wish, Prime Minister," and left. When I walked back to my Departmental office, I arrived to find that she had sent in the heavies even before she saw me, that they were already there packing up all the computers, to the shock and horror of the SpAds.' Classy, Mrs May, real classy.

A week is a long time in politics. It took less than two weeks for Michael to shoot up into the starry heights of British politics and, almost without stopping to admire the view from space, to plunge straight back down, deeper than before, into the Mariana Trench that is the backbench of a party in turmoil, with a government in place that no longer wanted anything to do with him. There was going to be jet lag for all of us in this rapid trajectory.

CHAPTER TEN

TOXIC FALLOUT

'At the heart of why Michael and I are getting divorced
is not that we hate each other, it's because I can't look
after my family and myself and be a wife of politics.'

Sarah Vine, talking to *Tatler* in 2022

In the early summer of 1986, I was back in Turin for the
summer before my first year at university. Most of my time
was spent loafing around by the pool up at the local tennis
club. Since the end of April, the news had been dominated by
the explosion of Reactor 4 at Chernobyl Nuclear Power Plant
in the Ukraine, which released various radioactive isotopes
into the atmosphere.

Between May and June – exactly when I was lying by the
pool in Northern Italy – those radioactive particles combined
with moisture in the atmosphere, forming what we now
know to be 'acid rain', a massive cloud of which drifted

across Europe, affecting soil, water and crops. It was that year's scare story, with fears of devastated 'ghost' forests across Scandinavia, of fish corpses piling up in the vast rivers of Russia, and that was before the winds changed and the acid cloud headed for the tourist hotspots of Greece and Italy. I remember reading an article in my Italian newspaper about finding levels of contamination of radiation poisoning in the wild boars in Piedmont that was ten times higher than a tolerable level – and imagining vast, tusked porkers with two heads rampaging through the hills around our village.

Many years later, when I was receiving specialist care for my thyroid and trying to get to the bottom of my hair loss, one of the professors I went to see sat me down and took a thorough health history. He wanted to know if there was anyone in my family with similar problems, where I had lived in my life and so on. When I mentioned Turin, his ears pricked up. There was, he explained, a higher than normal instance of low-level thyroid dysfunction in the region, almost certainly as a result of the unique climatic conditions that had trapped the toxic Chernobyl cloud over Piedmont for a good few weeks. As a result, Turin was something of a centre of excellence for the diagnosis and treatment of thyroid problems. He suspected I might have mild radon poisoning, and ran some tests. They came back inconclusive. But, somehow, I couldn't get the notion out of my head: was there just something inherently toxic about me?

Similarly, for years after the nuclear explosion of Brexit, I blamed the fallout from that for the slow poisoning of my own life. In the immediate aftermath, that summer, we fled to the Lot-et-Garonne in South West France for a long planned holiday, just the four of us, to hide and sleep and lick our wounds. And sleep we did: I have never been so tired and would fall asleep at every opportunity. I now know that extreme somnolence is one of the symptoms of ADHD when under extreme stress. Nowadays, when things get a bit too much, as they do from time to time, I still find the best course of action is to just curl up and go to sleep. Sometimes, a small part of me hopes not to have to wake up.

For his part, Michael took refuge in another room, listening to endless murder mystery books on tape – wallowing in the golden haze of Lord Peter Wimsey and Dorothy L. Sayers. But I had the kids to keep me busy and help me forget. When Eddie Vaizey and family popped in on their way to their own holiday, he confined himself to giving Michael a quick hug and saying gruffly, 'Terrible idea leaving a Remainer in charge.' Later we went to see Topaz and her husband in their French house for a few days. But otherwise we were alone, banished from the Court of Cameron for good, cut off from so many of our political friends, Michael fired by Prime Minister May and generally in the dog house. As we sat under those dark, star-lit skies at night, there seemed very little left to say. We were both too numb and stunned to talk about what had happened, or think about what to do next. My only consolation was that, while Michael was now effectively out of a job, I at least still had mine.

I blamed myself, because that has always been my default position, my masochistic comfort zone. If only I hadn't been so blasé with Dave on the sofas at Chequers; if only I could have persuaded Michael not to sacrifice himself on the altar of Europe; if only I had never written that article trying to justify ourselves to the Camerons; if only I hadn't gone to that party and been yelled at by Sam; if only I'd spoken up to

Michael about the madness of shoring up a rickety house of cards like Boris – so many 'if only I hadn't' notes to self, that I could have wallpapered my downstairs loo in them.

I've always been robust about regrets though, so, at first, I simply shrugged – and metaphorically and figuratively went back to work. We both did.

When it came to my work, here at least, I was cooking with gas. My role as columnist on the *Daily Mail* was by now delving more widely into socio-political issues, which is to say – what I wrote seemed to be what the readers wanted to hear. Dacre admitted to being pleased that I had engaged a broad and growing readership, and he commissioned me to write frequent opinion pieces and features outside the column.

My fury with Geordie Greig over on the *Mail on Sunday*, for running what seemed to be deliberately targeted cross-bow pieces by my own brother and Rachel Johnson, was boxed up and put in the grudge chest, along with all the other slights and hurts during the Brexit brouhaha. All's fair in love, war and politics, I reasoned, and tried to focus on the future.

Michael and I were both determinedly smiling and waving, keeping our noses clean and papering over the cracks with diligence and hard work. Michael himself was no longer hobbled by the ministerial code of conduct so he started writing for *The Times* again. I secretly – and fervently – hoped that politics would just quietly go away, that he would go back to journalism full-time and that the man I had married would slowly begin to emerge from his carapace, to strip off those layers of political camouflage, and shuck the armour to emerge, pink and smiling, as from his metaphorical Clarins bath; the same goofy, incorrigible genius I had first encountered all those years ago on the slopes of Méribel.

But politics casts a more baleful shadow than that. In January 2017, Michael went to America for *The Times*, to meet Donald Trump who was about to take office in his first term as president. The interview that resulted garnered criticism for not holding Trump to account, for not asking the difficult questions that we, the great unwashed, imagine we would, David-style, sling at the great Orange Goliath. Of course, anyone who has interviewed Trump knows that asking him difficult questions is like pushing blancmange through a letter box – it just doesn't go well; half of it slides down the outside, most of it ends up spattered all over you and everyone ends up in a mess.

Indeed, a close friend of mine was once dispatched to grill him for a travel piece, of all things, just after he had acquired Mar-a-Lago in the mid-Nineties. At the time he was married to Marla Maples, his second wife – an exquisite-looking creature with, my friend recalls 'femurs like a gazelle's'. Breakfast was by the pool, but before that there was a very hands-on (in the literal sense of the word) tour of the house, during which The Donald demonstrated his lack of boundaries by pinching her arse in every doorway, then sliding his arms around her waist when she stopped dumbstruck in front of a large painting of himself in all his radioactive glory, before exhorting her to 'check out' his wife's derrière. As my friend, determined not to be rattled, unfolded her napkin and reached for her first sip of coffee, she enquired whether, given the millionaire exclusivity of the venture, he was at all worried about the optics of the small shanty town that seemed to have sprung up around the entrance to the gates.

Bad idea. 'That does not exist and you are not taking this meeting seriously,' he snapped, and that was the end of that.

Anyway, among the many derisory write-ups of Michael's encounter was one by the lefty comedian Stewart Lee who, in an *Observer* article later that month, used the excuse of criticising the interview to excoriate Michael as an emasculated Brexiteer, an ill-born, meek man, self-serving nest-cuckoo and adopted misfit. But he saved his ultimate insult for me.

'As a student, David Cameron is rumoured to have put his penis into a dead pig. To outdo him as an adult, in an act even more bizarre and obscene, Michael Gove put his penis into a *Daily Mail* journalist.'

Just pause for a second and read that again. Imagine you have a little girl and are tucking her up in bed and, when she asks what you think she'll be when she grows up, you say, 'You will work really hard and get a really good job and then a man who you've never met but who hates you because you don't agree with his political views will say that the idea of having sex with you is more disgusting than having intercourse with a dead pig.' Or saying to your little boy, 'Make sure, when you grow up, to use all your brains and your ingenuity to craft insults to women that denigrate them professionally and make them feel like a fucked pork product.'

Even my father was shocked by that one. I just hope that when 'comedian' Lee meets his maker, his maker is a woman.

Quite apart from the personal hurt that the resulting gleeful coverage of Lee's comments caused me, I realised that for Michael, and by extension for me, there would be no quick escape. I had thought we might have been lifted out of the Petri dish of contempt by no longer being under the public microscope of politics but no: the referendum had stirred up lasting loathing beyond our ken.

Still, I was looking forward to having my brilliant husband back. Naively, I thought he would forget the siren call of frontline politics and reconnect with journalism and writing, enjoying the extra money and the freedom. The children, who had always been immensely proud that he had once worked for the BBC, thought he might land a gig making the tea for Nick Robinson on the *Today* programme, or similar, a bit like Ed Balls. As a brilliant public speaker, I thought he might go the Gyles Brandreth route (only without the colourful jumpers), and make a shilling or two regaling rooms full of claret-fuelled industrialists with his exploits. He had been working on a biography of Viscount Bolingbroke, the colourful seventeenth century Tory and political theorist once described by his contemporary and friend Jonathan Swift as a man who wanted to 'mix licentious orgies with the highest political responsibilities'; I couldn't wait to read it, and thought maybe Michael would now finish it.

For my part, I had my own recovery project: moving house. I loved Barlby Road – it had been our haven – but I felt so strongly that we needed to move from there now. The children were by this time beginning to be gangly teenagers and we lived in an area rife with gang pressures, prostitution and drug deals in the cul-de-sac behind our house and a general shadow of menace. I was permanently anxious that my young and impressionable, football-mad son would fall into the wrong crowd. Then Will was mugged on the way back from school – the standard West London heist of his phone, grabbed by a kid on the back of a scooter – and that shook me. I already felt unsafe there since the referendum:

because of all the paparazzi who had been there night and day almost throughout the Leave campaign, everyone knew exactly where we lived and I hated that.

From loving the 'rich tapestry' of life around us, of which we were a happy anonymous part, I now felt that we were all marked property, and could be singled out at any time, sworn at on the bus, or worse. Surrounded by anger on all sides, it felt like we needed a bigger fortress.

There was another, more practical, problem: we were in danger of being crushed to death – by Michael's books. Books, books, everywhere and not a word to say. They were multiplying like rabbits in springtime, teetering in corners, tumbling off shelves, gathering dust. Michael had always been insistent that 'books furnish a home' (and on occasion this became literally the case, as when the leg fell off one of the armchairs and a small pile of the more obscure biographies was pressed into service as support); but we were in danger of being driven out by them.

I found Lisgar Terrace, just south of the Olympia Exhibition Centre, between Hammersmith and Kensington. It was opposite a large council estate, and the house a few doors down was, I later realised, an HMO and brothel; but that's London for you. The house itself was big-boned and beautiful, with a faded Victorian grandeur that appealed to my Italian aesthetic. I loved the blousy, bosky, walled garden and the wrought-iron railings. It needed a lot of work (which we could never quite afford to do), but it was a fabulous space, and one for which I was immensely grateful later on down the line, during lockdown.

It was also closer to Will's school in Holland Park, easier for Bea to reach Grey Coat in Victoria and on the District

Line for Michael to get quickly to Westminster. I could walk to my office in High Street Kensington, or hop on a bus. It had a huge upper and lower ground floor and high walls just aching to be covered in bookshelves. It also had a large black front door, with a metal number 10 on it, the irony of which escaped no one. I loved it.

To my surprise and despair, Michael was dead set against us moving. I couldn't for the life of me understand why. Sam and Dave still lived around the corner from Barlby Road; Chris and Venetia were not far, in Queen's Park. Rachel Johnson lived just off Ladbroke Grove, Kate Fall too. All these people now hated us, as they never seemed to stop reminding anyone and everyone. I just didn't want to be around that anymore, forever worrying about bumping into them, everything a sad reminder of happier times. I felt it was time to move on and out, to focus on the road ahead, the next chapter. Michael felt differently: Barlby Road was still, despite everything, his happy place. Where I remembered the paparazzi blocking us in and the smell of their fag smoke snaking in poisonously through the windows on the morning of Brexit, he remembered the joyous suppers with Beth and the Henries, the lively parties with all our friends overspilling into our Moroccan tent-covered back garden, the children as tiny, sweet-smelling infants: the Belle Époque of both our marriage and his political career. Where I was determined to shut the door on recent disasters and make some new memories, he wanted to shore himself up with the bulwarks of the past. Much later on, after the divorce, a friend boiled this down. 'Michael, as a foundling, clung to Barlby in a more profound and symbolic way than many could comprehend. While your anchor was him and the kids, his was also about that place. Leaving Barlby crystallised for him what you already knew: that life had irrevocably changed.' But even he, I think, could see the advantages of a bigger space with growing teenagers – and so eventually, reluctantly, he acquiesced.

We both responded so differently to the traumas of the previous year. He wanted to stand still and take stock; I wanted to run for the hills. I thought that at Lisgar, away from the gaze and glare of those who knew where we lived, what we were doing, we could regroup. Up until this point, I hadn't actually thought that these differences might be the harbinger of a more particular doom, but it was actually on the day we moved, in the summer of 2017, that a chill entered our marriage.

Things didn't exactly get off to the best start. Barlby Road had been cleared, the contents stored overnight. I had booked us into the Royal Garden Hotel, opposite the *Daily Mail*, for a night, and parked the car across the road in one of London's poshest little corners, Kensington Square. We got up early and headed off to join the removals men – only to discover that the car had been broken into and the windows smashed. So much for the exclusive address. Foolishly, I had left a bag in there containing all our passports and other documents; that was gone, along with various other items.

Later, the police found the bag, with all the passports still in it, dumped in a bin in Marcus Garvey Park, just across the street from our new address. With hindsight, this might have been a bit of an omen about our new neighbourhood. But at the time I was so used to things going wrong, I hardly gave it a second thought.

When I say that the first removals pantechnicon was loaded entirely to the gunwhales with Michael's books, I'm only slightly exaggerating: there was only room for our bed, which the removals men duly unpacked and assembled. It was going to be a busy day: even with removals men doing the heavy lifting, we had four floors of a new house over which to distribute all our stuff: there were a lot of tiny decisions to be made. My mother had flown over from Italy to help, and my lovely cleaning lady, Maria, was on hand too. Despite the car break-in, I was incredibly excited.

Michael, by contrast, was not. He had been remote and a bit surly during the days we packed up Barlby Road, so I wasn't expecting much in the way of sleeves-up hard labour; but I was gobsmacked when, the removal men having put together the bed in our new bedroom and Maria having found the box of bedding, he opened up his briefcase, rifled around for a minute, removed a couple of books, kicked off his shoes and repaired to his side of the bed to read them. William joined him.

The second lorry arrived and he moved not a muscle, neither to help nor to direct, not even to give the removals men cups of tea and biscuits. My mother, busy in the base- ment kitchen helping Maria, was livid. 'I know it's probably not my place,' she said, through gritted teeth, 'but I'm sorry: what kind of a man lies on his bed reading a book while his wife and mother-in-law do all the work?'

He hardly moved for the rest of the day and certainly didn't unpack anything else. We did everything, and I do mean everything. I was entirely flummoxed and actually incredibly upset. Part of me wanted to rip his head off: how dare he not help me? What sort of lazy, selfish so-and-so could have lain there all day and simply ignored all the ruckus around him? What was wrong with him? But the greater part of me was the Pollyanna-ish part: the part that wanted this day to be a fresh start, a celebration, a coming together of the family.

So, in the interests of familial amity, I swallowed my rage and did my best to make the first night in our new home super-special, in among the chaos and the unpacked boxes, raising our glasses to our new Lisgar life. But I didn't forget – and the rage inside me continued to fester. I remember I hunted for days and days on Ebay to find enough bookcases to house his collection, eventually finding some huge ones (from a church in Wales) for the living room. Once they had arrived, I asked him to unpack the book boxes – of which there were at least a hundred – but he simply refused to do so. I kept asking and asking, and eventually he did so, but in such a way that only made the problem worse, stuffing the books in any which way. I had imagined that he would be delighted to finally have a proper library, a cherished home for all his beloved reading – but he just seemed to regard it as an annoying chore.

'I knew you could sense that I wasn't OK with the whole "New house, new life" idea,' Michael says, when I remind him of this day. 'I know I was reluctant and mulish, dragging my heels. I just hate admin and change.'

Gradually, this sense seemed to seep into other areas of family life too. Michael was always a firm believer in the importance of a to-do list, and it dawned on me that if the kids and I featured on his at all, we were a fair way towards the bottom. Suddenly I had become a bookkeeper of marital annoyances; noticed all the times he simply checked out of family life; noted the disproportionate levels of attention we gave our now tricky teenage children: he not enough, me too much by way of compensation; began to subconsciously log the amount of time he spent out in the evenings; couldn't help but be painfully aware of how little we were talking. I reasoned that he was probably just a bit depressed as a result of everything (I mean, who wouldn't be?) and tried my best to make him feel loved and appreciated. But it seemed as though not even my best efforts could make him care about anything but his one true passion: politics.

When in 2017, after the snap election in June, Prime Minister May realised she was losing her base support, the Westminster siren came calling once again. She invited him back in from the cold, offering him another cabinet position as Environment Secretary. I did not have the strength to lash him to my metaphorical mast: I could tell it was all he really wanted. Even though the naive part of me was secretly still amazed that, just like that, he could shrug off the memory of their last humiliating meeting and scamper back to Whitehall like a puppy, I could see how happy he was to be working on a complicated brief again. So, like a mother sadly packing away the infant clothes, I folded away my fantasies of a different type of life. He had clearly outgrown them.

I think it was around that time that the notion began to dawn on me that perhaps Michael and I no longer wanted the same things in life. It's sad to say, but I just didn't feel like I was part of his plan anymore.

Michael himself now acknowledges this. 'After the events of 2016, you must have thought that you'd finally nursed me out of the virus of politics,' he tells me now. 'You must have thought, "OK, I got him out before he was killed, he's slowly recovering, building up those antibodies, nicer life, nicer husband, better dad," then bam, I was re-injected, jamming in the needle as I rushed off, eyes blazing feverishly. I get that now.'

I kept going, of course, but from then on, I just felt like I was running out of rope to hold my marriage together. It was as if politics had smashed the vase of our relationship and while I was trying to pick up the pieces, Michael just wouldn't give me the glue. He just seemed so much happier elsewhere – but instead of addressing the problem, I did the opposite. I too found other things to occupy my time, throwing myself into work and children and spending more time with my parents, who were struggling post-Brexit.

Bea was having a tough time at school; during the referendum and through the long trudge towards Brexit afterwards, both classmates and teachers had discovered the joy of tormenting her for who she was, from passive aggression in the form of Remain badges and loaded debates; to actually getting into hair-pulling fights in the school playground. When she was in Year 9, in 2017, she tells me now, there was a bust-up between her and some other kids during Pride Week, during which Michael's name came up as 'not just an effing Tory but effing gay'. Bea reacted furiously every time and decided that if she was going to be hated anyway, she might as well play up to it by smoking in the courtyard and getting into fights – while secretly working hard. She ended up in permanent two-hour detentions – yet despite her dyslexia and undiagnosed ADHD, she got good GCSEs and flew through her A-levels.

She rolls her eyes about it now, 'One-hour detention for the length of my skirt, one hour for that day's answering back some cow in my class,' she says. 'It was magical to them and their parents that I was Michael Gove's daughter because it seemed to give everyone a springboard to attack me from. Well, I showed them.' Sometimes her acts of rebellion were rather joyous: like the time she heard someone muttering about her parentage at a party, whereupon she wrapped her arms around the friend she had come with and confronted the whisperers. 'So yeah, my dad's a spy and my girlfriend here is in the Mafia so you want to watch what you say,' she said and spun on her heel to go and top up her WKD.

She also discovered the anarchic joys of social media and dived straight in, flexing her muscles as a troublemaker, smoking, pouting like Lolita to the camera, showing off her tattoos, even badmouthing her poor father as 'Tory scum', albeit with a shit-eating grin. It was a textbook phase but, my God, it was a testing one, made infinitely worse by the fact that she was brilliant at it and garnered thousands of followers no matter how often her accounts were shut down for their inappropriate content. Anyone could – and did – hurl themselves similarly into the limelight but not everyone was tracked by the national press as they did so, with every teenage fracas up for grabs by pulpit pundits.

She looks rueful about it now, but shrugs it off. 'I didn't know it mattered until it mattered,' is all she will really say, not realising how heartbreaking that sounds.

Having been a deliciously nerdy little boy – his head bursting precociously with both facts and opinions, his ability to charm grown-ups unparalleled – William reacted very differently from Bea when it came to being a Gove kid. Instead of tackling the world head-on, he simply ran into the warm digital embrace of *FIFA* and gamed all the hours he was allowed to, which enabled him to largely ignore the real world where his parents were raising hackles. He tells us now that he had some friendship issues at his school – his best friend's older brother said that they couldn't possibly be friends, but they quietly ignored him – and he had always coped well with the inevitable jeers in the playground. But occasionally, the vitriol bubbled up, like when we were on holiday in Madrid with my parents in 2018 and Roger took out all his frustrations with his son-in-law on his grandson.

'Fucking Brexit bollocks,' he bellowed at Will, stabbing the air with his cigar while he tucked into a plate of chips. 'Your fucking father is going to make me pay extra fucking tax, extra fucking hassle, he can go and fuck himself.'

What was a 14-year-old boy supposed to say to that? Will says now that he reacted to this as he did to all such slurs by 'going into my head'. Again, my heart clenches when I hear him say this. Again, our children responded in very different ways to the pressures around them, Bea by externalising her rage, Will turning it inwards, on himself.

On Christmas Eve 2018, as I was picking up some last-minute supplies of spuds from Waitrose around the corner, my phone rang. It was Will. I answered in my usually breezy way: 'Hi, darling, everything okay?' As I wrote at the time, he responded with a howl of anguish. It took me several minutes to establish the precise details of his predicament, but in essence it appeared he had tripped over the Christmas tree and fallen through the plate-glass French windows.

I asked him to switch his phone to FaceTime and was confronted with a white-faced child with a huge gash on his shoulder – about 10cm long and deep enough so you could see the bone and tissues. On the same arm, a fat tongue of flesh was hanging off it, like something out of a horror movie.

I put down the spuds and ran. It took me about 10 minutes to get home, by which time he was sitting on the stairs with the front door open, shaking and covered in bloodied kitchen towels.

His lips were blue, and the hall was looking distinctly Quentin Tarantino. Both French door windowpanes were jagged, gaping holes. Carpet, presents, tree – all were covered in a fine spattering of blood.

On my dash back, I'd managed to call an ambulance. While waiting for it, I remembered a distant first-aid course and did my best to apply pressure to the gaping wounds.

His main concern, bless him, was that I would be cross because of the broken windows and ruined carpet. By the time the ambulance crew arrived the situation was a little more under control. My daughter – who had been upstairs with a mate smoking an illicit cigarette – had mopped up a lot of the blood and Will had calmed down considerably.

In fact, the crew seemed more concerned for my husband, who was gasping for air having also sprinted back from the Tube station, loaded down by last-minute Christmas shopping. Not until they saw the lacerations did they realise we weren't time-wasters. Their eyes widened, the paramedic visibly gagged at the sight of Will's arm and not long after we were on our way to A&E.

An ambulance ride, quite a lot of nitrous oxide (I still have the videos of him giggling while the surgeon, a very nice man from Iraq, went to work) and 64 stitches later, he was all fixed up.

It wasn't until a few years later that Will, who had initially told me he'd simply tripped over the Christmas tree, revealed the truth of what had happened. He had become so angry with losing a *FIFA* game that he had run at the glass in a fury, wanting to smash into something. Little did he know that the antique glass would shatter all too smashingly and impale his arm on the shards left behind. 'I just wanted to hit something. I didn't expect it to break.'

Every parent of every computer gamer knows how angry their kids can become with a game, but it didn't take a rocket scientist to work out that Will repressing his anger at everything else in his life might have been at play here. And the stakes had been so potentially catastrophic that my blood ran cold at what could have happened. This wasn't just anger management issues, this was actually life threatening.

Had he fallen an inch to the side either way, he could have severed a ligament or, much worse, an artery. If I hadn't been in Waitrose and had missed his call, as I so often did, I might not have got home in time. These outcomes played them-selves out in my mind for months – long after the patient himself soon rallied and started showing off his impressive scars.

Not that this was how some saw it. For some of the more cockroachy of Sarah Vine critics, this was just another way to attack me. 'Your son is obviously as stupid as you and your husband are,' some charmer messaged on social media. 'Do the human race a favour and remove your whole family from it by all of you jumping through a window.'

It was this that was so toxic about the fallout from politics. I wrote in an earlier chapter about how once you're in poli-tics you're no longer considered human, but this was someone actually wishing death upon us. I've had a lot of disagree-ments with people over the years – but would I wish them dead? Never.

Obviously, ours wasn't the first politician's family to receive death threats and I suspect we won't be the last; but that doesn't take away from the terror of being under the shadow of such intent. Lisgar Terrace certainly became less of a haven when the security services contacted us to tell us that someone had painted our home address on a wall in Derry, in Northern Ireland. We had cameras and a burglar alarm installed but it was menacing to think that people could be outside waiting for us, following us. For Beatrice's 18th, she received a card, postmarked Northern Ireland. With her name and address in multicoloured childish writing, it looked like something from a cousin or friend.

Excitedly, she opened it. Inside a card that read '18 today! Yay!' with a badge attached saying '18, Woo!'

And inside that, in letters cut out from a magazine or newspaper, the following message: 'Tell your dad that if he doesn't [and here I won't specify what he had to do, for security reasons] he won't live to see you turn 19. Do not make this public.'

That will always be my abiding memory of her 18th.

But we were lucky. Much later, in 2021, when David Amess, the MP for Southend West was murdered in a horrific attack by an Islamist extremist called Ali Harbi Ali at his constituency surgery in Leigh-on-Sea, our names came up in the police investigation that followed. Analysis of Ali's phone records showed that he had been standing in Lisgar for hours each day for a full week before he shifted his focus to Amess. He had tailed Michael on two of his morning jogs and had clearly followed me to work because his phone signal was located in Derry Street, the side street off Kensington High Street where Associated Newspapers is based. I shudder to think how close we came to being his prey – and simultane-ously feel guilty that the Amess family had to suffer such grief and loss themselves instead.

If I had thought post-Brexit that the game was probably not worth the candle, by now I was utterly convinced. By the time Michael went for the top job again, running for leadership directly against Boris this time, in June 2019, after Theresa May resigned for failing to secure a Brexit deal to which everyone could even vaguely agree (no surprise there), I was well and truly done. I really couldn't give a toss about his success or failure, to be brutally honest. Which was a shame because, as I now know – because I talk to my ex-husband far more than I ever did when he was my actual husband – this was the one moment when he allowed himself to get excited, the one moment when he himself thought he was within sniffing distance of actually becoming prime minister. 'I was just more confi-dent of my ability to do the job better than anyone else in contention, especially when it came to a Brexit deal,' he tells me now. 'I just had to persuade my fellow MPs to believe in me enough to get into the final two, because at that point the membership gets to vote – and that was my moment to clinch the deal.'

Boris was certainly the front runner at a national public level, but Michael was right, with the party faithful grass-roots, he was always very popular, even after the debacle of his first tilt at leadership three years before. If he could reduce the race to being a choice between go-get-'em Gove and a Bonkers Boris, he might just get there. Yes, he might just get there, I told myself sternly, ignoring the inner wails of horror. This was Michael's moment.

What happened next should one day feature in a *House of Cards*-style TV show. Except that people would tell the scriptwriter that, no, that couldn't possibly happen in real life.

And yet it did.

Remember Geordie Greig? The smiling gentleman villain? I don't know what Michael or I did to him in a former life, but yet again Geordie Greig, who had now moved across to be editor of the *Daily Mail*, unsheathed what he would doubtless now call his sword of truth – and stabbed Michael to death, using me to help drive the knife in.

The *Mail* had bought a book for serialisation called *Michael Gove: A Man in a Hurry*, in which the author, Owen Bennett, had attempted to claim that Michael had admitted to using cocaine 'on several occasions', decades before in his twenties. The story was based on a briefing he had held with his advisers back in 2016 when they had heard this confession, when they had then told him to keep deadly quiet about this. Despite this advice, it seemed, one of the very aides themselves – probably Beth Armstrong, sadly, who was now working for one of Michael's competitors in the leadership, Dominic Raab – had said this to the author but he couldn't make it stand up because the leak refused to verify it.

So far, so political biography. The story probably wasn't going to run in the book because of this stumbling block – but the *Daily Mail* is made of sterner stuff and, with Geordie Greig's say-so, that formidable machine cranked into action to make the story work.

Michael had apparently mentioned a party at his Mayfair flat in the 1990s which he shared with Ivan Massow. When questioned by the *Mail*, Ivan said honestly that he couldn't remember ever seeing Michael snort cocaine. 'I then couldn't believe my eyes,' he says now, 'when that clear rebuttal was somehow translated into "Former flatmate says Gove hid drug use from him" headlines. It was unbelievable.'

That was very much Greig's style of editing: he would take a rumour, and then twist it into a story. But on this occasion, he really outdid himself. He knew he couldn't stand up the cocaine story directly; but he figured he might get it via a pincer action.

Key to this was one of the paper's senior executives, whom Geordie knew I liked and with whom I had a good relationship. Greig rightly surmised that, if asked by this friend, I might hang Michael without realising. I was just going into my Pilates class when the *Mail*'s man rang. In his polite and gentlemanly way, he explained that this was a bit of an awkward situation, but there was this allegation in the Bennett book, and did I know anything about it?

Crucially – and this is key – he made no mention of the fact that the story had not been stood up or that, unless they could get confirmation of its veracity, it would not even appear in the final draft of the book itself.

I knew nothing of any of this at the time, of course, so I answered as I always do: by telling the truth. I pointed out the obvious, that I hadn't known Michael at the time of the supposed abuse, and indeed wasn't even aware of the conversation that had allegedly taken place with the SpAds. My friend pushed me but I stuck to my guns, despite a rising feeling of dread in the pit of my stomach. I was, after all, one of the newspaper's supposed star columnists; I worked hard and gave my all; I thought that, despite everything that had gone before, I had done my best to behave professionally and build a good relationship with Geordie. And now here I was, standing in the street in my leggings, being taken for a fucking fool by someone I considered not just a respected colleague, but also a friend.

LESSON TEN IN HOW NOT TO BE A POLITICAL WIFE:
trust no one.

My friend hung up, and I called Michael. He wasn't answering, so I called Josh Grimstone, his head of comms, and briefed him. He thanked me, said he would get back to me – and I trotted off to do my pelvic floor exercises.

By the time I came out, Michael had taken stock and decided to come clean: the story was out there, better to be honest about it. Yes, he had confessed to his team that he had used cocaine in his twenties; no, he was not going to deny that he had said it. Geordie had effectively bounced him into torpedoing his own leadership bid. They had their gotcha.

Again, with hindsight, I should have used my heft as a columnist and told my friend and Geordie to take a running jump – but I didn't. I was too worn down by it all, too tired really to put up a fight. And besides, with the departure of Paul Dacre and Ted Verity being moved to the *Mail on Sunday*, my livelihood depended on bloody Greig – and it was clear to me that my own future at the *Mail* depended on me standing by and waving past the assassin's car. For the first time ever, I was being forced to choose between my career and my husband: my remote, detached, lost-to-me, politics-obsessed husband and the one thing in my life that I was actually any good at.

I made my choice.

The story ran in the *Mail*. Michael apologised for his past drug use; was roundly accused of hypocrisy by the nation's press for having taken a tough political stance on drugs ever since; he was eliminated by his peers before the leadership vote reached the membership voting round, leaving the party faithful with the empty choice of Boris or Jeremy Hunt. Boris romped it and the rest is history: Michael was – yet again – called back into government, this time as Chancellor of the Duchy of Lancaster (in layman's speak, effectively the deputy prime minister); he and Boris duly got Brexit done with the compromised January 2020 Withdrawal Agreement.

By now I didn't care How to Be or How Not to Be a Political Wife, that was no longer the question. The question, by now, was what did I want to be, where did I want to be? Did I even, when all was said and done, want to be A Wife?

EPILOGUE

'Kindness, more kindness, and even after that more kindness. I assure you it is the only hope.'

E.M.Forster, *Passage to India*, as quoted in Sarah Vine
& Tania Kindersley, *Backwards in High Heels: The
Impossible Art of Being Female* (Fourth Estate, 2009)

On Thursday, 4 July 2024, Michael Gove left politics. He had announced his intention to stand down earlier in the year, whereupon Ed McGuinness was selected to stand in Surrey Heath in his stead, but in the election the seat went to Al Pinkerton of the Liberal Democrats, ending nearly three decades as a safe Tory seat. In one sense, I wish I had been with Michael that night, though maybe my skip for joy at seeing him finally uncoupled from the juggernaut of politics would have been deemed insensitive. His subsequent master stroke of moving back into journalism and editing *The*

Spectator would have also brought me some delight: this was the job – I think – that he was always meant to do. It actually made me chuckle when I heard he'd got it because I remember his mother Christine telling me about him asking her for a *Spectator* subscription for Christmas – aged 7.

But I wasn't with him anymore. I had clinched the How Not to Be gold medal and I was no longer a Political Wife. In July 2021, Michael and I had announced that we were separating, and by January 2022 we were divorced.

During 2019, I had moved out of our bedroom and into the little box room up at the top of the house. Nothing was said. The children hardly commented. I felt so detached from reality by now that I didn't even wonder at that. When we finally talked to them about the split in 2021, they seemed unnervingly unsurprised. 'You never fought,' says Bea now. 'The divorce was very, very calm – to be honest, you were kinda divorced for years.' Apparently, she and Will had discussed us divorcing back in 2019 and from then on, as Will later said in the Richard Coles podcast, 'We knew it was just around the corner.' His first reaction was very Will – yay, two Christmases – but he did admit in the same podcast that our split was the closest Michael ever got to breaking his heart.

When we talked to our friends, they were just sad that our marriage had been gently eroded away. There was no scandal; being locked together in lockdown had simply unlocked us once and for all.

We sold Lisgar Terrace; Michael moved into a grace-and-favour flat in Carlton Gardens and I have been renting in West London ever since. The children are no longer children but they are still based with me. As a family, we are still close. It is, as they say, a good divorce.

Was there a sliding door moment here? If, back in 2003, when all our political friends were persuading him to stand, I had realised what awaited us and stood in the way of Michael's decision? If I had persuaded him to stay at *The Times*, would our lives have been different? Would our marriage have survived?

On balance, I think probably yes. That's not to say it would have been untroubled – no marriage ever is. What is ironic is that these days I can speak to Michael far more frankly and intimately than I ever could when I was married to him. Back then everything was clouded by emotion and drama. Even more bittersweet is the realisation that in trying to be a good political wife, I increasingly thought I couldn't question him or challenge him, so I just shut down and stopped trying: thereby failing, not just at being a political wife as I have demonstrated here, but at being a good partner at all. Add to that the suppressed trauma of an early life being told how fat and useless I was – and his very different ways of reacting to his own traumas – and it was no surprise that we stopped functioning as a couple. Nowadays, we are so much better at being not married but still a family; hence his and the children's own very personal observations throughout this tale. Will puts it very well: 'The thing that most surprises people about us is first how normal we are, compared to so many other "political" families, and second, how well you and Dad get on.'

The real divorce here was between me and politics; as Will said to Michael in that podcast, 'You *are* politics.' Ultimately, I don't think many couples would have survived what we went through, to the degree that we went through it. George and Frances did not; Boris and Marina did not; Kate Fall and her husband did not; Matt Hancock's marriage did not. The mechanisms by which these marriages fell apart may all be different; but there is one common denominator: politics.

The real villain of the piece is not Michael, or me, or Dave, or Geordie, or Dom, or any of the vast cast of characters in this book: it's politics, and the toxic culture that surrounds it. It's the way the quest for power – and crucially the desire to hang on to it at all costs – corrupts hearts and minds. It's like a virus that gradually invades every cell in the body, or an addiction that creates a hunger that can never be sated.

One of my favourite books as a child was *The Lion, the Witch and the Wardrobe* by C. S. Lewis. I was always struck by the character of Edmund, who is stolen away by the White Witch after she offers him a box of 'the best Turkish Delight'. It is enchanted, and Edmund cannot resist its intoxicating, addictive effects, sinking deeper and deeper under her spell, willing to do anything on the promise of more until, ultimately, he betrays his siblings, Lucy, Susan and Peter, all for just one more morsel.

That, in a nutshell, is politics. And you're welcome to it.

ACKNOWLEDGEMENTS

Grateful acknowledgements go to:

My father for fucking me up so brilliantly.

Susannah for giving me the courage to write all this down and showing me the way.

Beatrice and William for contributing their unique wisdom and insights.

Michael Gove for being the best ex-husband a girl could ever ask for.

My agent Eugenie and editor Ajda for having such faith in this project.

Imogen, Santa, Lucy, Claudia, Topaz and Joanne for always being there for me.

Ted for always having my back.

Boles for bullying me (with love), Simone for the wise counsel, Eddie for the lolz, Henry for humouring me (and for being so incredibly handsome).

My family, and especially my beautiful mother, for
  enduring.
My grandmother Ruth, who saved me, and without whom
  none of this would have happened.
And last but not least, Samantha ... for being a good friend,
  while it lasted.